FULL
HOUSE

FULL HOUSE

JANET EVANOVICH

St. Martin's Paperbacks

This is a work of fiction. All of the characters, organizations, and events portrayed in this novel are either products of the author's imagination or are used fictitiously.

This book is a revised and enlarged version of a book which was published under the same title by The Berkley Publishing Group with the author writing under the name Steffie Hall.

FULL HOUSE

Copyright © 2002 by Evanovich, Inc.

All rights reserved.

For information address St. Martin's Press, 175 Fifth Avenue, New York, NY 10010.

ISBN: 978-0-312-53154-6

Printed in the United States of America

St. Martin's Paperbacks edition / September 2002

St. Martin's Paperbacks are published by St. Martin's Press, 175 Fifth Avenue, New York, NY 10010.

25   24   23   22   21   20   19   18   17

This book is for my fans—for those of you who have been with me since the very beginning, and who have asked me to get one of my early (1989) romance novels, *Full House*, into print again, and for all of you who wanted to see what my early books looked like, and who have asked me to put *Full House* into print so that you can read it for the first time. As I read this book again, it was interesting for me to take a trip down memory lane and see my writer's roots. Some things haven't changed—I still like a good slapstick joke, and I'd rather laugh than cry. Some things have—I'm a lot sneakier, my plotting is a lot more intricate, and my characters spend a lot less time kissing and a whole lot more time dodging bullets these days. I've gone back and enlarged and enhanced this book with the help of my good friend Charlotte Hughes. And Charlotte and I will continue to work together on future stories. All of you fans asked me for it—so here it is. Just for you—enjoy!

CHAPTER ONE

Nicholas Kaharchek surveyed his seven new polo students moving across the sandy practice field. He grinned as he watched an especially entertaining female named Billie Pearce.

In the four years since Nick had started the polo school, he'd seen his share of companionable stable bunnies and eager polo groupies, but he'd never seen anything like Billie Pearce. She was neither a stable bunny, nor a polo groupie, nor a rider, by any stretch of the imagination. From what he could determine during their brief conversation following the classroom part of the program, she was a housewife, smelling like fresh-baked chocolate-chip cookies and looking good enough to eat in her brand-new black riding boots and cream-colored pants. A woman like that could make a man forget all his troubles. Well, almost.

She had "girl next door" written all over her, what with those large hazel eyes and a mouth that was a smidgen too wide for her face. She wasn't wearing a ring; he'd noticed that much right away. But she had an aura of well-rounded maturity and general satisfaction that he associated with a happy homemaker and motherhood. Not that he considered himself an expert on women, although, by God, he did his best.

Nicholas Kaharchek knew *horses*. It was said he'd inherited his horse sense from his Cossack ancestry. It was also rumored that the Cossack blood ran hot beneath the calm exterior of his personality—a rumor many of the local ladies testified to be true. Nick had actually learned a lot about women while handling horses. He knew precisely what tone of voice to use on a high-spirited filly and how to lull even the most temperamental of them into a sense of well-being when startled. He knew how to move his hands just right over horseflesh—slowly, deliberately, but feather-light, until the muscles quivered like those of a satisfied woman.

Yeah, he knew how to play females, and the fact he had money—lots of it—didn't hurt. He genuinely liked women, enjoyed their individual uniqueness. He liked the way a woman smelled, enjoyed the feel of her downy hair when he pressed a kiss on the back of her neck, the way she looked sitting across a candlelit table or lying naked on the thick rug in front of his fireplace. And women liked him. They liked being seen on his arm, liked the fact that he was generous to a fault, and they liked the way he treated them. At least most of them.

But Nick had a habit of moving on after only a few dates. Less complicated that way, and he was a man who did not like complications. He'd learned the hard way.

He caught sight of Billie Pearce and suspected he was wasting his time, at least as far as polo was concerned. She had about as much business on a polo field as he did at a Tupperware party. He had a feeling teaching Billie Pearce to play polo would be like spitting into the wind.

Her horse ambled up to the red, white, and blue beach ball that served as the beginners' game ball, and stopped. His ears drooped slightly, his eyes half closed, and he gave a huge horse sigh. The animal obviously had other places he'd rather be.

"Listen up, horse," Billie said, "I'm paying forty dollars for a morning of polo. Forty bucks, you got that? That would pay for a pedicure. The least you could do is pretend to enjoy this."

The horse snorted.

"My sentiments exactly," she muttered.

Billie aimed carefully at her beach ball, swung the mallet in a loop over her head, and completely missed her target. The mallet slipped from her grasp and hurtled halfway across the field. "Dammit."

Nick took in the sight with a mixture of disbelief and curiosity. The woman had absolutely no idea what she was doing, and she seemed to be lecturing a horse about polo, though sadly enough the horse probably knew more about the sport than she did.

Still, she was cute in an old-fashioned way. She made him think of nice things: the way grass smells after it has just been cut, the feel of crisp sheets against his body, window curtains billowing in a soft breeze, and the smell of something tasty baking in the oven. He retrieved her mallet and guided his horse to her side.

"Mrs. Pearce," he began in a patient voice, "there's a little leather strap attached to the mallet. If you slip your hand through that strap, it will prevent you from slinging it across the field and committing involuntary manslaughter."

Billie felt a rush of embarrassment. She must look foolish to someone with his expertise, and it wasn't easy taking criticism from a man who looked as though he belonged on the cover of *GQ*. He wore custom-made Argentine-style boots and polo wear that seemed tailor-made to fit what could only be described as the perfect body.

She met his gaze. "Sorry, it was an accident. I was hoping this would be easier, but it's all I can do to stay atop this horse. I had no idea the ground would be so far away."

Nick raised an eyebrow. "I seem to remember you wrote on your application that you'd been around horses all your life."

"That's right." She wasn't about to tell him the truth: that she'd simply lived next door to someone who owned horses. "It's, uh, been a long time. I've gotten a little rusty. And the horses are shorter where I come from."

He nodded as though it made perfect sense, which it didn't. His saddle creaked under him as he put weight on his stirrups. "Mrs. Pearce, I don't mean to discourage you from playing polo, but maybe it would be a good idea for you to take a few riding lessons first. To sort of get back into the swing of it."

Billie looked around and had to admit she was lacking. The other students were much more skilled at managing their horses.

One woman in particular had caught her eyes, a stunning brunette whose long hair draped her shoulders like a silk shawl. She wasn't a student; that much was certain from her perfect posture, and an air of confidence that came from years of training. She and her horse moved across the distant riding arena with such fluidity it looked choreographed.

Billie realized Nick was waiting for an answer. "The ad in the paper said you didn't need to be an expert rider," she offered as explanation.

"That's true, but it helps if you know *some* of the basics." Such as which end of the horse you're supposed to face, he thought. Was this woman for real? He glanced at his watch and moved his bay gelding away from her. "This session is almost over. Why don't you take Zeke back to the barn and wait for me? I'll give you a lesson in tacking and horse care."

"Um, okay, sure." Billie glanced down at the stubborn animal, wondering how to coax him toward the barn. "Go, Zeke," she whispered.

"Nudge him," Nick said. "Like this."

It looked easy enough. Billy very gently pressed both heels against the horse's side, prodding him forward.

Nick nodded his approval. He had to admit watching Billie Pearce was more interesting than anything else going on in the field at the moment. "That's right."

Zeke ambled forward as Nick watched. Like most of the polo-school horses, Zeke had been donated. At one time he might have been the pride of the circuit, but he was retired now, and he took his retirement seriously. In his three years' tenure at the school stable, he had never been known to move faster than a shuffle. Yet, despite being incorrigibly lazy, he was by no means stupid. If forced, he knew when to take the field, when to follow a ball, and when to return to the stable, the latter of which he managed at a faster pace. He carried Billie to the apron of hard-packed dirt in front of the stable, gave a snort, and came to a dead stop, jolting Billie forward. She grasped his mane to keep from falling off. Zeke craned his neck, giving her a look of pure disgust. Nick smiled and dismissed the class.

Billie watched the other women guide their horses to the barn and dismount with ease. Stable hands appeared out of nowhere, took the horses, and led them inside the barn. A couple of the stable hands looked to be high-school age, obviously working summer jobs. An older man in a baseball cap appeared, and he barked orders at the boys as they rushed about in their work.

Billie tried to block out the man's harsh voice as

she sat very still on the horse, waiting, because she had no intention of climbing off Zeke while there was another human being within a twenty-five-mile radius. She had no desire to further embarrass herself and give Nick Kaharchek more conversational fodder for his evening meal.

The July sun was high in a cloudless blue sky, and the gentle hills of Loudoun County, Virginia, stretched in front of Billie like a giant, undulating patchwork quilt of field and forest. Horses stamped their feet and whickered softly in their stalls. The air was heavy with the smells of horse, oiled leather, and baking straw, prompting Billie to think of her childhood in Lancaster, Pennsylvania. Her father had been a small-business owner, but they'd lived side by side with Mennonite farmers. Good, sturdy people, who weren't afraid of hard labor. They revered their land and their marriages and worked to make them successful. Billie respected them for that, and she envied them because she'd had to give up on her own marriage. She'd had no choice. It took two people to make a relationship work, and her former husband had wanted no part of it.

Her gaze shifted once more to the brunette woman and her horse, now moving at a faster gait, perfectly attuned to each other. Damn, but the woman was good. Her hair lifted and fell gracefully against her shoulders and back, making Billie think of a shampoo commercial. Would she ever be able to ride like that?

Billie momentarily closed her eyes and enjoyed the feel of the sun on her back while she listened to the lulling buzz of cicadas singing in the distance. At least she'd held on to the house after the divorce, she reminded herself, thinking back to her disastrous marriage. Her children might have to make do with a part-time father, but they sure as hell weren't going to lose their home and the sense of stability Billie had fought to give them.

"Mrs. Pearce, what are you doing?"

Billie jumped at the sound of Nick's voice. She watched in awe as he approached the stable on his own horse. He reminded her of a centaur, that mythical creature who was half-man and half-horse. His riding was so fluid it was difficult to distinguish where the man left off and the horse began. He was as skilled as the woman she'd been watching. Billie envied them both.

"I was waiting for everyone else to finish up so you could give me my lesson," Billie said, trying to avoid looking directly into his brown eyes or noting how the sun had bronzed his olive complexion. She did not need to be caught up by his good looks. Kaharchek was definitely not her type.

The silent declaration drew her brows together in a frown as she pondered exactly what kind of man *would* be her type. Well, there *was* that chemistry teacher with the tortoiseshell glasses who'd made it plain months ago that he was interested. She suspected he would already have asked her out had she returned his interest. And the manager of the Kroger store made it a point to speak to her several times when she was in the store, pointing out various sales, saving coupons for items he knew she purchased with regularity. But she hadn't given either man much thought, because she simply didn't have a lot of time for romance, what with teaching, her children, housework, and gardening, and the list went on and on. *But* if she *had* been able to squeeze in a little time for a man, it certainly wouldn't be for someone like Nicholas Kaharchek.

For one thing, they had nothing in common. His father had amassed a fortune in his lifetime and provided well for his only son. It was common knowledge that when the elder Kaharchek had retired, Nick had been content to let a number of talented second cousins run the empire while he concentrated on raising horses and being a hands-on owner of Loudoun County's most widely read newspaper. Billie respected the paper, but having heard rumors of Nicholas Kaharchek's various liaisons, she wasn't sure she respected the man.

Nick dismounted and handed his horse over to a groom as he regarded her. "You can dismount now."

"Easy for you to say."

It amazed him how little she knew. "Just swing your right leg over the horse and hold on to the saddle with both hands."

She hesitated. "That sounds risky."

He saw the doubt in her eyes. "Mrs. Pearce, are you afraid of horses?"

"Of course not. I'm not afraid of anything. I killed a spider yesterday. It was big and black and hairy." She suppressed an involuntary shudder.

"Uh-huh."

"Okay, so maybe it wasn't hairy, but there was a

time I wouldn't have entered the same room with a spider. I've grown," she announced with aplomb. He just looked at her, and she suddenly felt dumb for mentioning the spider. Nick Kaharchek had probably never been afraid of anything in his life.

"I just wasn't expecting this horse to be so big," she said, getting back to the subject at hand. "I feel like I should parachute from the back of this animal." She took a deep breath, closed her eyes, and swung her right leg over the horse. The saddle slid through her grasping fingers, her arms flailed at the air. Nick reached for her, trying to break the fall. She grabbed at his shoulders, twisting slightly in mid-air, and fell against him. There was an exchange of grunts as they both hit the ground with a loud, bone-jarring thud. Somehow, she'd managed to knock the man off his feet. Worse, she'd landed right smack on top of him. On top of him, for heaven's sake! She simply lay there for a moment, sprawled across the polo god on the hard-packed dirt, breast to chest, zipper to zipper, thigh to thigh.

Everything touching.

Billie blinked and looked into Nick's startled eyes. Lord, Lord, he would think she was an idiot for sure, and he would have every right. She had no idea what to do. How would Miss Manners suggest she extricate herself from such a delicate situation without making it worse? All she could do was apologize profusely and hope he didn't press charges for assault and battery.

If only the man didn't feel so good. She tried to remember the last time she'd been so close to someone of the opposite sex and couldn't. All her nerve endings tingled, and something low in her belly tightened and coiled and sent a rush of pleasure through her.

Lord, don't let me go and do something stupid like have an orgasm right now, she prayed.

"Sorry," she whispered. "I lost my balance, and then my knees went weak."

"I know the feeling."

"Are you okay?" Billie asked. "I hope I didn't hurt anything."

"Nothing I'd want to tell you about."

She gave a mental wince. She'd made a spectacle of herself in front of him and everyone else by flipping her mallet out like a Frisbee. Now she'd gone and made a eunuch out of the most eligible bachelor in Loudoun County.

"Well, now," a feminine voice said. "Isn't this cozy?"

Billie glanced up. It was *her,* the gorgeous creature she'd watched earlier. Only the woman was even more beautiful up close. She appeared to be only a few years younger than Billie, but her skin was flawless, as though she pampered it on a regular basis.

Nick looked in her direction. "Hello, Sheridan."

The woman tossed Billie a look. "I see Nick has taught you how to dismount."

She had the smile of a movie star. Billie decided somebody had spent a fortune on braces. She searched for her voice. "This is my first lesson."

"I would never have guessed."

Billie suddenly felt small as she took in the mocking smile. Sheridan was the kind of woman who made all other women feel as though they had a huge wart on their nose.

Nick gestured. "Sheridan, meet Billie Pearce, my new student. Mrs. Pearce, this is Sheridan Flock, an old, uh, friend."

Billie nodded at the woman and carefully lifted herself to her feet. She made a production of brushing dust from her britches, too embarrassed to look at either of them.

"It's nice to meet you, Miss Flock," she said, finally making eye contact with the woman, refusing to be intimidated. "I watched you riding earlier. You're magnificent."

"I learned from the best." Sheridan eyed Nick in such a way it was clear that horseback riding wasn't all he'd taught her.

"I'd best be running along," Billie told Nick.

"Not so fast. Your lesson isn't over."

Sheridan pressed her lips together in annoyance. "Oh, let the poor girl go," she said. "Can't you see she's had enough for one day? Why, it's obvious she's not cut out for this sort of thing."

Billie immediately stiffened, but her voice was pleasant when she spoke. "It's true I'm not as adept as you, Miss Flock, but then, we're not in competition, are we?"

Sheridan's smile faltered, but she pretended to ignore Billie. "Nick, I've only been back from Europe for a few weeks, and this is the first chance I've had to ride Clementine. Daddy has been entertaining nonstop since I arrived, so I've been forced to play hostess. I thought we might go riding like old times."

Nick wore no emotion. "I can't, Sheridan. I'm working."

"You call that work?" She laughed. "Besides, you're the boss. You set your own hours."

"Sorry, I'll have to take a rain check."

Their gazes locked. Billie felt like an intruder. Finally, Sheridan dismounted and handed over her horse to a waiting groom. She left without comment, although Billie sensed her anger, boiling inside.

Billie looked at Nick and noted the strange twist to his lips. "Are you laughing at me?"

"This is called a grimace." Nick demonstrated while he talked. "Let's start with the basics. Now, this is a saddle."

Billie's look was deadpan.

Nick had no idea why he was taking up his valuable time. There was no telling what was going on back at the house, and seeing Sheridan again after all these months had left him shaken. He had enough problems, and Billie Pearce was only adding to them. "This is a stirrup."

"Mr. Kaharchek—"

"Pay attention. Now, you slide it up snug against the saddle like this. This is a girth. You unhitch the girth and the saddle slides off. You can take the saddle pads off the horse at the same time." He motioned for a stable hand lurking just inside the barn. From the look on the kid's face—bafflement and amusement— he'd witnessed the whole thing. Nick avoided eye contact. Instead, he handed the saddle to the youth and in turn took a blue nylon halter from him.

He pulled Billie toward Zeke's head. "Always leave the reins over the horse's neck while you're removing the bridle." He placed her hand behind Zeke's ears. "This strip of leather is called the 'crown piece.' You gently slide it over the horse's ears and—" He paused when Billie's face suddenly registered pain. Her face went white. "Something wrong?"

"He's . . . on . . . my . . . foot! The dumb—son—of a horse—is on my—foot!" She tried to shove Zeke, but it was like trying to move Mount Everest. Tears smarted her eyes.

Nick reacted quickly; one firm touch, and the big chestnut gelding calmly shifted away from Billie. She stared wide-eyed at her brand-new riding boot, perfectly branded with the imprint of Zeke's shoe. She gasped in pain. "My foot is broken. It's probably shattered." She glared at the horse. Was she just imagining the smug expression? She'd seen that same look on Sheridan Flock's face. "You did that on purpose," she accused. She shot a glance at Nick. "He obviously finds it amusing."

Nick had to agree. It did look as though Zeke were smiling. "I'll have the stable hand shoot him immediately." He signaled for the hovering boy to take Zeke away and brush him down before putting him into his stall.

"That's not a damn bit funny," Billie said as she watched the horse walk away with a jaunty sway of its hips. If body language was anything to go by, the animal clearly thought it was the victor in their little encounter. As for her, jaunty swaying was out of the question. She couldn't put any weight on her foot. "I'll never walk again," she wailed.

"Mrs. Pearce, please calm down." Nick sighed. Just when he thought things couldn't get worse. The woman was really hurt. She'd probably managed not to sign a release form and would likely sue the pants off him. His insurance company would cancel. His polo school would be history.

And she was hurt. That was the worst part. His protective instincts snapped alive. Her pretty eyes were swimming with tears she refused to shed. He purposefully lowered his gaze, focusing instead on the belligerent set to her chin, and decided she probably was brave, even if it didn't look that way at the moment.

He scooped her into his arms and turned toward the barn. Her mouth popped open in surprise, but he felt her arms circle around his neck as though she realized she had no choice. She pressed against him for support. Just what he needed after having her fall full length against him, coming in contact with him in all the right places.

He envisioned her children and their friends coming home at the end of the day to the smell of home-made cookies and tall glasses of milk. He envied them, wondered if they realized how lucky they were. Having been raised by one of the wealthiest and most powerful families in the state, he'd had little opportunity for warm, straight-out-of-the-oven cookies and cold milk.

Billie shifted, and the soft material of her tank top brushed against his bare arms. She felt soft and curvy and feminine, a nice contrast to the women he'd dated who felt they could never be thin enough.

He owed Zeke a nice red apple.

Damn. He had no business thinking how soft and warm Billie Pearce was. She had "room mother" and "PTA spokesperson" written all over her pretty face. She would never consider a three-day weekend filled with sun, fun, and great sex. She was different, and she wouldn't appreciate knowing he was aroused just thinking about her.

Inside the barn, Nick plunked her down on a bench. "How does it feel?"

"Smushed."

"Smushed?"

Lord, she was talking like her sixth-graders. "How do you think it feels?" she snapped. "It feels like a horse crushed it to smithereens."

"We have to get the boot off."

"Oh, no you don't! Not without ordering me a morphine drip."

He almost smiled. "Mrs. Pearce, I need to examine your foot. That means I have to pull off the boot."

"Okay, fine. Perhaps after that you can have me drawn and quartered." Billie sucked in her breath and gripped the bench as he gingerly worked the boot off her injured foot. She closed her eyes, trying to remember the breathing techniques she'd learned in Lamaze class years before as she prepared for labor and delivery when her children were born. She took a deep cleansing breath and concentrated on the top of Nick's head.

She wanted to touch it, run her fingers through the

silky strands. It was the color of black coffee, thick, satiny, falling in lazy waves across his forehead and curling over his ears.

Another deep breath. He probably had hair all over the place. Something fluttered in her stomach. She was delirious with pain; that was the only excuse she could come up with for allowing her mind to run amuck with thoughts of his body. Another cleansing breath. She blew out through her mouth.

"What are you doing?"

"Huh?" Billie blinked and found Nick watching her curiously. His mouth was set in a grim line. She wondered if he had a sense of humor. Not that the occasion called for it. "I'm trying to get my mind off the pain."

His look softened. "I'm sorry." He eased the boot from her foot and peeled back her sock as she continued to grip the sides of the bench. She really was trying to be brave. He stood, hands on hips, and uttered an expletive. "It's swollen."

"Imagine that." Nevertheless, she was relieved to have the boot off. Her foot *was* beginning to swell and change color, seemingly right before her eyes. Not very attractive. Her only saving grace was that she had taken the time to paint her toenails the night before. That and the fact that Miss High-and-mighty wasn't there to witness her second accident of the day. Who was she to Nick anyway? Billie wondered. "It's turning purple," she said.

Nick shook his head. It was her right foot. She wasn't going to be able to drive. Someone was going to have to take her to the hospital to get the foot

X-rayed. He could ask Arnie Bates, the older stable groom, but the man's disposition had soured considerably since Nick had caught him smoking in the stable, something that was forbidden. The only reason Nick hadn't fired him on the spot was that Arnie's wife was pregnant, and they needed the money. And because Arnie had needed a break.

Someone was going to have to take her home as well, Nick reminded himself. He felt his stomach sink at the possibility that it would, most likely, be him. He could already hear himself volunteering. Not that he was averse to being in the company of a beautiful woman, but he had his own worries—his cousins. Deedee was alone in his house, and Max was wandering about the property, up to God knew what. Nick would have almost preferred having Zeke step on his foot to leaving the pair unsupervised.

Deedee was not his greatest concern. She might be a little harebrained, but she wasn't dangerous. Not like Max.

Nick glanced at his watch. Eleven o'clock. Chances were, Deedee was still sleeping. He'd left her a full pot of coffee. Everything should be fine . . . unless she decided to make herself lunch. Slim possibility, he decided. It wouldn't occur to her to prepare her own food, even if she ate on a regular basis, which she didn't, because she was more interested in keeping her model's figure. Max, on the other hand, was hiding out and could do a lot of damage if left to his own devices. Nick gave a weary sigh. He would simply have to take his chances where the boy was concerned. At least for now, since there didn't seem to be any choice in the matter.

"You're not going to be able to drive with that foot, and you need to see a doctor."

Arnie started past them.

"Can you cover for me for a bit?" Nick said. "I need to take Mrs. Pearce to the emergency room."

The other man glanced at Billie's foot. "Yeah, sure."

Billie didn't think the groom looked very happy about it.

Nick reached for the boot, handing it to Billie, and, once again, lifted her in his arms. They exited the barn. "What's his problem?" she whispered, motioning to the stable groom.

Nick shrugged. "He's having a bad day. Don't mind him."

Most of the students had left, with the exception of a few who still lingered, talking among themselves, probably comparing notes on their first lesson. Nick looked at the cars remaining in the field beside the barn. "Which one is yours?"

Billie fished in her pocket for her keys. "The green minivan."

A mom-van, he thought. He could almost picture her with a van full of youngsters, laughing, their metal braces flashing in the sun. He was sure he'd find animal crackers and a box of Wet-Wipes in the back seat.

A simple hospital run, he told himself. They'd be in and out in no time. Max wouldn't have time to do much damage. Maybe. In the meantime, Nick would take the first opportunity to convince Billie to give up polo. He had his hands full in more ways than one, and the last thing he needed in his life was a woman like Billie Pearce.

Even if he was a man who enjoyed a good challenge.

CHAPTER TWO

Two hours later Nick turned into Billie's subdivision: a small cluster of fairly new, large brick colonials on the outskirts of Purcellville. The houses sat on nicely landscaped quarter-acre lots. Each yard contained its share of flowering dogwood, cherry, and crabapple trees. The nether parts of the houses were cloaked in azalea, boxwood, spreading juniper, and holly. Silver-dollar-sized cedar chips kept order around the trees and where beds of impatiens, phlox, and begonia grew.

Everything looked neat and orderly, Nick thought. So normal. Quite fitting for a woman like Billie Pearce.

She pointed to a house nestled in the cul-de-sac. "That's mine."

Nick parked the minivan in the driveway and, ice pack in one hand, helped Billie hobble to the door on a single crutch that she'd insisted she hadn't needed but now seemed grateful for. X-rays had not detected any broken bones, but the foot would be sore for a few days. It was badly swollen and tinted a bilious green and purple.

"You'll need to call for a ride home," Billie said, standing aside as Nick unlocked her front door. She was glad she'd straightened the kitchen before she left. There would be clutter; there was always clutter in a house where children lived, but at least the place was presentable.

Nick nodded. He did need to call for a ride, but he wasn't in a hurry. Sheridan had probably already phoned by now, and he wasn't eager for the conversation that awaited. He almost preferred having Max and Deedee run amok than facing his ex-fiancée. Besides, he and Billie had spent the past couple of hours at the hospital together, and he hadn't once mentioned she try another hobby. He wanted to do it in a way that wouldn't hurt her feelings.

Who was he fooling?

He was suddenly curious to see how Billie Pearce lived. It didn't matter that he could almost see the words "hands off" stamped across her forehead, or that she was the complete opposite of what he wanted in a woman; there was an alluring side of her that made him want to take a closer peek.

He turned the knob and pushed the door open wide

enough for her to enter. "I'll bet you have a dog with floppy ears, and a cat that sleeps curled up in a wing-back chair all day," he said.

"Um, well, she doesn't sleep there *all* day." Billie stepped inside and he followed. "The phone is in the kitchen. Would you like a cup of coffee?" Now why had she gone and done that? she asked herself.

He saw the doubt in her eyes and knew she had offered the coffee more out of a sense of politeness than a need for him to hang around. That made it all the more desirable to accept.

"Sure." He closed the front door behind him and, once again, followed her, this time into a large country kitchen with an old-fashioned round oak table and four upholstered chairs. It was situated in front of a large bay window that overlooked the backyard, where a vegetable garden had been planted. The room looked inviting. He grinned at the sight of a little-bear cookie jar.

"Just as I thought," he said and lifted the lid. It was filled with chocolate-chip cookies.

"Help yourself," Billie said.

Munching his cookie, Nick glanced at the rest of the house. Her carpet, a mushroom color, had been chosen out of practicality, to accommodate children and pets running about, just as her beige walls would not show handprints as easily as white ones. She had added color in comfortable-looking overstuffed furniture of plaids and prints and bright throw pillows. Tasteful watercolors adorned the walls, as well as pictures of her children in various stages of growth.

"I like your place."

Billie headed for the coffeemaker, taking care with her foot. "It feels empty with my children gone. I can't seem to get used to being alone." She put in a fresh filter and reached for her coffee canister.

Nick helped himself to another cookie. "Off at camp?"

"Off with their father," she said, giving a disparaging frown. "He took them to Disney World."

Nick pondered it while she put the coffee on to brew. He was being nosy, but he didn't care. He noted the look on her face and wanted to learn more. "Unfriendly divorce?"

Billie slouched into a chair at the kitchen table and propped her injured foot on the one beside it. "The divorce has been great. It was the marriage that had problems." Why had she told him that? she wondered. She almost never spoke ill of her ex, especially in front of the children. She was feeling sorry for herself, that's all.

Nick looked at her expectantly.

Billie saw the look and shrugged. She'd probably never see the man after today, so what did it matter? "An early mid-life crisis," she said, waving her hand in the air as though to make light of it. As though it hadn't mattered, when, in fact, it had mattered very much. "He hit thirty and took a nosedive. I should have suspected something was amiss when he got a membership to a tanning salon."

"And after he got a tan, he got a sports car and a girlfriend?"

"Something like that." Billie sighed. In retrospect, the marriage had never been that wonderful. She'd married a man who wasn't ready for monogamy. He'd made an effort in the early years, but as time passed, he'd felt more and more confined, restless. She had blamed herself. Perhaps she could have done more. After having been divorced for four years, she found that time had dulled the trauma of rejection. Still, it hadn't completely erased the occasional pang of guilt.

She straightened her shoulders. She was not one to dwell on the past, but she had certainly learned from it. She might not have been the world's greatest wife, although she knew in her heart she'd given it her best shot, but she was a terrific mother. And she was a good teacher—the best darn teacher at Purcellville Elementary the previous year. She had an award that said so. And she had a green thumb that kept fresh vegetables on the table for two growing children.

Nick saw the slight tightening of her mouth and knew his prying had opened old wounds. He decided to change the subject. "You didn't take your pain pill."

No wonder her foot hurt like the dickens, Billie thought. It throbbed as though, well, as though a damn horse had stepped on it. "I try to avoid medication, even aspirin if I can help it. I'm overly sensitive to it."

She was trying to be tough again, Nick thought, just as she'd balked at the idea of using a crutch. "The doctor wouldn't have given it to you if he didn't think you needed it." He glanced at the sample packet they'd given her. "My dentist has prescribed this pain-killer to me before. It's very mild." He found a glass and filled it with water.

Billie hesitated for a moment before popping the pill into her mouth and following it with the water.

Nick realized he might have acted too quickly. "You probably shouldn't have taken it on an empty stomach."

"Now you tell me."

The coffee had finished dripping through. He'd only planned to grab a quick cup, dissuade her against her polo career, and be on his way, but he couldn't just leave her. She needed food, and she probably wouldn't go to the trouble with her bum foot.

Face it, Kaharchek, he told himself, you're in no hurry to leave.

"How about some lunch?" he said, turning to her refrigerator. "I bet there are great leftovers in here."

Billie had to shake her head at the sight of Nick Kaharchek, renowned playboy and newspaper mogul, with his nose in her refrigerator. He was one of those people who never looked out of place. He'd seemed perfectly comfortable in the hospital, doing his best to reassure her and asking the doctor all the right questions so that Billie didn't have to try to concentrate in her state of discomfort. He was obviously a man who had no trouble taking control when the situation called for it; he was taking charge of her kitchen as though it were completely natural.

"Help yourself," Billie said, wondering at the change in him. Was this the same man who'd been so aloof on the polo field? She studied him as he moved about the room with an ease that surprised her. "You know, you're much more mellow in a kitchen than you are on a horse. Do you always experience

this change of personality when confronted with a refrigerator?"

"Cookie fumes," Nick told her, hauling out a platter
of lasagna. "They go straight to my head." He located
plates and put sliced squares of lasagna onto them,
stuck one inside the microwave and turned the timer
to three minutes. "So, how many kids do you have?"

"Two. A son and daughter, ages eight and ten."
Billie continued to watch him. He seemed to be moving about slowly and deliberately, as though he had
all the time in the world. Was he stalling? She suddenly wondered why he was hanging around. The
man wanted something. She'd cut her teeth on sixth-
grade con men. What was *Kaharchek* after? Surely he
had better things to do. She thought of Miss Sheridan
Flock who, no doubt, was waiting by the phone for
his call. The come-hither look she'd given him had
left no doubts in Billie's mind that the woman was
ready, willing, and able.

Her mind searched for answers. Was he afraid of
a lawsuit? Was he trying to butter her up with lunch
and that knockout smile in hopes of winning her over?
It probably worked on most females, but she wasn't
buying. The man was a known womanizer. A hunk
with money. He could have any woman he wanted.

So why was he spending time with a divorced
mother of two? He'd given no indication that he even
liked her. Okay, she had to admit there was a slight
physical attraction. Well, maybe the attraction was
more than just slight, she told herself, remembering
how her body had reacted when she'd fallen on top
of him and all their body parts had touched.

She had her reasons. She still believed the old-fashioned notions that sharing a bed with a man meant love, commitment, and ultimately marriage, beliefs that sent ice water through the loins of most men nowadays. But she'd made up her mind long ago never again to settle for less.

"You miss them, don't you?"

"Huh?" Billie realized she had been lost in her own thoughts. Her shoulders slumped. "Yes. I should have signed up to teach summer school like I usually do, but I wanted to have time with my children. I should have taken into account they'd be gone. Not only that, most of my friends are teaching, so I don't see them much." Lord, she sounded downright pathetic.

"Is that why you decided to take polo lessons?"

She was beginning to feel light-headed. "That's one of the reasons."

"Why'd you choose that particular sport?"

"You mean why did I choose something that I'm really no good at?" She didn't give him a chance to respond. "You'll think it's silly."

"Try me anyway."

"I want to be good at something. Anything. My children's father excels at sports. Big football star in high school, hockey star in college. He skis like he was born wearing them, he has a cabinet full of tennis trophies, and now he has taken up skydiving. The kids think he's some kind of superhero."

"Surely you're good at something."

"I've tried bowling, but I had a bad habit of throwing the ball into the next lane. I think the manager was thankful when I turned in my shoes. I couldn't hit a tennis ball if my life depended on it, and I was such a klutz the few times my ex-husband took me snow-skiing, he began insisting I stay inside by the fire and drink hot chocolate. The one time I tried sailing, I fell in the water and had to be fished out."

Nick found it hard to believe that she could be so bad at everything, but the earnest look on her face convinced him she was telling the truth. He was thoughtful. "I'll bet your ex can't make chocolate-chip cookies. And where do your kids go when they need help with their homework or have a bad cold?" He thought of his own mother. She could have organized a dinner party for fifty at a moment's notice, but she couldn't have made a simple grilled-cheese sandwich if someone had been pointing a gun at her. "Not all mothers are good at that sort of thing, and some just don't take the time." He saw that his words were having very little effect on Billie. But how could he expect to help her when he had so much else on his mind?

"How long will they be gone?" he asked, changing the subject.

"Huh?" Billie realized that she had lost her train of thought again.

Nick noticed the dazed look in her eyes, and wondered if it was the medicine already at work. "Your children? How long will they be away?"

"A month."

He perked. "A month?"

"May as well be a year."

At first he just stared, but his mind was already

beginning to race. He didn't like what he was thinking. "A whole month? That *is* a long time, considering there are almost five weeks in this month."

"Thanks for making me feel better," she said, annoyed as she watched him put the lasagna aside. He removed lettuce, tomatoes, and whatever else he could find in her refrigerator, and began preparing a salad. Talk about a man knowing his way around a kitchen, and this wasn't even his kitchen. She didn't quite know what to make of it, except that he seemed to be finding ways to hang around longer than necessary. He was being too precise with the salad, tearing the lettuce into perfect bite-sized pieces and quartering the tomatoes so carefully that Martha Stewart would have been impressed. She was glad she didn't have radishes on hand; probably he would have made florets out of them.

Yes, he was definitely killing time.

Billie rearranged her foot, studying the look on his face. He had something on his mind, but what? She could feel the pain pill taking effect already, making her woozy-headed. If he did have an ulterior motive for being there, for preparing her lunch, she was at a clear disadvantage.

Perhaps he was simply concerned about her, she thought, trying to give him the benefit of the doubt. She had become more suspicious where men were concerned since her divorce. "After Disney World, they're going down to the Keys," Billie said after a moment, "and I'm miserable." Had she confided too much? Her eyelids felt heavy, gritty. She propped her elbows on the table. One slipped, surprising her, throwing her off balance. She began to topple.

Nick was there to catch her. "Whoa. Are you okay?"

"I'm fading fast. I knew I shouldn't have taken that pain pill. I warned you."

"You definitely need food." He helped her straighten in the chair. "Can you hang on just a minute?"

"Shur."

Nick grabbed the plate of lasagna from the microwave and began searching for flatware. He wouldn't worry about the salad at the moment, he just wanted to get something in her stomach, at least keep her coherent until he got what he wanted.

What he wanted.

He really was a cad, as so many women had pointed out once they got that certain look in their eyes—the one they wore while daydreaming about bridal gowns and wedding bands and babies—the look that sent him racing for the hills like a champion sprinter. But he was a desperate cad. And Billie Pearce had the answer to one of his problems. Fate had obviously sent her his way—it was the only possible explanation. He had a twinge of guilt over the rotten thing he was about to do to her but brushed it aside. It was necessary. And for a good cause, he reminded himself.

He joined her at the table and cut the lasagna in bite-sized pieces. "Okay, open up."

"What are you doing?"

"Getting food into you."

"I'm perfectly capable of feeding myself." She made a swipe for the fork and missed. When she managed to grab it, the fork slipped through her fingers and clattered onto the wooden table.

"Maybe not," he said, wondering if the medication would work for or against him. "Let me help you."

Billie was too sleepy to argue. She opened her mouth, and he forked a piece of the warm lasagna inside. "Okay, chew."

She did as she was told. "I need something to drink."

Nick jumped from the chair and opened the refrigerator. He found a diet soft drink inside and grabbed it, then threw open the freezer door and reached inside an ice bin.

"The ice maker doesn't work," Billie said. "Hasn't worked in years and nobody can seem to fix it."

He pulled out an ice tray instead.

"I'll drink it from the can."

Nick popped the metal top and handed it to her. He waited until she took a long sip before coaxing more food into her mouth.

"You're very handy in the kitchen," Billie managed. "Do you like to cook?"

"I like to eat. Eating necessitates cooking. Here, take another bite."

"I'm full."

"You only ate three bites."

Billie cocked her head to the side, trying to understand what made the man tick. Nicholas Kaharchek was a strange one, indeed. He owned a string of polo ponies, a newspaper, and a huge patch of prime real estate. He'd arrived at the barn in a custom Mercedes 550 SL. Not someone you would expect to find preparing his own food. "You don't have a cook?"

"I have a male housekeeper, of sorts. But he hates to cook." Nick looked around the kitchen. "You know, this is a big house, lots of doors and windows in the place. Have you ever been robbed?"

The question took Billie by surprise. "No."

He tried to coax her into taking another bite, keeping his eyes averted. "You probably have an alarm system."

She shook her head.

"You really should have one. Especially since you're here all alone."

Surely he wasn't trying to sell her an alarm system, she thought. The man was already a millionaire.

"Of course, it would probably take weeks to get it installed."

Billie shifted uneasily in her seat. Odd that he should bring up alarm systems at a time like this. There *had* been some strange noises in her backyard since the children left, sounds she would probably have attributed to a stray cat digging through her trash or a simple breeze rustling the bushes outside her window, had she not been alone in the house. She gave a sigh of disgust. She was being ridiculous. He was making her nervous.

"This is a safe neighborhood," she said. Sure, there'd been a minor burglary some weeks back, but that was all. Besides, she added silently, Raoul, the bug man, made it his business to keep an eye on things.

Nick had seen the momentary flash of doubt in her eyes. Time to make his move. "It just occurred to me that we might be able to help each other."

Billie focused on his face. Here it comes, she thought, fighting grogginess and the strong urge to close her eyes. Here's the pitch.

"I have a friend who's looking for a place to stay for the next two weeks. You could rent one of your empty bedrooms to my friend, and then you wouldn't be all alone in this big house."

Billie pondered it as best she could in her present state. The idea was certainly appealing—the extra money would come in handy and having someone else close by might ease her night jitters. But a stranger in the house? The idea didn't sound appealing. "Why doesn't this friend stay with you?"

"That's the problem. She has been staying with me, but it's not working out."

Billie's eyebrows rose inquisitively. Not an easy task, considering it felt as though each lash were weighted. "She? Are you trying to dump a girlfriend on me? Boy, that's tacky." She shoved the plate of lasagna aside, folded her arms on the table, and put her head down.

Nick leaned down as well, trying to look into her eyes. He was losing her. He didn't want to sound desperate, but he had to move quickly. "We're related. Cousins," he added.

Billie yawned.

"She's nice, but she's a little, well . . . disorganized right now. She's getting married in two weeks, and she inadvertently canceled her apartment lease too soon. She literally found herself, luggage and all, on the street. I took her in."

"Nice of you," she managed.

"Uh-huh. But her fiancé isn't happy about her living with me. Thinks I'm a poor influence. Silly, huh?"

Billie gave up the fight and closed her eyes. " 'Magine that."

"And she doesn't want to move in with him before the wedding. Scruples and all that." Nick almost choked on the lie. Deedee wouldn't know a scruple from a truffle. After going through four husbands in five years, she knew enough not to move in before the marriage. Two weeks of living with Deedee and you were ready for the Foreign Legion.

"So, what do you say?"

Billie peered at him through one eye. "About what?"

"Will you let her stay for a couple of weeks?"

"Will you leave and let me go to sleep if I agree?"

He smiled. "After I finish off the lasagna and toss back a couple of cookies."

"Deal." Billie closed her eyes, too drowsy to move from the table to a more comfortable spot.

Relief flooded Nick, and for the third time that day, he hauled Billie into his arms and carried her to what looked to be the master bedroom. He was only vaguely aware of his surroundings, the smell of some flowery scent, the feminine decor. He'd just solved a major problem, and that was all that mattered at the moment.

Very gently, he laid Billie on her bed. She was so damn cute, with that turned-up nose that made her look more like a college girl than the mother of two. He felt like a real rat foisting Deedee on her, but he had no choice. It was dangerous for Deedee to stay at his place now. Max was out of control.

Besides, it would give him a chance to spend more time with Billie Pearce, and with her children gone, he might just be able to take her mind off missing them. And give him a chance to get his head on straight where Sheridan was concerned.

Of all times for Sheridan Flock to show up in his life again, it had to be just when he had come to terms with the end of their relationship.

CHAPTER THREE

Billie sat at her breakfast table, drinking coffee, wondering what had gone wrong. She hadn't intended to rent out a room. She hadn't intended to get spooked by all that talk about alarm systems. And she definitely hadn't intended to give in to Nick's soft brown eyes and thousand-watt smile. But she had. Somehow, he'd conned her into doing exactly what he'd wanted, and now she was sitting there, waiting for her boarder to arrive and dreading the thought.

It had to have been the pain pills; it was the only excuse she could come up with for taking a perfect stranger into her home. In fact, she only vaguely remembered agreeing to the whole ridiculous notion.

Having dispensed with her bothersome crutch, Billie hobbled to the door when she heard a vehicle pull into her driveway. She had a morbid desire to see the woman she would be living with for the next two weeks. She peered through the tiny window in the door.

A whirlwind of a woman hurled from the cab of a pickup truck and slammed the door. She was a tall redhead with milk-white porcelain skin and a model's figure that was emphasized in her spandex shorts and halter. Billie could hear the string of expletives pouring from the woman's mouth; they seemed to be centered around the fact she'd had to rise before noon. Billie didn't know which annoyed her most: the fact that the woman cursed like a truck driver or that she looked so good in spandex.

Either way, Billie wasn't happy to see her.

She swallowed hard and opened her front door to Nick, who was balancing three packing boxes in his arms.

He eased his cargo through the door and smiled warmly at Billie. "Good morning. How's the foot?"

Billie responded with a frown. She'd been had. He looked too happy, almost euphoric. In contrast to his passenger, who stood, arms folded across her ample chest, tapping her foot and glaring at him.

Nick made the introductions. "Billie, this is my cousin Deedee Holt. Deedee, this is Billie Pearce."

Deedee made an acknowledging noise that seemed to emanate from the back of her throat. The best Billie could manage was a nod.

"Well, I can see you two are going to get along

just fine," Nick said, backing toward the door.

"Not so fast," Billie said, then smiled prettily at Deedee. "I'd like to have a word with Nick. Would you excuse us?"

Deedee shrugged, headed for the sofa, and curled up, tucking the longest legs Billie had ever seen beneath her. "I need a nap anyway."

Billie shoved Nick outside. "We need to talk."

"Deedee is really very sweet," he whispered.

"Which is why you're in such an all-fired hurry to get rid of her."

"I've already explained everything. Trust me, you'll love her. Right now, she needs coffee. She's not used to getting up this early. Once she tosses back a couple of cups of caffeine she can charm the skin off a snake."

Billie recognized the man from the stable unloading the pickup. He wore the same disgruntled look as before, only this time she couldn't blame him. Two trunks, seven garment bags, thirteen cartons, and twelve pieces of matching luggage were efficiently stacked in Billie's foyer. He gave a grunt of disgust before making his way wordlessly toward the truck.

"Your stable hand is obviously having another bad day," she said.

Nick glanced over his shoulder. "Yeah, he's definitely got an attitude problem. Guess I need to talk to him. This would probably be a good time to do it."

"*After* you explain the meaning of all this." Billie pointed to the mountain of luggage.

"Deedee isn't what you'd call a light traveler," Nick said. "We'll bring the rest over tomorrow."

"The rest?"

"Only a few more things. Mostly shoes. My cousin is a bit of a clotheshorse." He checked his wristwatch. "Oops, got to run."

He was gone. Billie closed her eyes and took a deep breath, then opened them slowly. She went inside and regarded the woman on the sofa, who opened her eyes and gave a semblance of a smile.

"I guess you're stuck with me, huh? But don't worry, I can afford to pay my share. I'm rich, and I have a rich fiancé as well."

Deedee's voice was high-pitched and squeaky, making Billie think of Betty Boop. "Well, that certainly works to your advantage," she said, wondering if the woman had ever held a job. "Would you like some coffee?"

"I'd kill a Boy Scout for coffee."

Billie believed it. She hurried into the kitchen with Deedee on her heels. As she filled a mug, she searched her brain for innocent conversation. "Nick said you're cousins?"

Deedee lifted impossibly long, thick black lashes. "Yeah." She didn't sound particularly thrilled about it. "My mother is his father's sister. Nick and I practically grew up together. He used to do some of the most outrageous things. Made his father so mad. It was the only time the man ever noticed he had a son." Deedee inhaled her coffee. "Nick's father was heavy into making money."

"What about Nick? Is he into making money?"

Deedee shook her head. "Nick never gave much thought to money, but when you're filthy rich you don't have to think about it. All he cares about is his newspaper and those smelly horses. He gets up every morning at five-thirty to take care of them, even though he employs people for the job. Have you ever seen a horse up close?" Deedee shuddered.

Billie inadvertently looked down at her foot. The swelling had gone down during the night, and it wasn't as sore, but it would take a while before the discoloration went away. "Yes, unfortunately, I *have* seen a horse up close."

Deedee followed Billie's eyes to the foot. *"Ee-yeuuw,"* she said, wincing. "What happened to your foot?"

"You know Zeke? The big brown horse with the attitude? He stepped on it."

"Oh, honey, that's worth a lawsuit. And Nick is so rich he wouldn't miss the money."

Billie tried to hide her amusement as she sipped her coffee. Deedee was obviously annoyed at Nick. "I don't think I could get very much. Nothing's broken."

"Gee, that's too bad."

Billie decided the woman had a strange way of looking at things. She wiggled her toes. "I hope it's better by next weekend. I paid for three polo lessons in advance."

"You're taking polo lessons? Are you one of those horse-crazy people?" She looked distressed. "Oh, jeez, I hope you're not taking lessons just to get closer to Nick. There are a least three women in every class of his who want to marry him. Let me tell you, it's not worth it. I know Nick's handsome and charming and wealthy, but the man steps in poo, for God's sake. Horse droppings, you know? Who'd want to live with a man whose shoes always smell?"

Billie smiled. She was beginning to like Deedee. "Actually, I took a class for the exercise." That was only partially true, of course, but she wasn't ready to tell Deedee how much she wanted to impress her children.

"Exercise? *Eeyeuuw*. I hate exercise. It's easier if you don't eat."

"I can't afford to starve myself. I need energy."

"For what?"

"Well, I teach sixth grade all day, and then I come home and cook and clean and take care of my own two kids, and then after supper I iron or do lesson plans, and then I watch a little TV and go to bed."

Deedee's eyes opened wide. "You do all that? In one day?"

"Yes, but you see, I never get any real exercise. Pretty soon the cellulite will take over and my only alternative will be liposuction."

"Gross."

"Mmmm. Well, I'm going to whip myself into shape this summer. I've started jogging, too." Billie refilled their cups.

Deedee wrinkled her nose. "I tried that once, but I got sweaty. I hate to sweat."

Billie took a peek at Deedee over her coffee mug. "I don't mind sweating. I bought weights, too. And then I signed up for the polo lessons. I figured all that bouncing around would be great for my backside."

"Too bad you have to do it on a horse."

"I kind of like horses. At least I did before I met Zeke. I still have a lot to learn. Like how to mount and dismount."

"You want to learn how to mount? You've come to the right place, honey."

Billie was almost certain they weren't talking about the same thing. She watched Deedee sip her coffee. The woman had a great body. "You don't exercise at all?"

"I don't have to. Like I said, I don't eat. That's another thing about Nick. He eats all the time and never gets fat. After a while, you find yourself hoping he'll choke on his damn doughnut." Deedee sighed. "I haven't had a doughnut in five years. I figure I won't eat until I'm sixty-five, and then I'm going to let myself go. I'm going to eat boxes of candy, and fast food, and a ton of Twinkies."

"Sounds like a good plan to me."

Deedee swiveled in her seat and looked at her luggage in the hall. "I guess I should unpack. I don't suppose you have a housekeeper?"

Amazingly, the woman was serious. Billie shook her head. "I can't seem to keep good help these days." She limped to the foyer. Her foot was beginning to ache from being on it all morning. "I'll show you to the guest room. It's upstairs. Sorry I can't help you carry anything."

Deedee picked out a medium-sized suitcase. "I'll just take this one for now."

Once upstairs, Deedee stopped at the doorway to her bedroom. "*Eeyeuuw,* colonial. My bedroom is always French provincial. Don't you have any guest rooms that are French provincial?"

Billie was thankful for the patience she'd gained from teaching. "No. I'm not really a French provincial person."

Deedee dropped her suitcase on the bed. "Nick isn't, either. Once I redecorated his whole house. It was between my second and third marriages. No, wait, it was between my third and fourth." She waved her perfect ruby-red fingernails. "Anyway, I was staying with Nick for a while and he had to go off on a business trip, so I hired a decorator, and we worked overtime to have it finished before Nick got home." She sat down and tested the bed. "You should have seen the look on Nick's face. Megasurprise."

"Did he like it?" Billie already knew the answer.

"The man went berserk. Honestly, such a fuss over a few sticks of furniture. He has no taste." She opened the suitcase and looked petulant. "I thought I had my makeup in this one."

Billie cast a cursory glance at the bag. "Looks like lingerie."

"Damn." Deedee stomped off down the stairs, and began opening luggage. Finally she stood, hands on hips, and tossed her red hair over her shoulder. "It's not here. Nick must have left it with my shoes. He probably did it on purpose, knowing him."

"But you're wearing makeup."

Deedee shook her head. "This is my morning makeup. I have to change into afternoon makeup, and then when five o'clock rolls around I put on my evening makeup. There's a difference, you see."

"I would never have guessed, but I'm not exactly on the cutting edge when it comes to fashion and cosmetics." Billie's own makeup consisted of foundation, blush, and mascara.

"I'm an ex–beauty queen, honey. I *had* to learn these things at an early age."

"A beauty queen. No kidding."

"Won my first pageant when I was four years old. Went on to win—" She paused and her pretty brow furrowed in thought. "Oh, I have to stop doing that," she said, immediately raising her brows so the wrinkles disappeared. She smoothed her forehead with her fingers as though to wipe away all traces. "Anyway, I don't actually remember how many I've won, but you should see all my trophies." She hitched her chin proudly. "I know how to work an audience, bu-lieve-you-me."

Billie nodded. "I'm impressed."

"Which is why I need my makeup. I can't afford to let myself go." She sighed heavily. "I know Nick did this on purpose. First, he literally dragged me out of bed at dawn and ordered me to pack my clothes with the help of some field hand with the disposition of a troll. That didn't stop him from leering at me every chance he got, mind you. Then, if that weren't bad enough, Nick threw me *and* my designer luggage in the pickup he uses to haul hay and horse feed and only-God-knows-what. Are you believing this? I was literally traumatized by the whole thing." She paused and shuddered. "I would never have agreed to any of it had my little sports car not been in the shop. No telling when I'll get it back. That's the price you pay for driving foreign cars.

"I'll bet Nick's having a good laugh over it right now," she went on without stopping for air. "He knows damn well I can't do without my shoes. Why, I wouldn't think of walking out of this house without the right shoes. I need to borrow your telephone, honey. Nick either brings my stuff or I'm going to pitch a fit the likes of which this town has never seen."

Billie immediately reached for the portable wall phone and handed it to her. "Here," she said. There was something in Deedee's voice that told her the woman meant business, and Billie was in no mood for fit-pitching.

An hour later, Nick arrived with five cartons of shoes and three more pieces of luggage. "How's it going?" he asked Billie, making a special effort to keep his tone light.

She cocked an eyebrow. "I'd like to see you in the kitchen."

"I really should be getting back to the stable. I had to fire a guy, and he didn't take it well."

"In the kitchen, Kaharchek." It was the voice she used to order her students to the principal's office when she caught them playing doctor in the utility closet. No one walked away from that voice. Not even Nick Kaharchek.

He followed her into the kitchen and stood with his back supported by the refrigerator, his hands stuffed into the pockets of well-washed jeans, his feet crossed at the ankles in fake nonchalance. Billie looked at his moccasins and noticed they were clean. Deedee should be excited about that. "You wanted to see me?" he said.

She hobbled to the coffeepot, poured herself another cup of coffee, and took a sip before answering. Another technique she'd learned as a sixth-grade teacher. Authoritative stalling. Never give your victim the upper hand. Always make him wait for that dreaded first sentence. Yessir, everyone knew Mrs. Pearce could make a twelve-year-old squirm, if the situation required it.

Nick didn't squirm quite so easily. He continued to watch her with a steady gaze that was tempered by a slight curve at the corners of his mouth. He wasn't sure if she was working herself into a frenzy, or calming herself down to be civilized; but damned if she wasn't cute, with her discolored foot and flattering running shorts. She had the most perfect legs he'd ever seen. Slightly tanned, smooth-skinned, shapely. He could only imagine those legs wrapped around his waist.

"You're not using your crutch," he said, hoping to chase away his lewd thoughts.

"It's bothersome. I don't need it."

"But the doctor said—"

"That's not why I wanted to talk to you." He simply stood there, his gaze fixed on her legs. Her scare tactics weren't working, Billie realized. Sixth-grade boys were usually quaking by now, but Nick was looking at her as if she were lunch. "Hello!" she called out, trying to get his attention.

He dragged his eyes back to her face. "Mmmm?"

"This was really rotten of you. That woman—" She pointed toward the stairs which led to the bedroom where Deedee was presently napping. "She's going to drive me right over the edge before dinnertime."

"Who, Deedee?" He feigned a look of surprise.

"Don't give me that innocent look. You just didn't want to live with her, so you foisted her off on me."

Nick sighed. She spoke the truth. He was relieved to have Deedee out of his house—she tended to get on his nerves at times—but he would never have dumped her on Billie if it hadn't been absolutely necessary. Max made it necessary. And he had other things on his mind as well.

"Admit it."

Without waiting for an invitation, he poured himself a cup of coffee, and Billie ground her teeth, peeved because he was making *her* wait, using one of her manipulative devices to his own advantage.

"I really do feel bad about it," he said, trying to sound remorseful, "but you have to understand, I just can't serve any more time with her. I was stuck with her for three months between husbands two and three . . . or was it three and four?"

"Well, I don't want a stranger in my house so you'll just have to take her back."

"Oh, no." Nick sipped his coffee. "Possession is nine-tenths of the law. You have her. You're going to have to keep her. I'm willing to pay."

"There's not enough money in the world." Billie

leaned forward with determination and stuck her face an inch from his. She could see the stubble on his jaw. "Listen up, Kaharchek. This is my vacation, and I don't intend to spend it listening to someone squealing *'Eeyeuuw'* all the time, cramming all that luggage in my foyer, and complaining because my furniture isn't French provincial."

"I can arrange to have a new bedroom suite delivered in an hour."

"That's not the way things are done around here. I make do with what I have."

"She's not a bad person, you know. She's just difficult to live with. She's very . . . um, unique."

"I want her out."

Nick, usually quick on his feet, had trouble concentrating with her so close. He could smell her shampoo, the soap she'd used when bathing, and the light talcum powder she'd sprinkled on herself after toweling dry.

Once again he tried to clear his mind. "Look, I'll make a deal. I'll give you free riding lessons if you'll keep her. By the time your kids return you'll be playing polo like a professional. I can even have you jumping fences." It was a lie, of course. He couldn't imagine Billie Pearce *climbing* a fence without hurting herself.

Billie pondered his offer. Free riding and polo lessons? Jumping fences? She could almost see the looks of awe on her children's faces. "How many free riding lessons?"

Nick thought for a moment. "Three." Three lessons would give him the time he needed to woo her into his bed. Lord, but he could be a jerk at times.

"Do I have 'stupid' written across my forehead, Kaharchek? I can't possibly accomplish all that with three lessons. Forget it." Once again she pointed toward Deedee's sleeping quarters. "Take her back."

She was tough. "All right, then. You can have as many lessons as you want."

As many lessons as she wanted? At no cost? And Deedee was paying rent to boot. *Now* he was speaking her language. Surely she could put up with some prissy, empty-headed ex–beauty queen for two weeks.

"Name the horse."

"You won't have to ride Zeke."

"I want a gentle horse, and a promise from you that you won't laugh if I throw my mallet halfway across the field. No wisecracks, not from you *or* your friend, Miss Flock."

Nick set his coffee cup on the counter and looked at her. "You're pushing it. Besides, I have no control over Sheridan."

"Take it or leave it."

Nick pondered it. He hated being outwitted. He never would have become as successful as he had if he weren't a good businessman, a good negotiator. But Billie Pearce had him by the short hairs, and she knew it. How he would keep Sheridan away was another matter since she boarded her horse at his stable. But he would promise anything; he was just that desperate.

"Okay, deal." Nick offered his hand, and they shook. Giving in had been his first mistake, touching Billie his second. The gentle stirring beneath his belt reminded him of what it had felt like having her fall on top of him. He tightened his grip on her hand, noted the flash of surprise in her eyes, and decided what the hell. If she slapped his face it would be well worth it.

He pulled her hand to his mouth. "Deal," he repeated, kissing the soft center of her palm while fantasizing running his tongue between each finger with tantalizing slowness. There was more to Billie Pearce than chocolate-chip cookies, and despite their obvious differences, he wanted to explore her, taste her on his tongue and savor her.

Billie stood there, stupefied and transfixed, as Nick moved his lips up her forearm, kissing the sensitive inside. What did the man think he was doing! Had he lost his mind? Was he as crazy as the woman in her bedroom? Not that she was any better because she was allowing it!

Billie licked her bottom lip, preparing to give him the verbal beating of a lifetime when he raised his head and brushed his lips across hers.

All thinking ceased.

Nick knew he was a goner the minute he touched Billie's mouth. What on earth had possessed him to do such a thing? Nevertheless, he couldn't seem to stop himself. He pulled her closer, slipping one arm around her waist so he could feel her body against his. One thing was certain, he liked making deals with Billie Pearce, even if she'd gotten the upper hand this time. She felt good in his arms, her skin smooth and cool in her air-conditioned house. His mind ran amok at images of her hot and rumpled in his bed.

Billie finally regained her wits and jerked away. "This isn't part of the deal, Kaharchek. I'm sure most women would be flattered, but I don't do business this way."

He simply smiled, which unnerved her. If she'd been a violent woman she would have slapped the smirk right off his face.

"Perhaps we can work out a few more deals. I like negotiating with you." Actually, he enjoyed her lively banter.

She tossed him a suspicious look. "What kind of deal?"

Nick grinned and pressed his lips against her ear. "I could teach you other things," he whispered.

Billie felt the beginnings of a gigantic shiver at the base of her backbone, and tried to suppress it as best she could. She grabbed a wooden spoon from a jar on the counter and whacked him with it. He gave her that bone-melting grin. She took another swipe at him, but he jumped away. "Careful now," he teased. "You don't want to risk another injury."

She gave him her most menacing look as he gazed back at her calmly, still smiling, as though he knew something she didn't. Like how his kiss had affected her. Oh, but the man was smug. He knew what he did to women, and he played them like a tune. He winked at her, and she was tempted to grab her cookie jar and throw it at him.

"You're just lucky I'm at a disadvantage!" she shouted to his retreating back. "You're just lucky I can't catch you. You're lucky I can't send you to the principal's office!" He chuckled and called out a goodbye before closing the front door behind him.

Billie stared dumbstruck at her palm and the inside of her arm. He'd kissed her! Nick Kaharchek had just kissed her as though he had every right. And he had done a fine job of it if the quivering in her stomach was any indication. She touched her lips. It had been all she could do to keep from crumpling into a heap at his feet. No one had ever kissed her and left her weak-kneed before. No wonder his students went goo-goo-eyed over him. Even Miss Flock, who seemed as cool as a cucumber, had given him the come-on. And no one had ever offered her such an outrageous suggestion in her ear . . . not even her ex-husband who, toward the end, had come up with some pretty bizarre ideas.

"Eeyeuuw," Deedee called from the living room. "There's a dog in here."

Billie jumped, startled. She hadn't heard Deedee come down the stairs. "That's Buffy. She's a cocker spaniel, and she's very friendly."

"I've never lived with a dog before. Nick has dogs, but they stay outside or in the kitchen, and I try to stay out of those places."

"You don't go outside or into the kitchen?" The woman was becoming weirder by the moment.

"I avoid the outdoors because I can't risk having the sun on my face. I'd rather bake my face in a 350-degree oven than lie in the sun. As for the kitchen, I try to stay as far away from food as possible. The only time I allow myself near one is to pour a cup of coffee." She looked at the dog and shuddered. "Does it shed?"

Billie limped into the living room. "I brush her every day. I've always had a dog. When I was a kid I had a big old collie."

"Was its name Lassie?"

"Nope. Her name was Annie. She used to sleep at the foot of my bed. Hardly left any room for me."

"Does Buffy sleep at the foot of your bed like Annie used to?"

Billie shook her head no. "Buffy sleeps with my ten-year-old daughter, Christie. And Spot, the cat, belongs to my eight-year-old son, Joel."

"You have a cat, too? Oh, I hope my allergies don't start acting up. There's not a face concealer on the market that will hide a red nose."

Billie made a note to stop brushing the cat, then immediately felt guilty.

"Nick said your kids were at Disney World. Boy, I love Disney World. I've been there seven times. I always wear a hat, of course. And plenty of sunscreen."

"I've never been to Disney World. I'm not much of a traveler. I guess I'm a homebody."

Deedee looked at her seriously. "I think it's cute that you're a homebody. I bet you're a great mother."

Billie smiled. It was the first nice thing Deedee had said. "Thanks. I try to be, but sometimes it's hard when you're on your own. I keep thinking to myself, if I'm such a great mother, then why don't my kids have a great father?"

"Gee, that's deep. How long have you been divorced?"

"Four years."

"Four years! Honey, what are you waiting for?" she cried. "I've gone through three husbands in the past four years. A woman can't afford to wait around forever, you know. One day you'll wake up, and find your butt sagging to your ankles. You need to get moving, honey, before gravity takes over."

Billie slumped in a chair. She felt the beginnings of a headache and considered taking another pain pill. She almost preferred being knocked out to spending the rest of the day listening to Deedee. Two weeks suddenly sounded like a life sentence.

"Hey, I know," Deedee said. "I could help you find a husband. I'm good at that sort of thing. I just have trouble hanging on to them. That's why I absolutely refuse to sign a prenuptial agreement. Trust me, I live quite well on alimony checks."

Billie almost laughed out loud at the thought of Deedee's husbands trying to buy their sanity back during divorce negotiations. And she could only imagine the kind of man Deedee would choose for her. "It's nice of you to offer, but I think I'd rather find my own husband. It's, um, personal, you know?"

"How do you plan to meet a man if you're a homebody? Mr. Perfect isn't going to come knocking at your door and sweep you off your feet, you know? And I'm very discreet at this sort of thing."

Billie suspected Deedee was about as discreet as a runaway train. "I have my own idea of what I want in a man," Billie said, wondering how she would worm her way out of Deedee's matchmaking scheme, but the woman wore a look of sheer determination that told Billie it wouldn't be easy. "And to tell you the truth, I'm kinda, sorta interested in a man already." She thought of the chemistry teacher who was about as interesting as a week-old newspaper. She could always play him up.

Deedee rolled her eyes. "Tell me it's not Nick."

Billie stared at her. "Nick?" She hadn't thought of using Nick as a way out.

"Like I said, all the women are hot for him. You should see how his students simper when he passes by. It's downright disgusting the way they carry on."

Billie pondered it. Deedee had just given her the answer she needed. Nick Kaharchek was the perfect man to fend off any unwanted matchmaking on Deedee's part. Besides, what man in his right mind would go up against one of Loudoun County's wealthiest and most successful citizens? Not to mention Nick's looks. And Nick would never have to know.

Besides, he owed her.

Billie pressed her hand against her forehead and gave a dramatic sigh. "I must tell you the truth, Deedee," she said, "although I trust you'll keep this in the strictest confidence. I'm no better than the other women who lust after Nick. I can't help myself."

Deedee answered with a blank look. She was obviously clueless. "What are you saying?"

"I'm hot for him, Deedee. I'm like a volcano on the verge of erupting." Damn, she was good. "Every time I see him I can feel this fiery heat in my belly, coiling and twisting like a giant tornado, so fierce and tumultuous I fear it will spew forth like molten lava and spit fire toward the heavens."

Deedee gaped at her. *"Eeyeuuw!"*

CHAPTER FOUR

Billie studied the inside of her freezer and wondered what frozen dinner she could microwave herself for lunch. She had a choice. Low-fat chicken and vegetables, low-fat chicken with fettuccini noodles, or fat-free chicken soup. She closed the door and leaned her head against it.

She would have given her good foot for a juicy, medium-rare steak, seasoned fries, and a tossed green salad, swimming in thick blue-cheese dressing. And something chocolate, of course. A meal was not a meal without some sort of chocolate for dessert.

The house was quiet. Deedee was taking her second nap of the day, this one due to a migraine brought on by Billie's confession of her feelings for Nick. Okay, so she had overdone it a bit talking about lava and spewing fire, but Deedee had gotten the message loud and clear. Billie hadn't counted on giving her a headache; she had simply tried to put the quietus on Deedee's plan to find her a man.

Billie turned as someone tapped on the back door. She was almost relieved to see the familiar face of Raoul the bug man. She let him in. "How goes it, O Great Insect Warrior?"

His blue-black hair was combed neatly in place, and his lime-green tank top—worn to emphasize the muscles he'd earned as a construction worker—advertised Hernandez's Pest Control Service.

"What the heck happened to your foot?" he asked.

"A horse stepped on it during my first polo lesson."

"I warned you it was a dangerous sport. You planning on suing?"

"I don't think this particular horse has any money. He's retired."

"Very funny, Pearce. I meant the owner. I handle Nicholas Kaharchek's pest control account. You ask me, he's more interested in the women who flock to his stables wearing those tight britches than he is teaching polo. The fact you hurt yourself under his, uh, tutelage, makes him responsible."

Billie suppressed a smile. Raoul's vocabulary was less extensive than that of her sixth-graders, but he surprised her now and then by spouting off a word that made her wonder if he picked them out randomly from a dictionary in order to impress her. "I'll be okay," she assured him. "Besides, Mr. Kaharchek took me to the hospital personally. He was very concerned."

" 'Course he was, but you can bet he had ulterior motives. He's either trying to get into your pants or see that you don't sue his ass off."

"Raoul!"

"I'm just telling you the way it is."

Billie did not want to think about whether or not Nick was using his polo classes as a way to seduce women, especially when she could still taste his kiss. He had been all business during the class; she had not witnessed any improprieties between him and the other women, but then, she'd been preoccupied with Zeke, and she had no idea what he did in his private life. Deedee talked as though he had a veritable harem. Probably, she should have smacked him harder with that spoon.

"May I offer you something to drink?" she asked Raoul, hoping to change the subject. He could be fanatical at times, especially when it concerned her or her children. He was obviously a good husband and father to his own wife and children and resented Billie's husband for "doing them dirty" as he called it. A proud father, he thought nothing of pulling out his wallet and flashing pictures of his three children.

"A glass of iced tea would certainly go a long way toward restoring my faith in humankind." He took a seat at her kitchen table.

"Bad day, huh?" Billie opened the refrigerator and pulled out a plastic pitcher. It was not unusual for Raoul to stop by after servicing a house in the neighborhood, which he seemed to be doing a lot of these days due to a strange epidemic of spiders and other creepy-crawly things that made Billie shudder just to think about. "What happened?"

"You know Mr. Callahan from two streets over? I found German roaches in his walls. You got any idea how hard they are to kill off? Our Defense Department isn't equipped for German roaches." He accepted the glass of tea she handed him and drank it down in one gulp.

Billie refilled his glass and sat in the chair opposite him. Raoul took his job seriously—sometimes obsessively so—but he was a darn good pest-control professional, as he preferred calling himself. Yet, lately it seemed nothing he did worked. That didn't keep him from trying, and his customers would never think of hiring anyone else.

Raoul was not only a great bug guy; he knew the houses well and kept an eye on them when the owners vacationed. The minor burglary that had occurred in the neighborhood the past week had him snapping pictures of anyone who looked suspicious to him. He immediately delivered them to the police station and insisted they keep them in a file.

He would never have accepted pay for looking after her neighbors' houses, but he was not opposed to asking for souvenir ashtrays of the places they visited. He built shelves in his basement and put in special lighting to show off his collection as one would fine art. Billie thought it a bit strange, but if Raoul enjoyed it, that was good enough for her. She suspected his wife tolerated a lot.

Raoul also insisted on making home repairs for Billie, although it didn't seem to be his area of expertise. It would have been simpler to call an expert, but Billie knew she would hurt Raoul's feelings if she did. So she allowed him to tinker with her plumbing and appliances to his heart's content, even though he never managed to get them running properly.

"Have you tried speaking German to these roaches, Raoul?" she asked. "Maybe they don't understand English or Spanish."

He gave her a look. "Very funny. You just better hope they don't get inside your walls."

Billie shuddered. "That's your job. I just feed you and keep you in iced tea and coffee."

"How's the toilet?"

"Still making that funny noise."

"Damn. I'm probably going to have to drain the tank and—"

Billie shook her head. "You've already got too much to do these days what with this strange insect infestation, not to mention half the neighborhood gone on vacation. I'll call a plumber." She held her breath.

A look of pure indignation crossed his face. "I'm going to pretend I didn't hear that. Who tuned up your van and taught you how to check the oil when you came close to burning up your engine?"

"You did, O Great One." She wouldn't mention that it took him several days to do her tune-up when she could have taken it to a garage and had it done in a fraction of the time. In return, Billie baked cookies for his children or sent him home with a meat loaf so his wife wouldn't have to cook dinner that night.

"Eeyeuuw!"

Billie and Raoul jumped simultaneously at the sound. They glanced in the direction of the stairs where Deedee stood wearing a short hunter-green satin wrapper that made her fair skin look like fine alabaster.

"What's wrong?" Billie asked.

"Your cat jumped on my bed and got hair all over me." She hurried closer. "Are my eyes puffy? Is my nose red?"

Billie looked closely. She was vaguely aware that Raoul was gawking at the woman. "Not that I can tell."

"I should probably take something just in case. I have a big night tonight." She looked at Raoul, her lip curling in distaste at his shirt and tattoos. "Who are *you*?"

Raoul was obviously annoyed by the look on her face. "I kill bugs."

Deedee opened her mouth. *"Ee—"*

Billie cut her off. "This is Raoul," she said quickly. "A friend of mine."

Deedee blinked several times. "For real?"

"And who might you be?" Raoul asked.

"I'm Billie's new housemate."

He glanced at Billie, eyebrows raised.

"Deedee only moved in today."

"Not by choice," the other woman said. "My cousin kicked me out of his place, the selfish goat."

Billie noted the question in Raoul's eyes. "Deedee's cousin is Nick Kaharchek. She's staying with me for a couple of weeks."

Raoul shot her a look of disbelief. "She's actually living here? Kaharchek's cousin?"

"Just until I get married," Deedee added. "I'm marrying a wrestler. You've probably heard of him. Frankie the Assassin?"

"You're marrying Frankie the Assassin?" Billie said, having heard the name come from her son's mouth a number of times. Raoul did not look impressed.

"Yeah, isn't that great? Wait until you see him. He's such a hunk." Deedee lowered her voice and gave Billie a meaningful look. "I'm partial to athletes. Their bodies are always so fit, you know what I mean?"

"I think so."

"And he's loaded."

Billie shifted in her chair. Deedee seemed to have forgotten that Raoul was in the room. "You don't say."

Deedee widened her eyes. "I've got a terrific idea. You could come to the match with Frankie and me tonight. Frankie isn't wrestling. He got a concussion last week. So we're just going to watch the show. You could come with us and look the guys over and pick one out for yourself. The Greek Gods will be there, and Slimeball, and Dirty Deed Dan." Her face lit up in a smile. "Oh, I have just the man for you. Big John is wrestling tonight." Her tone grew reverent. "They call him Big John because—"

"Raoul, would you like more iced tea?" Billie cut in.

He stood. His lips were pressed into a grim line.

"Nah. I've had just about as much as I can stand." He started for the door.

"Excuse me, Deedee," Billie said, following him out. She closed the door behind her.

Raoul picked up his gear, turned, and shook his head. "I know this is none of my business, but why would you allow that lunatic in your house?"

Billie's mouth fell open. "Deedee is not a lunatic. She's just different."

He shook his head as though he couldn't believe what was happening. "How long have I known you?"

Billie thought. "A year. Maybe longer."

"Right. And I've seen firsthand how hard you've tried to give your children a loving, secure home. I respected you for that, especially after what their old man did. Now I find out you're cozying up to the biggest shyster in town, and taking in his crazy relative who seems intent on introducing you to a man who's hung like a—"

"Raoul!"

"Miss Harebrained in there introduced the subject, not me." He planted his hands on his hips. "If it was money you needed—"

"I'm not doing it for the money." She paused, hating to admit her weaknesses, even to Raoul. "I've been lonely without my children, and I can't sleep at night for hearing weird noises."

"What weird noises?"

"In my bushes by my bedroom window."

"How come you didn't say anything? You know I make it my job to keep my eye out for the people in this neighborhood."

"I didn't want to burden you. You already do too much for all of us."

"Maybe I like doing it. If my wife and kids were alone, I would hope someone would look out for them now and then."

Billie appreciated his sentiment. "Deedee will be long gone before the kids return from their vacation. And Nick Kaharchek has not given me any reason to believe he's a shyster, so stop worrying."

"You really are naïve, you know that?" He shook his head sadly. "I've got bugs waiting. See you later."

Deedee was sitting at the table blowing her nose into a tissue when Billie reentered the kitchen. "I'm sorry I wasn't very friendly to your pest control man," she said. "I always get this way when my allergies act up or I'm PMSing."

Billie looked at her. The woman's eyes were watering and her nose was red. "Do you have something you can take?"

She nodded. "I shouldn't have made such a big deal of your cat. This is your house, after all. I'll just make sure to keep my bedroom door closed."

Nick was right, Billie thought. Deedee was actually very sweet. A little dim-witted at times, but sweet.

"I really wish you'd go with us tonight. Looks like you could use some fun."

Billie pointed to her foot. "I'd like to go," she lied, "but my foot is swollen, and I can't get it into a shoe."

Deedee studied the foot. "It doesn't look nearly as swollen. I bet it will be fine by tonight."

Billie glared at her foot. Damn. Of all times for the swelling to go down. She would almost prefer having

Zeke step on it again to attending a wrestling match. "I'm not much of a wrestling fan."

"Honey, after you see Big John in his black satin briefs you'll be a fan for life. He might be just the man to take your mind off Nick."

Billie felt her left eye twitch. "Would you excuse me for a minute? I have to make a phone call."

"What's wrong with this phone?" Deedee pointed to the portable on the kitchen wall.

"I have to call my therapist."

"You're seeing a therapist? And what's wrong with your eye?"

"It's a nervous twitch. That's why I'm calling my therapist."

Deedee stood. "No problem. I have to find my allergy pills." She paused and gave a sly smile. "You know, Big John could work off some of that stress."

Twitch, twitch. Billie hurried toward her bedroom.

She closed her bedroom door, made for her night table, and dialed Nick's stable. She felt her heart skip a beat when he answered. Get right to it, she thought, steeling herself. Lay it all in his lap. "It's me." She tried to make it sound like a warning, but her voice wavered. Shit.

"Let me guess. Billie Pearce?"

"You have to do something about this situation. You have to help me. This was really a crummy thing to do to me, Nicholas Kaharchek."

"Okay, calm down. What did Deedee do? Did she explode something in your microwave? You're right, I should have warned you about that. I'll buy you a new one."

"It's not the microwave."

"You didn't let her drive your van, did you? She has a problem with stop signs. Why do you think her car is always in the shop?"

"This is much more serious."

Nick sounded exasperated. "Well, what the hell did she do?"

"It's not what she did, it's what she's going to do. She's determined to take me to a wrestling match tonight and fix me up with some anatomical freak named Big John." Billie had to stop talking long enough to catch her breath. From the other end, there was a long pause and a muffled sound apparently caused by a hand being clamped over the phone. "Nick, are you laughing at me again?"

"No."

"You are! I can hear you. This isn't funny. The man wears black satin briefs. He grunts and rolls around on the ground."

"Just tell Deedee you don't want to go."

"It's not that simple."

Nick sighed, understanding the problem. It was never simple to say no to Deedee. "All right, what do you want? I guess I could throw in a custom-made saddle with the free lessons."

"I don't want a saddle. I called you because you're devious and sneaky and completely unscrupulous. I want you to think of a way to get me out of this." She paused in thought. "You can pretend to drop by to discuss my polo lessons. It'll take five minutes out of your precious time. You can be on your way as soon as they leave."

"I don't think they're going to fall for it, Billie."

"Listen to me, dammit! I'm a mother who happens to prefer making brownies to having a blind date with Big John—I am *not* about to spend an evening with a guy who measures his manhood by the foot."

Nick stared at the toe of his boot and admitted to himself that he didn't want her spending the evening with that kind of guy, either. In fact, he didn't much like the idea of her spending the evening with *any* kind of guy. Not that he had any right to feel that way. His interest in her wasn't exactly altruistic.

He sighed. It had seemed like a good plan at the time: getting rid of Deedee and maybe spending a little free time with Billie on the pretense of checking on his cousin. Most divorcées appreciated an evening out and a little attention, and they were quick to show their appreciation. He knew a couple of them who would have welcomed Deedee with open arms if it meant seeing more of him.

Billie Pearce obviously didn't feel that way.

"Don't worry about it," he said, knowing he couldn't just walk away when he was responsible for getting her into such a jam in the first place. He might be lacking in scruples where women were concerned, but that didn't mean he was irresponsible. "Go along with the plan, and I'll make sure you're rescued."

"Rescued?"

"Just think of me as your personal white knight." He hung up, thinking how ridiculous that sounded, even to him.

Billie stared at the telephone. Her white knight, she thought. Nicholas Kaharchek was about as close to being a white knight as Deedee was a choirgirl. She hung up. Raoul was right. She had gone and gotten herself involved with a family of lunatics.

Several hours later, Billie stood in front of her mirror and took a quick survey. Tailored white shirt, crisp, pleated khaki slacks, and brown moccasins— the only shoes she could get on her injured foot. It was about as unsexy as she could get, and she hoped it would get her safely through the evening. It was a little like wearing a cross to ward off Dracula, or a necklace of garlic cloves to scare away the plague. Dammit, where was Kaharchek? The Assassin was scheduled to arrive any minute and the promise of rescue was growing slim. She looked at her foot, only slightly swollen, and contemplated taking a hammer to it.

She jumped and put her hand to her heart when the doorbell rang. Be calm, she told herself as she limped down the stairs; this couldn't be as bad as she was making it out to be. Big John was probably very nice. And going to see a wrestling match would be a new experience that might impress her son even more than polo lessons.

Probably when you put a wrestler in street clothes he looks like a real person, she told herself.

Billie opened the door and took a step backward. Frankie the Assassin was almost seven feet tall with long, black, slicked-back hair. His eyebrows formed a thick black line straight across his forehead, as though someone had drawn a line across it with a marker. He wore a custom-made tux, black tie, and no shirt. Billie's jaw dropped as she stared at the massive chest and pectoral muscles. They had to be real; she'd never heard of men getting implants.

"I'm Frankie," he said, holding his hand out. "You must be Billie."

His hand was the size of a rump roast and Billie feared her own would be crushed, but he was unexpectedly gentle as they shook. "Nice to meet you, Frankie."

"Deedee speaks very highly of you."

As if acting on cue, Deedee came clacking down the stairs on three-inch magenta satin sling-backs. She wore a skin-tight, spaghetti-strapped sheath with plunging neckline, a skirt slit to mid-thigh, and decorated top to bottom with glittering magenta sequins. She had matching glitter on her heavily lined eyelids and dangling diamond earrings that Billie suspected were about equal in value to her own four-bedroom colonial.

Billie swallowed and smoothed an imaginary wrinkle from her khaki slacks. "I didn't realize this was formal."

"It's not," Frankie said. "Deedee and I just like to make an entrance."

"Yeah," Deedee said. "We don't want to disappoint the fans. They like to see the Assassin and me dressed up."

Nick knocked on the open door. "Excuse me. Am I interrupting?"

Billie felt herself sag against the chair rail in giddy relief. She'd been saved. Nick had kept his promise. Big John was going to have to impress another woman with his largesse.

"We were just going out," Deedee said, her little-girl voice surprisingly authoritative. "We're taking Billie to see a wrestling match."

Nick grinned affably. "That sounds like fun. Mind if I tag along?"

Billie felt a wave of panic. Oh, no! That wasn't part of her plan. She had about as much business spending an evening with Nick Kaharchek as she did with Big John, and the absolute last place she wanted to spend it was at a wrestling match! She vigorously shook her head no behind Deedee's back, but Nick ignored her.

"As a matter of fact, I do mind," Deedee said. "You'll ruin everything."

"No he won't," Frankie said. "I like Nick. Nick's a good guy. Besides, he looks just like Billie. Don't you think they make a cute couple?"

Nick was wearing a starched white shirt, open at the neck, sleeves rolled to his forearms; perfectly creased, European-cut, pleated khaki slacks; and his brown moccasins.

"They look like the Bobbsey Twins," Deedee said, giving Nick a disparaging look. "People will think they're a tag team."

"Yeah," Frankie said, laughing. "You guys ever consider wrestling?"

Nick splayed his hand on the small of Billie's back and rubbed his thumb across her spine as though he had every right. He gave no indication if he noticed her reaction. Her back went ramrod stiff. "It's crossed my mind," he said.

His voice made Billie's stomach flutter, at the same

time as it set her teeth on edge. What did he think he was doing? This was not at all what she'd had in mind, and it wasn't like she hadn't been specific. Nick Kaharchek was playing a game. At her expense. She inched away.

Deedee must have suspected Nick was trying to pull something as well, because she shot him a look of pure venom. It was obvious she didn't trust him as far as her heavily made-up eyes could see him, and that she was mad as hell that he'd managed to foil her plans for the evening.

"Everyone ready to go?" Nick asked innocently.

Billie had no choice but to follow. What did it matter? she told herself. In little more than twenty-four hours, her life had been turned upside down and inside out. The fact that there was an expensive Mercedes and a sinister-looking black stretch limo in her driveway didn't faze her. Her neighbors would think nothing of it once they caught sight of Deedee in her garb, walking beside a seven-foot giant whose chest was literally bursting from his tux.

"Maybe it would be best if we went in separate cars," Nick said, his hand possessively curled around Billie's neck. "I'm afraid I can't fit four people in mine."

"Forget it," Deedee snapped. "We'll all go in the limo. And watch your hands, Kaharchek."

Billie shot him a look that echoed Deedee's words. Nick simply grinned in response. He was enjoying himself.

"This white-knight stuff is tough," Nick whispered to Billie. "Nobody appreciates me. Here I am rescuing you, as promised, and all I get is abuse."

Billie looked at him coolly. "You didn't follow the plan."

"Perhaps Big John is not the man from whom you needed rescuing."

Damned if he didn't have the sexiest eyes, she thought. She'd heard the term "bedroom eyes," but she only now grasped the full meaning. "Don't think I haven't taken that into consideration, but I have Mace in my purse, and I'm hell-bent on using it before the expiration date."

His fingers slid along the nape of her neck and tangled in her short silky hair. "Okay, so I lied. I'm not a hero, and I don't know the first thing about being a white knight."

"Now, there's a big surprise."

A chauffeur dressed in formal livery held the door as Frankie and Deedee settled into the luxurious back seat. Billie solemnly crept into the dark, cool interior and took a seat facing Deedee. Nick took the seat next to Billie and swiveled toward Frankie. "What, no bowling alley?" he asked.

Frankie smiled. "I didn't want to be ostentatious."

An hour later they pulled up to an auditorium in D.C.

"We've got front-row seats," Deedee said. "You're gonna love this, Billie, honey. Sometimes they come right over the ropes at you, and when they put Big John in a body slam it makes your heart jump."

Billie gave her a weak smile. "I'm not going to get hurt, am I?"

Deedee blinked. "Do you know what the odds are of something like that happening?"

A roar went up when they entered the auditorium, pushing Billie back into Nick's chest. "It's for Frankie," Nick shouted. "He's very popular."

"Oh, yeah? Why are some people booing and yelling obscenities?"

"I guess he's not popular with *everyone*. He lost a match last week."

Deedee turned, obviously having heard the exchange. "It wasn't Frankie's fault," she whispered to Billie. "He pulled a groin muscle putting his opponent in an overhead spin, and after that—well, it was awful that he then got dropped on his head. Fortunately he has me to feed his ego, and I'm an expert when it comes to that sort of thing."

The auditorium was brightly lit, and stuffed to capacity with screaming fans. Big John entered, dropped his floor-length fur coat, and paraded about.

"He's fat!" Billie said. "Why would you try to set me up with a fat man?"

"Honey, that's muscle," Deedee whispered.

It looked like flab to Billie. Big John turned to the crowd, grasped his meaty hands together and held them high in the air. The audience roared and whistled and stomped their feet. Big John paused and smiled briefly when he caught sight of Frankie and Deedee, and his gaze automatically slid to Billie as though he'd been expecting her. He opened his mouth and wiggled his tongue at her in a taunting gesture. He mouthed the word "Later."

Billie shrank back in horror. *"Eeyeuuw!"*

"He likes you," Deedee said. "And don't think he doesn't know how to use that tongue. I've heard rumors."

Big John's opponent, Snakeman, climbed between the ropes with a twenty-foot boa wrapped around his body, the snake's head resting in his hand. The man's arms were tattooed in snakes.

Billie closed her eyes. "It's a real snake, isn't it? Tell me when it's over."

"Billie, open your eyes!" Deedee said. "You're going to miss the best part, where Snakeman shoves the snake in Big John's face and the snake's tongue lashes out at him."

An earsplitting roar erupted from the crowd as the boa arched its massive head and its tongue whipped in and out of its odd-shaped mouth. Billie decided she would have preferred facing the boa's tongue than Big John's.

Big John squared his shoulders as if trying to quell the hint of fear on his face as Snakeman arrogantly taunted him with the boa. A referee ordered the wrestler to deposit his boa into an enormous canvas sack held by an animal handler. Billie sighed her relief. Still, it was too much for her—the noise, the impending violence, the thought of Big John so much as putting a finger on her. It was going to be a long night, considering she would probably sit there with her eyes closed for the most part.

She could only hope the snake didn't find its way free of the sack.

"It's okay," Nick whispered in her ear. "Don't be afraid."

His warm breath against her neck sent shivers down Billie's spine and raised goosebumps along her arms. He pulled her closer, enveloping her in his scent, warming her from the heat of his own body. Billie couldn't find the wherewithal to pull away.

"I'll protect you," he added.

Suddenly, Big John and the snake didn't seem so formidable.

CHAPTER FIVE

By the time the show ended, Billie was thinking wrestling was sort of fun. Not the snake part, of course. Mostly she liked the fan enthusiasm and the flash of the extravaganza. And her mood heightened considerably when the limo driver pulled in front of a reputable steak house. She had been there before and knew they served the best beef in town. Her mouth watered, and her stomach growled, a Pavlovian response to the smells as they walked through the double glass doors leading inside.

She wasn't nearly so thrilled when Nick slid into the booth beside her, so close his thigh pressed against hers. The booth seemed to shrink to half its size. She tried scooting closer to the wall and discovered she was already as close to it as she could get without being on the other side.

"Could you move over a little?" she whispered.

He shifted in the booth but didn't so much as move a smidgeon. Instead, he slid his arms along the back of it, dropping his hand possessively on her shoulder. On the surface, it seemed casual enough, but there was nothing casual about the way Billie's body responded to his simple touch. Her stomach tightened, and she held her breath, afraid to release it in case it came out in a loud gush. He began drawing tiny imaginary circles along the base of her neck, his thumb rotating lazily. Billie's stomach did a tiny flip-flop. Once again, she caught the subtle hint of his cologne.

"What would you like?" he whispered.

Billie blinked several times. "Excuse me?" Her voice sounded like a croak.

"For dinner." His mouth curved into a half-smile, and there was a look of genuine amusement in his dark eyes.

He knew exactly what he was doing to her, she thought. The man oozed sensuality. He had flirting down to an art, and he was obviously enjoying making her squirm.

But why? she asked herself. She was hardly the sort of woman a man like Nicholas Kaharchek would desire. She did her own nails, had her hair trimmed by the next available operator at a no-frills salon, and purchased her clothes off half-price racks or sidewalk sales. She was an ordinary woman, an average housewife, probably nothing like the women Nick normally dated.

Perhaps Nick thought he was doing her a favor, she thought suddenly. Probably he thought she would get all starry-eyed and tongue-tied over a drop-dead gorgeous millionaire who only had to crook his finger at a woman to capture her heart. If Nick was interested, there was only one reason why, and the thought wasn't especially flattering.

If only her body were as determined to steer clear of him as her head.

Billie wondered if Nick knew what was going on inside of her, and the thought that he might indeed be attuned to her building attraction was unsettling. He only had to look at her a certain way, touch her lightly with those expert hands, to send her thoughts into a tailspin and create a heat wave low in her belly. In a very short time he'd managed to spin a web of intimacy around them, the likes of which she had never known. It was simultaneously provocative and completely nerve-wracking, and like a fool, she found herself waiting in anticipation for his next touch.

She reached for a cracker, tore open the cellophane, and took a bite. Anything to keep her mind off the man beside her, she told herself.

Nick noted Billie's discomfort and knew she was as aware of him sexually as he was of her. Instead of feeding his ego, as it would have in the past, he found himself utterly confused. The oh-so-proper mother of two who baked cookies and taught sixth-graders was the sexiest thing he'd ever come up against. What was this power she had over him that made him desire her?

She was adorable, with her fresh-scrubbed look and hair that made him think of spun silk. She had the prettiest legs he'd ever seen on a woman, and her curves enticed him. But he was accustomed to pretty women. What he wasn't accustomed to was her simple nature. The women he dated were sophisticated, traveled in the right circles, knew where to vacation, how to play the game, and how to please a man in every sense of the word. Like Sheridan. His smile faltered.

Billie Pearce didn't even seem to like him. She didn't put on airs, didn't try to be witty and charming; in fact, she didn't seem to care that she was getting cracker crumbs all over the white tablecloth. Perhaps that was it. She was unpretentious. She was just Billie.

"So what did you think of Big John?" Deedee finally asked, looking up from her menu. "Isn't he wonderful?"

Billie felt Nick's eyes on her, sensed his knowing smile. "Big John? Uh, he was . . . um, awesome."

"He definitely likes you," Deedee said, following the length of Nick's arm with her eyes. Some of the glitter had fallen to her cheek. It was clear she didn't appreciate her cousin putting his hands on Billie. "And wasn't it romantic the way he got thrown out of the ring, almost at your feet?"

Billie nodded solemnly. "Very romantic. I especially liked it when he did that thing with his tongue again, and the woman beside me fainted."

"I told you he was hot. And believe me, Big John

knows how to treat a lady. Unlike some men who go through them quickly, and then toss them aside without a second thought."

Nick didn't miss the look Deedee shot him. She did not want Billie to become involved with him. He merely smiled. Deedee was still sore at him for hauling her out of her bed in her nightie and insisting she leave his home immediately. She'd had no idea he was trying to save her pretty neck. For now, she would just have to think the worst of him. And cad that he was, he would enjoy participating in the game.

"We're going to a formal reception at some embassy tomorrow night," Deedee said. "How about if we get you a date with Big John, and we can all go together?"

Billie formulated a mental list of preferred things to do: a basket of ironing that needed tending to, that kitchen drawer that was overflowing with junk and begged to be straightened, the spots on her carpet she'd been meaning to clean.

"A date with Big John could get you noticed by a lot of important people," Deedee said.

Billie pondered it. A date with Big John was just behind cutting off her thumbs with a carving knife. "That's nice of you to offer, but I don't think so. I think Big John is . . . ah, well, how do I put it? Far too big for someone like me," she said at last. "I'm sure it would be uncomfortable." She looked up and found three pairs of eyes staring. Deedee was blushing, something Billie had not thought possible. Beside her, Nick chuckled. Frankie's thick dark brows were arched high over his forehead, forming an upside-down V.

"What'd I say?"

Nick did his best to control the laughter that threatened to overtake him. The funniest part of all was that Billie truly had no clue how her words had sounded. Later tonight, when she was tucked into bed in her sensible mother-type pajamas, she'd remember the double entendre and throw the covers over her head out of embarrassment. He'd give anything to be there, next to her, when it happened.

Too late, Billie realized how her words had probably sounded to the others. "That's not what I meant," she insisted. "I just don't like staring into a man's navel when I speak to him."

Deedee sighed. "He's not *that* big."

"I'd feel dwarfed beside him." Billie glanced around frantically. "Would somebody please call a waiter?" She glanced up and froze when she caught sight of a familiar face. Sheridan Flock was headed their way, followed by a man who looked to be a good ten years younger and model-handsome. She felt Nick stiffen beside her.

Sheridan paused at their table and her eyes fell on Nick. "Well, what have we here?" Her gaze flitted about. "Slumming tonight?"

Nick shrugged. "I might ask you the same thing, Sheridan," he teased, although Billie could sense the tension in his body language. "I thought you preferred French restaurants."

Billie wondered if the woman was following Nick, then told herself she was being paranoid.

"Not at all," Sheridan said. "You know me, I'm quite the adventuress."

Suddenly, there was silence. Billie shifted in her seat as Sheridan's gaze swung in her direction. She knew how ordinary she must look compared to the beauty wearing a simple black dress that hugged an absolutely perfect figure. Thin spaghetti straps emphasized her slender shoulders and shapely arms.

Finally, Deedee broke the silence. "A steak restaurant is right where she needs to be," she said. "Got to feed that growin' boy."

Billie suppressed a smile but Frankie laughed out loud.

Sheridan regarded Deedee. "Hello, there," she said. "I don't believe I've met the new man in your life, Deedee. Is this husband number six or seven?"

Deedee shrugged. "Actually, I've lost count, but nobody can ever accuse me of being always a bridesmaid but never a bride. Sheridan, honey, meet Frankie. He's a famous wrestler."

Frankie offered his hand, but Sheridan didn't take it. "I'm afraid you have me at a disadvantage," she said. "I don't get the opportunity to attend many wrestling matches these days."

"Sheridan, you'll have to pardon us for not inviting you and your friend to join us," Nick said politely, "but we obviously don't have room."

"Actually, I was on my way out," she said.

Deedee chuckled. "Probably past your boy's bedtime."

Sheridan laughed. "I see you still have that great sense of humor, Deedee. I admire a woman who can still hold her head high despite what others think of her."

"We simply must do lunch, honey," Deedee replied. She waited until the woman walked away before looking at Nick. "What a bitch."

"You held your own."

"I can't believe you almost married her. My God, she's wicked."

"Don't be so hard on her," Nick said.

Billie, who'd decided it was best to remain silent instead of swapping barbs, looked at him quizzically and wondered why he was defending the woman.

Deedee made a tsking sound. "Poor thing probably resents us for being able to stay out late. After all, she has to take that child home and tuck him in for the night."

When they finally left the restaurant more than an hour later—once Billie had eaten her steak and part of Nick's, much to his amusement and Deedee's disbelief—they found that a small crowd had formed around the limo, drawn by the license plate held in place by a fourteen-karat-gold frame with THE ASSASSIN printed in black relief. Frankie waded into the middle of the crowd. He signed a shopping bag and an arm cast. He wrote his name in black felt marker on the foreheads of several fans who were without paper products.

Finally, Frankie pulled Nick aside and whispered something into his ear. Nick nodded as Frankie grasped Deedee's hand and started down the street, turning once to give Billie a broad smile and wink.

Billie didn't like the looks of the wink. "What did Frankie say to you?" she asked Nick.

Nick ignored the question as he ushered her into the limo and gave directions to the driver. He settled his lean frame onto the plush back seat and patted the place next to him. "Come sit here. It's more comfortable."

"I'm comfortable enough. Where are Frankie and Deedee going?"

Nick sighed and reached out, hauling her off the opposing jump seat so that she was sitting beside him. "Frankie and Deedee want to spend some time alone. He keeps a condo just a few blocks from here."

"What about Deedee and her scruples?"

"I never said Deedee had scruples about sleeping with Frankie. I said she had scruples about *living* with him."

Billie's gaze narrowed into mere slits. "You planned this, Kaharchek. Just when I think there might be some human decency in you—"

"Think of me as a knight with tarnished armor." Nick pressed a button, closing the dark, soundproof panel that separated them from the driver. "Actually, I had nothing to do with it, but it's just as well. You've been giving me the come-on all evening. Now's your chance to act on it."

Billie's jaw dropped open. She closed it. "You're delusional. You have serious problems. You need help."

He liked getting her riled. "You're right, I do have a serious problem, and it's got your name written all over it. You could help. Face it, Billie. You want me."

"What I want is out of this car."

"Afraid you'll lose control?"

She stared at him, unable to speak. There was a hint of amusement in his eyes, but Billie sensed he believed every word he was saying. The man had probably never had no for an answer. He looked so smug, relaxed, with his legs stretched in front of him, casually crossed at the ankles. "You've got to be kidding," she said at last.

"On the contrary, I'm fairly good at reading people, especially the opposite sex. I sense a very passionate woman beneath that Goody Two-Shoes exterior of yours. I'll bet you're hot stuff once you get going."

"I hate to blow your fantasy and ruin your good time alone in the shower tonight, but I am *not* hot stuff."

He had to admit she could hold her own. "You're not hot stuff? What are you, warm stuff? Cold stuff?"

"It's none of your business what kind of stuff I am."

He slid his finger through the wave of hair above her ear. "Suppose I make it my business?"

Billie's eyes narrowed. "You can't imagine how many times I've heard that line."

The beginnings of a frown creased the area between his brows. "Lots of boyfriends?"

"Lots of television."

"Does it work on television?"

"Usually," she admitted.

"You think it'll work tonight?"

"Get real."

Nick grinned. "Mothers are pretty tough, but polo

players are even tougher. I usually win."

Billie looked at him levelly, a hint of amusement in her large hazel eyes. "You don't scare me, Kaharchek. Nothing scares me. I teach sixth grade, remember?"

He continued to smile at her. It was an easy, affable smile, completely without guile and pleasantly intimate. His voice was soft and husky, a bedroom voice compatible with the smile. "You can cut a wrestler down to size with a look, and punch ornery horses, but you're not so brave about acknowledging the attraction between us."

Outwardly Billie struggled to seem calm, but the tension building between her shoulder blades was tight as a rubber band stretched to its limit. And Nick knew exactly what he was doing to her.

She willed her voice to be steady and spoke softly but distinctly. "My attitude toward you has nothing to do with bravery or acknowledgment. It has to do with common sense and a little self-discipline. Simply put, I refuse to be one of your little playthings." Having seen the way the beautiful Miss Flock had looked at him had convinced her to maintain a safe distance from the man.

His gaze slid the length of her. "Is that why you wore this prim white shirt? So you wouldn't turn me on?"

She didn't respond. He'd obviously broken his share of hearts and she wasn't about to become his next victim.

"You failed dismally because you look extraordinarily sexy in it. You have this don't-touch-me look that makes me want to touch you all the more." He leaned over and kissed her gently on the lips, then very calmly folded his arms, leaned back in the seat, and closed his eyes.

Billie stared at him, gaped at him actually, eyes wide with surprise. "That's *it*?"

"Hmmm?" He didn't open his eyes.

"You're not going to make a pass at me?"

He opened one eye. "You sound disappointed."

"Isn't that what this whole thing was about? I'll bet you talked Frankie into letting us use his limo so you could plan this big seduction scene."

"Frankly, I just wanted to spend some quiet time with you." He took her hand in his and held it. "Relax."

A very confused Billie leaned back in the plush seat. What was going on? she wondered. Here she was with Loudoun County's biggest stud, and he wasn't going to make a pass at her after all? Was it some kind of game meant to confuse her? She understood games about as much as she did her VCR. She simply sat there wearing a perplexed look.

Was she disappointed? she asked herself. Perhaps she *wanted* Nick to desire her, despite the flash of pain she'd seen in Sheridan Flock's eyes, despite knowing how quickly Nick went through women. As ridiculous as it sounded, even in her own head, she knew there was still some small part of her that would never fully recover from her ex-husband's rejection. The fact that Nicholas Kaharchek found her sexy had bolstered her self-confidence and made her feel like a woman again instead of a mother and a schoolteacher.

Nick noted the play of emotions on her face and wondered at them. He couldn't begin to decipher her feelings when he was clueless as to his own. He picked up a phone and gave the driver Billie's address. "And how about stopping by the Dairy Queen on the way home?" he said.

"We're going to the Dairy Queen?" she asked.

"I'm hungry. You ate part of my dinner."

She blushed. "I only had a few bites of your steak."

"You ate more than half of it. Heaven only knows where you put it."

"I've been wanting a good steak for a long time. All I eat is low-fat frozen dinners."

"Why?" His brow wrinkled. "Never mind, I think I know."

"Know what?"

"You don't feel comfortable with your body."

"Excuse me?"

"And we both know the reasons."

Billie stared at him, stunned. Was the man a mind reader? "You don't know what you're talking about."

"Your ex-husband wouldn't recognize quality if it slapped him in the face."

Billie's own face flamed. Nick had seen right through her insecurities, the nagging doubts that sometimes flared when she remembered what it had felt like being tossed aside for another woman. Was he backing off out of pity? The thought sent a hot flash of anger through her. "Don't bring my past into this. I feel perfectly comfortable with my body and who I am, thank you very much. You just can't handle the fact that I'm not the least bit interested in an affair with a man who uses women, and then walks away once the newness rubs off."

"You've certainly got me pegged." He looked amused.

"I, on the other hand, still believe in old-fashioned values. Love and marriage and family."

"Man, you really play hardball, don't you?"

"You don't believe in marriage?"

He shrugged. "I think it's great in theory but not at all realistic. Everyone I know has been divorced at least once, including my parents."

"Is that why you broke it off with Miss Flock?"

He looked at her. "What makes you think *I* broke it off?"

"Give me a break. I know your type. Mister Love-'em-and-leave-'em. I'm surprised you actually went as far as buying an engagement ring."

"Yep, you've got me all figured out," he said.

"Uh-huh. I've got your number, Kaharchek. You and a dozen other men just like you."

"What about you? Did you like being married?"

"No, but that doesn't mean it couldn't be good. That's why next time I'll be smarter when it comes to choosing a husband."

"Oh, yeah? What will you do differently?"

Billie saw the twinkle in his eyes and knew he was playing with her. She composed her face and tried to look deadly serious. "I'm going to marry an older gentleman."

"How old?"

"A man who is well past his midlife crises. And he's going to drive a Volvo station wagon instead of a sports car." She ticked the remaining qualifications off on her fingers. "He will not be into snakes, wrestling, sequins, nor will he have enlarged body parts."

"You know, enlarged body parts sometimes work in a lady's favor."

Her look would have shattered reinforced concrete. "He will absolutely, definitely not have a membership to a tanning salon. He will not own a hot tub, a gold chain necklace, or designer underwear." She pressed her lips together primly. "He'll wear plaid flannel boxer shorts. The big ugly baggy kind."

Nick smiled and raised his eyebrows, knowing there was an element of truth buried in the humor. "So, that's your ideal husband, huh?"

"Yup."

"I think you just described my Uncle Henry. He's in a nursing home in Falls Church. They let him have visitors on Sundays. I could fix you up with him."

"Very funny, but I'm almost serious. I'm not marrying another immature, insecure Romeo who'll only end up straying like the last one, without a care as to what it means to tear a family apart, including two young children."

Nick felt something tug at his gut as he remembered his own parents' divorce. They had been so caught up in their own anger and misery, they had given little notice to their son's feelings. Instead of allowing her to see how her words had affected him, he merely grinned.

"I don't suppose you'd want to have a wild fling with no strings attached before you meet Mr. Right?"

"When pigs fly, Kaharchek."

The limo had stopped moving. They'd arrived at the Dairy Queen. "Then allow me the pleasure of buying you a banana split with all the fixings while there's still a little life left in you."

Billie allowed him to help her out of the limo. She caught sight of the grim line of his lips and thought he looked disappointed. She had told him what she wanted out of life, and he'd accepted it, knowing that, while their paths had crossed and they'd enjoyed a few moments of sexual awareness and camaraderie, they had very little in common when it came to the important stuff.

"Mind answering a personal question?" Billie asked once they'd ordered their sundaes.

"Shoot."

"Why'd you break off the engagement? I mean, it's obvious the woman is still in love with you."

"You think so?"

"Damn, Kaharchek, it's written all over her face."

Nick paid for the sundaes. "You've got it all wrong, Billie. Sheridan dumped *me*."

She gaped. "For real?"

"Three days before the wedding. Broke my heart into a million pieces, left for Europe, and the rest is history. She spent eight months over there. Yesterday was the first time I've seen her since her return to the States." He handed her the sundae she'd ordered. "Any more questions?"

Billie was embarrassed for asking. Nick, despite his

reputation with women, was still pining away for Sheridan Flock. It made Billie all the more determined to steer clear of Nick. "No more questions," she said softly.

CHAPTER SIX

Deedee sprayed her flame-red hair and postured in her slinky black dress. "I don't know why you won't let me get you a date for tonight," she said to Billie. "Embassy parties are always so much fun. Especially when you're on the arm of a seven-foot wrestler. Everyone notices you." She pouted at the mirror and outlined her lips in glossy red lipstick. "I like being noticed." She shot Billie a look in the mirror. "Sure beats sitting at home waiting for Nick to call."

"I'm *not* waiting for Nick to call," Billie said defensively, at the same time thinking Deedee didn't need to be on the arm of a wrestler to be noticed. The woman was stunning all by herself, six feet tall in spike heels, with enough cleavage to give Dolly Parton a run for her money. The shimmering black material clung to her slim-hipped figure like plastic wrap while she rummaged through a huge chest of jewelry. "I plan to have a nice quiet evening at home. Besides, Nick is still hung up on that Flock woman."

"That bitch from hell?" Deedee exclaimed. She turned and made a sound of disgust. "What gave you that idea? They split up months ago."

"Did you know she was the one who broke the engagement? Broke Nick's heart."

Deedee turned back to the mirror. "I find that hard to believe. Nick began seeing other women the minute Miss Hoity-Toity boarded the plane for Europe. We're talking about my cousin here. Trust me, he's not cut out for celibacy." Deedee winced. "Oh, shoot, I shouldn't have said that, what with you having the hots for him and all."

"It's okay," Billie said, pretending she was trying to hide her disappointment. "Nick is way out of my league."

"I hope you're not comparing yourself to Sheridan, honey, because let me tell you, you've got her beat by a mile. She's not half the woman you are. She's shallow."

"Thanks, Deedee."

"I'm not just saying that to make you feel good. I've known her since grade school, and she's nothing but a spoiled daddy's girl. Got worse after her mother died. What Sheridan wants, Sheridan gets." Deedee paused to catch her breath. "Her daddy is a retired three-star general with power and money who isn't opposed to throwing his weight around when it comes to his little girl. Sheridan is just like him."

"Maybe she wants Nick back."

"Nick is smarter than that."

Deedee threw her hands into the air. "Oh, hell. It's not here. The limo is on the way, and I haven't got my Stargio."

"What's a Stargio?" Billie asked, although she was still curious about Nick's relationship with Sheridan. Was Nick still in love with her, and if so, why was he kissing Billie?

"It's a necklace," Deedee said. "Stargio is the name of the guy who designed it for me. Diamonds and emeralds. Dammit, I got this dress just for the Stargio. I know where I left it, too. It's at Nick's. It's in the little safe in the guest room."

"Nick has a safe in his guest room?"

Deedee dialed a number on the bedside phone and waited impatiently. "No answer." She dialed another number, got an answer, and asked for Nick. "He isn't home, and he isn't at the barn. He's in Upperville looking at a horse," she told Billie, hanging up the phone. "You see what I mean about him? He's unreliable. Now what am I going to do? I can't possibly go to that party without my Stargio."

Billie wondered if Nick had made the trip alone, then chided herself. It was none of her business. Just because he'd kissed her silly didn't mean he was ready to choose a china pattern. She was overreacting. Men kissed women all the time.

"Maybe he'll be home in a little while."

"I can't wait." Deedee took her black satin evening purse from the dresser. "I'll just have to go over to

Nick's house and get it. Can I borrow your minivan? Mine is in the garage getting fixed. People keep smashing into it."

Billie remembered Nick's warning about letting Deedee drive. "Maybe I should take you. It might be hard to drive in those heels," she added tactfully.

"That'd be great." Deedee hugged her. "You're such a good friend. We'll leave a note on the door in case Frankie gets here before we get back."

Fifteen minutes later Billie pulled into the circular driveway of Nick's stately country house. The ivy-covered, redbrick house sat a good distance from the road, hidden from sight by a small hill, and separated from the stable by a copse of evergreens. It reminded Billie of the Governor's Palace in Colonial Williamsburg.

"Is this the first time you've seen Nick's house?" Deedee asked as if noting Billie's look of awe.

Billie nodded her head. "It's very nice."

"Nick bought it from some earl. This earl person had the bricks brought all the way from England."

Billie and Deedee walked to the door and knocked. "No one home," Deedee said. "And the door's locked. Damn." They walked to the back of the house where they tried several more doors. All locked. "Nick was robbed four years ago," Deedee explained. "Now he keeps everything shut up tighter than a clam at high tide." She sighed. "If Max were around, he could get us in. There isn't an alarm system that Max can't decode."

"Who's Max?"

"Maximillian Holt. He's my bratty kid brother, the

sixteen-year-old genius who keeps blowing up things around here."

Billie took a step back. "Blowing up things?"

Deedee seemed more interested in figuring out a way to get into the house than discussing her little brother. "Don't worry, he wouldn't hurt a fly, and he doesn't blow up big things. He just does it to get Nick's attention," she added.

"That would work for me." Billie shook her head sadly. Nick was living in a house with a kid who blew up things? Was anyone in the family normal? "Uh, Deedee?"

"Don't worry about Max, honey. He hasn't been seen in days."

Billie was relieved to hear it. "Does anyone know where he is?"

"Probably hiding in the woods. Max is very self-reliant." She carefully stepped into a bed of begonias and tried a window. "Any normal millionaire would have this house staffed with servants, but not Nick. He makes do with a part-time cleaning lady and a caretaker. And Fong, but he's pretty much retired. Nick even does his own cooking. Can you imagine not having a *cook*?"

Billie had never wanted a cook. "I like to do my own cooking," she said. She glanced about as she talked. "What does Max look like?"

"He's dark and skinny. Nothing to write home about, but you mark my word, that kid is going to be a hunk when he grows up. I can tell these things." She backed up several feet and pointed to an upstairs window. "That was my room. That's where my Stargio is."

Billie was beginning to feel nervous about skulking around in the bushes. It wasn't in her nature to peek into other people's windows, and the thought of running into Max was unnerving. "Maybe we should try up at the stable. Maybe there's a spare key."

"No way am I going to deal with Arnie the jerk. He gives me the heebie-jeebies. Besides, would you leave your house key with a man who looks like he belongs on the FBI's Most Wanted list?"

"Nick mentioned firing someone. I think it may have been Arnie, but I'm not sure." She wondered why Nick had hired the man in the first place.

Deedee didn't seem to be listening. "Come on."

"What are you going to do?"

Deedee marched to the patio at the back of the house and set her sights on a pair of French doors. "I'm getting my necklace." She took an insulated metal coffee carafe that had been left sitting on a lawn table and swung it into one of the small panes in the patio door. Shards of glass tinkled onto the slate floor and an alarm went off both inside and outside the house.

Billie had a moment of heart-stopping immobility and then planted her feet in sprint position. "Let's go!"

"Don't be a wimp," Deedee said. "It's just a silly alarm." She reached inside the broken pane and unlocked the door. "Come on, this will only take a minute."

"This is breaking and entering!"

Deedee waved her red nails. "Nick won't mind. He's always telling me I should be more resourceful. He'll be proud of me."

"Do I hear dogs?"

"Oh, my God, I forgot about the dogs!" Deedee pulled Billie inside the house and slammed the patio door shut just as a pack of assorted dogs came bounding through the patch of evergreens.

"Terrific," Billie shouted over the alarm. "First the alarm goes off, then a herd of attack dogs descends on us. Not only that, there's a madman running loose, or should I say *kid*, who plays with explosives. What next?"

Deedee clacked across the terra-cotta tile floor of the solarium and looked out a front window. "Oh, crud, it's the police. I swear, you'd think they were watching the place." She shrugged. "Probably worried that Max will go off the deep end." She turned on her heel and started up a broad central staircase. "You explain all this to them while I get my necklace."

Billie stared at the flashing lights. Don't panic, she told herself, at the same time wondering how they'd managed to arrive on the scene so quickly. She felt as if she were right smack in the middle of a bad dream, only her eyes were wide open. She licked her dry lips. She'd never been arrested. She'd never had a traffic ticket. She'd led an exemplary life. And now she was going to have to explain to the police that her friend was upstairs breaking into a safe.

She opened the front door and gave a tentative wave to the inhabitants of three squad cars. Deedee had gone too far this time. Billie only hoped their prison wardrobe came in orange because Deedee had claimed she looked hideous in that color.

"This is all a mistake," Billie said, knowing it would never fly.

"Hands in the air, lady," an officer shouted, aiming his gun at her.

Her stomach took a nosedive. Billie immediately raised her hands over her head. "Please let me explain," she called back loudly, trying to make herself heard over the noisy alarm. "I'm not a real burglar. See, Deedee, Mr. Kaharchek's cousin, needed her Stargio. It's some kind of jewelry designed specifically for one of her evening gowns," she added in case the officers wondered what she was talking about.

One of them rolled his eyes. "Deedee Holt, the ditsy redhead?"

Billie nodded and expelled the air that had been trapped in her lungs. It gushed out like a hot furnace. "Deedee insists her shoes and jewelry match her clothes. I personally don't care about such things."

The officer came forward. "You can put your hands down."

Billie almost wept her relief. They knew Deedee. It was going to be okay.

He punched a code into the small wall computer and silenced the alarm. "This isn't her car," he said, pointing to Billie's minivan.

"It's mine," Billie said.

"Don't ever let her drive it."

Deedee clattered down the stairs in her heels and squeezed through the doorway, next to Billie. A collective gasp issued from the police while Deedee, resplendent in her bejeweled cleavage, preened and smiled for them. "Well, hello, gentlemen. I hope I didn't cause another little ruckus."

"Where's Mr. Kaharchek?"

Deedee grimaced. "In Upperville looking at some dumb horse, where else?"

Frankie's limo pulled around the circular driveway and he got out. "I saw the note," he called out as he closed the distance between the limo and the officer. "Deedee had to get her necklace," he explained to the uniform at the foot of the porch stairs. "She can't wear that dress without her Stargio."

The officer just looked at Deedee. "Have you ever considered asking your cousin for a key?"

"She has trouble keeping up with keys," Frankie answered for her. "Don't worry, I'll pay for any damage."

Deedee jiggled to the limo and slid in, exposing a healthy length of leg to the observant eyes of the law. "Thanks, honey," she called to Billie. "Don't wait up." Frankie followed.

The officer standing in front of Billie shook his head. "She's something else, isn't she?"

"Uh-huh."

"Is Fong at home?"

"I don't know this Fong person or where he is at the moment."

"What did Deedee break this time?" he asked, writing on a form attached to a clipboard.

"A window in the French doors."

He handed the clipboard to Billie. "You'll have to make a statement. Just sign at the bottom. Is Nick coming home soon? We can't leave the house unattended and unsecured."

Billie scribbled a brief explanation on the sheet of paper, signed it, and handed it to the officer. "I'm not sure when Mr. Kaharchek will return. I'll stay. I'm a personal friend." She regretted it the moment she said it. What if Max showed up? What if he were lurking about just watching and waiting to make his next move? Damn Deedee! The woman should be forced to sit in jail for a week without her makeup kits.

The officers were already climbing into their patrol cars. Billie watched them drive single-file down the driveway, turn onto the road, and disappear around a bend.

She sat on the porch steps for a while after they drove off. Birds sang night songs and the sky darkened. An animal lowed in the distance and Billie guessed that Nick kept cattle as well as horses. One by one the dogs ambled around the house and sat beside her. Hardly guard dogs. They probably had come running, hoping to get fed, she decided. She smiled. There wasn't a pedigree among them.

Nick Kaharchek was a strange person. Not at all what she had originally expected; and the more Deedee complained about him, the better Billie liked him. He'd actually been a lot of fun at the wrestling match. She liked it that he could make himself at home in a kitchen. And he obviously liked animals.

"Just like me," she told the dogs. The thought saddened her. Not only did they live in separate worlds; there was another woman in the picture. Billie suspected there would always be a woman in the picture where Nick was concerned, whether it was Sheridan or not. He liked women and they liked him.

Billie heaved herself to her feet, went into the foyer with the dogs following close behind, and discovered another thing she liked about Nick Kaharchek—his house. It was a home. Warm and inviting without being ostentatious, though he could afford to decorate it like a castle if he wished. Roomy and spacious but still very simple and private. The couches were big and overstuffed. The tables were genuine Shaker. Fresh flowers sat in pots and vases on oversized window ledges and on the raised fireplace hearth of the great room. She turned on a few lights and found the kitchen.

It was a cook's kitchen. Iron skillets and copper pots hung from the ceiling beams, side by side with sprays of dried herbs, ropes of red onions, clusters of garlic, and wire baskets of potatoes, squash, and turnips. An oak table polished to a high gloss invited people to eat in front of the large stone fireplace and enjoy the aroma of food fresh from the elaborate black iron-and-stainless-steel restaurant-sized stove. Billie located the pantry and the dog food and filled five red bowls labeled Spike, Snuffy, Otis, Daisy, and Beans. Tails thumped the wood floor while they waited patiently.

Billie could not imagine Sheridan taking the time to feed Nick's dogs any more than she could imagine her cooking at his stove when he could easily afford to hire a full-time cook and housekeeper.

"Dig in," she told the hungry dogs. Billie suddenly realized she hadn't eaten dinner. She was starved. She looked into the massive stainless-steel side-by-side refrigerator and her mouth watered at the sight of a thick steak and the fixings for her own homemade creamy macaroni and cheese. There was a God.

She glanced about. Should she? After all, this was Nick's house. Yes, but she was protecting it until he arrived home. True, but she had driven Deedee there and watched her break in. That made her an accomplice, didn't it? She had absolutely no business going through Nick's refrigerator or coveting his food.

Fifteen minutes later, the steak was sizzling on the kitchen barbecue, the macaroni and cheese was bubbling in the oven, and Billie was busy sautéing onions, mushrooms, and sweet peppers when Nick stole into the kitchen.

He wasn't prepared for the emotion that caught in his throat at the sight of Billie working at his stove. He couldn't even name the emotion, but he knew it was very different from the usual rush of physical attraction he felt for her. He leaned against the doorjamb for a moment, letting his heart rate slow to a steady beat now that he knew she was safe.

He'd raced from Upperville as soon as he'd gotten the message about the break-in. He had a fourteen-thousand-dollar security system, which Deedee had crippled in thirty seconds. Not for the first time, either, he thought ruefully. But this was the first time it had frightened him to this extent, because crazy Max was out there somewhere . . . waiting for precisely the right moment to blow up something. It didn't matter that Nick had two round-the-clock security guards hidden on the surrounding hills; so far

Max had managed to elude them, leaving his threatening notes and paradoxically thoughtful presents on a doorstep or window ledge.

And then there was Arnie Bates, the parolee he'd hired because the man had needed a second chance and nobody had seemed inclined to give it to him. Not only had the man ignored the needs of Nick's horses, the fact that Arnie continued to sneak smokes in the stable after being warned was more than Nick could tolerate. He'd had no choice but to fire him. Arnie had left muttering threats, which seemed a lot more menacing after Nick discovered that the police were looking to pick up the man for questioning about a burglary.

He pushed aside thoughts of Max and Arnie and allowed himself the pleasure of watching Billie unobserved. Her face was flushed from the heat of the frying pan, her mouth tipped at the corners in some small secret smile. He guessed the smile was satisfaction in the simple task of preparing a meal. It was nice, and he felt a compelling need to be physically closer. He knocked on the mahogany molding and called, "Hi, honey, I'm home," in perfect Dagwood Bumstead fashion so she wouldn't be startled. He leaned over her shoulder and sniffed at the onions, then kissed her in a husbandly fashion on the back of the neck.

Billie smiled in good-humored tolerance and maneuvered away from him. "I bet you're wondering what I'm doing here."

"Nope. George called me on the car phone and explained about the alarm going off."

"George?"

"George Scanlon, the officer who took the statement from you. He sort of keeps an eye on the place." Nick tried to keep his voice light. He would not tell her why Scanlon was watching the place.

Billie wondered if Scanlon was keeping an eye out for Max. Sounded like Max needed to be under constant surveillance. She waited for Nick to say more, but he didn't. She took the macaroni and cheese from the oven and set it on the table. "I got hungry waiting for you, so I helped myself to some food. Hope you don't mind." She speared the steak, dropped it onto a heated platter, and garnished it with the sautéed vegetables.

"Looks good."

Billie smiled at his obvious interest in the steak. "I made enough for two."

Nick stooped in front of the fireplace and struck a match to the kindling. "This seems like a meal that deserves a fire."

"A fire in the middle of summer?"

"Sure. All we have to do is boost the air-conditioning a little."

He grinned at her, brushing a lock of hair from his forehead, and Billie's stomach quivered. That was the smile that had gotten her stuck with Deedee. Absolutely irresistible and very dangerous. It was the kind of smile that made a woman feel special, and Nick had a way of making her feel as though she were the only person in the world he wanted to be with.

Billie was still warning herself to ignore both his

smile and his charm as they shared the meal in front of a cozy fire.

"Your cheese sauce is great," Nick said. "You'll have to show me how to make this. Why are you frowning?"

"I'm thinking." Actually, she was trying to imagine a man sharing an intimate dinner with Sheridan Flock and complimenting her cheese sauce.

"About macaroni?" he asked.

Billie stabbed a slice of pepper. "No. About your smile. It's really something."

"It got me my first million."

Billie raised her eyebrows in silent question.

"Three days after I was born I flashed this smile on my dad and he deposited a million bucks in my name. It wasn't until later that a nurse told him I probably just had gas."

"A million dollars for one smile?" Billie mused aloud. "That was generous of him. Why do you sound so ungrateful?"

Nick shrugged. "It was easy for him to give me money. He had a lot of it."

"What would you have preferred over money?"

The answer came slowly. "Time. I was one of those neglected rich kids." He smiled at her again. "It could have been worse. I could have been a neglected poor kid."

"Doesn't look like you turned out so badly."

Nick helped himself to more macaroni and cheese. "I was lucky. I was literally dropped into Fong's lap."

"The manservant?"

Nick nodded. "He was mother, father, tutor, and

tyrant. And he's still all those things," he confided. "He doesn't let me get away with much."

"I'll have to meet this Fong."

Nick looked into her eyes for a long moment. "I'd like you to meet him. He would approve."

He slouched in his seat and loosed an exasperated sigh. "Can I level with you?" When she merely nodded, he went on. "You instill the strangest feelings in me. There's a lot of lust, but I can handle lust. It's this other stuff. I never tell anyone about my first million because it makes my father sound so crummy. Why did I tell you?"

"It's probably the mother in me. Encourages people to speak confidentially."

She changed the subject. "This is a great kitchen."

"One of the reasons I bought this house was because I fell in love with the kitchen. I like being able to eat right here in front of this fireplace. When it's light out you can look through those big, wall-sized windows and see the countryside rolling away from you. And the best part about the place is Mrs. Duffy. Jack and Ida Duffy live in the stone cottage you passed about a mile down the driveway. They're in charge of the house and grounds. Ida comes up to keep the house clean, and when I get too busy to do my own cooking, she jumps in to save Fong and me from starvation."

"Where is Fong now?"

"I sent him on a well-deserved vacation. Deedee was driving him crazy."

"Sounds like you're happy here."

"Sometimes."

Their gazes met. All the teasing had gone out of Nick's eyes. Billie looked away and reached for their plates. "I should be going."

Nick put his hand on hers. "You can't go yet."

Once again she found herself looking into his compelling eyes. And wishing she weren't so drawn to him. The heat from his hand was both comforting and discomfiting. "Why not?"

"You haven't had dessert."

Billie thought about her getting-in-shape program. "Maybe I'd better skip dessert," she said.

"I'll bet I can convince you otherwise."

Billie arched one brow. "Oh, really?"

"Once you taste my homemade ice cream you'll never turn down my offer of dessert again."

Billie cocked her head to the side. Had she heard him correctly? "You're kidding, right?"

He shook his head as he got up from the table. "I thought it would be fun to make ice cream." He pulled a stainless-steel contraption to the front of the counter. "Fong bought me this a couple of years ago. It's supposed to be the Cadillac of home ice-cream makers." He opened the refrigerator and took out a glass bottle of cream. "I even have real cream. Not the kind they sell in the supermarket with emulsifiers and diglycerides. This cream came from my own cow."

Billie just stared back at him. The man never failed to amaze her. "Okay," she said at last. "I'll stay on one condition."

"Name it."

"Tell me about Max."

CHAPTER SEVEN

Nick's smile faded instantly as he took a can of chocolate syrup and a bottle of vanilla extract from the overhead cabinet. "How do you know about Max?" He paused. "No, don't tell me. Deedee."

"Was she not supposed to say anything?" Billie asked, hoping she didn't end up causing problems between Nick and his cousin.

"No, it's okay. You were bound to find out about him sooner or later." He sighed wearily. "How do I even begin to explain Max Holt to you? He's a misdirected sixteen-year-old kid with an IQ that's totally off the charts. Unlike his sister Deedee, who doesn't have enough sense to get in out of the cold."

"I understand Max blows up things. Is he danger-ous?"

"He might be if he weren't so smart, but he knows what he's doing. He blasted a wooden tub of geraniums to smithereens and sent a solid brass weather vane to the moon, but I'd have to say the fireworks display made it almost worth it."

"Well, we should always consider the positive," she said. "How on earth does he find the material he needs to create these explosions?"

"He has a laboratory of sorts in the kitchen of a guest cottage on the property. These aren't regular bombs, you understand. He makes them with things he finds in the kitchen and garage. We're talking someone who could probably build a generator large enough to support the entire town during a blackout, simply by using wire and tubing and a few other odds and ends. I know it sounds wild, but it's the truth."

Nick sighed. "I could clear out his lab, but he'd only set up another in a different location. He's dev-ilishly clever, remarkably so."

After meeting Deedee, Billie was ready to believe anything about Nick's relatives. "Does Max have a reason for doing what he does, or is he just bored and using it to pass the time?"

"Oh, Max always has a reason. He believes in causes. A champion of the underdog, you might say. He was the only six-year-old I know of who had a bumper sticker that read "Save the Whales" on the back of his bicycle. He actually got his mother to quit smoking by quoting statistics when he was five years old, and once he became an animal activist, she and her friends were afraid to wear furs in his presence."

"So, what is his latest cause?"

"He came to spend summer vacation with me and discovered there were plans to develop some marshland east of here."

Billie nodded. "I know about that, I read about it in your paper. They're putting in a shopping center, a billion condos, and a light industrial park right in the middle of an important stop on the North Atlantic flyway. It's going to endanger millions of birds en route to breeding grounds. It's a national disgrace."

"That's pretty much what Max said. He wants me to use the paper to fight the project."

Billie raised her eyebrows. "And?"

"I don't want the marsh destroyed any more than you do, but it's against my philosophy as a publisher to slant the news. We've come out against it on the editorial page, but that's as far as I'll go. I feel compelled to report both sides of the issue, and there definitely is another side here. That development will bring in revenue for schools and roads and hospitals. The developer claims he's setting aside a significant number of acres for the birds and has taken safeguards to protect it."

Billie snorted.

"Yeah, I know. Anyway, Max has taken a very strong stand and has resorted to his own brand of persuasion to enlist my help. He always leaves a cryptic message beforehand, but he believes if you want to be heard, you have to make a loud noise."

"Like *boom*?"

"Precisely." His brows knitted together in a frown.

"I'm really worried. If I could just get hold of him maybe I could talk some sense into him, but I can't find the kid. He's doing this guerrilla number, skulking around in the woods, leaving candy-bar wrappers all over the place. I've hired security guards, but they can't catch wily Max."

"Are you sure he's nonviolent?"

"He's violently nonviolent. He's just trying to make my life miserable in order to get my attention." Nick paused. "You must think we're a whole family of fruitcakes. I'd feel a lot better if you had a few skeletons hanging in your closet. I don't suppose you'd want to tell me an amusing anecdote about some weird relative of yours?"

"I'm sorry," Billie said, laughing. "My relatives are boring. My family has trouble blowing up balloons. By the way, where are Max's parents?"

"Europe. They flew over for the Irish Derby and went on to the south of France. They're clueless where Max and Deedee are concerned because they were seldom around when the two were growing up. You have to understand, Max came as a complete surprise, which explains why he's ten years younger than his sister. Deedee is the endearing airhead and Max is the eccentric genius. He taught himself to read when he was two and graduated from high school when he was twelve. For the past four years he's bounced around from one major university to the next because they were too boring.

"Max needs to be challenged on a daily basis. Oddly enough, I seem to be a favorite of his because he asks to spend summers with me. Which means I'm in charge at the moment." He made an imaginary gun with his hand, put his index finger to his temple, and pulled the trigger.

"You like him, though, don't you?"

"Yeah. He's not a bad kid. He just doesn't know what to do with all the gifts he's got, and his parents never nurtured or even acknowledged his genius. They just see him as bothersome."

"I think what Max needs most right now is a big hug, and a better way to focus his energies."

Nick's mouth curved at the corners. Only Billie would suggest a hug for Max, which was probably what the kid needed most. He looked at her, feeling an unfamiliar sense of tenderness steal over him.

Half an hour later they took their ice cream to a small den off the solarium and Nick loaded *The African Queen* into the VCR.

Billie's eyes opened wide in surprise. "How did you know I'm a Bogart fan?"

"Lucky guess."

"I bet I've seen *Casablanca* a million times."

Nick slid his arm around Billie's shoulders and snuggled her next to him on the big overstuffed couch. "Listen, sweetheart—"

"Oh, no. Not a Bogart impersonation."

"No. Bogart impersonations are passé. I do Woody Allen impersonating Bogart. Listen, sweetheart—"

Billie couldn't suppress her laughter. "Stop! That's awful."

He pretended to look offended. "Most women go wild when I do my Bogart impersonations."

Billie scraped the bottom of her bowl and licked

her spoon to get the last smidgen of ice cream. "They were merely humoring you, Kaharchek. You'd be better off to find someone who appreciates your ice cream."

"Someone like you, maybe?"

"You're not my type."

Nick propped his feet on the coffee table. "How do you know I'm not your type?"

"Do you wear big, baggy boxer shorts?"

"Oh, yeah, I forgot about the boxer shorts. I'm willing to make a few concessions, but I'd have to draw the line at boxer shorts."

"Do you think Frankie is Deedee's type?"

"You're changing the subject."

"Yes, I am."

He looked thoughtful. "I think he's more her type than any of her other husbands."

"Marriage is very serious. Deedee shouldn't just rush into these things."

"You're not thinking of butting in, are you? Remember, if Deedee doesn't get married, you're the one who's stuck living with her."

"She's not so bad. Like you said, she's really very sweet. Maybe she should get counseling."

"If you really want to know, I think Deedee is happy with her lifestyle. She sort of bumbles along in her endearing innocence, but she thrives on change."

"You think I should mind my own business, huh?"

"Definitely."

Billie curled her legs under her and tried to turn her attention to the movie, but Bogart seemed pale in comparison to Nick Kaharchek. She could literally feel the heat from his body, sense his vitality and maleness. She wanted to lean into it, give in to the sheer pleasure of being in his arms. As if reading her thoughts, he suddenly pulled her close. Close enough for his breath to tangle in her hair. Close enough for his fingers to play along her neck. She swallowed against a rush of desire and knew it was time to go home.

She gave an enormous fake yawn and stretched. "Boy, I sure am tired," she said. "I'd like to see the rest of this movie, but I'm going to have to hit the road."

Nick grinned. "Feeling sexy, huh?"

She met his gaze. "Maybe a little."

He smiled knowingly.

Oh, but he was smug, so pleased with himself. She tried to conjure up some honest-to-goodness anger but wasn't successful. Instead, she burst out laughing.

"What?"

"Men and their egos."

"Hey, it's a small price to pay for the pleasure of our company." He grinned, enjoying their banter. "Know what else? I think you're starting to *like* me. Maybe more than you know." He sifted his fingers through the wavy hair at her temples and lowered his mouth to hers. Her kiss filled him with sweet longing. He wondered if she felt the same. "I like you, too, Billie."

"Nick, I—" Billie couldn't think of a response.

He shifted on the sofa, knowing if he weren't careful he could easily get carried away, and she would rush home in a fit of indignation like the world had never before seen, and probably thwart his future attempts at seduction.

Nick sighed. "I guess you should go home now." Besides, he'd kept her in his house longer than he should have. It had been selfish and dangerous, but he couldn't help it. Max was still lurking about, and the police feared Arnie Bates might create problems, as well.

"I'll walk you out."

Billie spied the headlights through the trees the minute she stepped outside the door with Nick on her heels. "Looks like company is on the way." A white Jaguar slipped through the trees, coasting in their direction.

"Yeah," he said, his tone flat.

Billie was not surprised to find Sheridan Flock behind the wheel. She climbed from the car, resplendent in skin-tight designer jeans, and a knit shirt that exposed her midriff and clung to every curve. If she looked surprised to see Billie, it didn't show on her lovely face.

"I hope I'm not interrupting anything," she said, her features tight.

"What can I do for you, Sheridan?" Nick asked.

She sighed and tossed her head back, her dark hair fanning one cheek. "I was restless and thought I'd ride Clementine."

"In the dark?" Billie blurted.

"I have a lighted arena," Nick told her. He regarded Sheridan. "It's fine with me. You know where to find the light switches."

She looked surprised. "No, I don't recall seeing them."

"I was just leaving anyway," Billie said. "Thanks for dinner, Nick. The ice cream was wonderful."

Sheridan laughed gaily. "Oh, don't tell me he prepared his famous homemade ice cream."

It was the first time the woman had acknowledged her. "Yes," Billie replied. "It was very good."

"Nick is real handy with his ice-cream maker. I'll bet he even pulled out his old Bogart movies and did impersonations."

Billie sensed Nick's embarrassment. She plastered a smile on her face. "Actually, we were so preoccupied with other things, we never got around to watching videos." She had the pleasure of seeing the woman's smile fade from her face. She was irritated with herself for letting Sheridan get to her. She was a thirty-eight-year-old mother of two who had better things to do than stand there swapping snide remarks with Nick's ex-fiancée. But damned if she would let someone like Sheridan Flock try to demean her. She hitched her chin high and turned for her minivan, missing Nick's amused look.

Billie drove home very carefully. She was afraid if she didn't concentrate on her driving, her mind would wander to thoughts about Nick and Sheridan. It was unrealistic to think Nick had not entertained other women in his home, had not prepared homemade ice cream or watched videos with them as he had with her. He'd lived a full life, and women had played a large part in it. She wasn't by nature a jealous person, but she didn't entirely trust Nick Kaharchek. He was too handsome, too charming, too sexy, and too rich. And she suspected he was saddling two horses right now so he could ride beside the woman he'd loved enough to propose marriage to. The fact that Sheridan had broken it off might make a man like Nick even more determined to win her back.

The thought wrenched Billie's heart. She already cared for Nick more than she should. She cared enough that she wanted him to be happy, whether it meant continuing his lifestyle as a womanizer or convincing Sheridan to give him a second chance. She would, as impossible as it sounded at the moment, offer him her friendship for as long as he wanted it, because wanting the best for your friends was what truly mattered. Now all she had to do was convince her heart.

The following morning Deedee shuffled into the kitchen at eleven-thirty and stumbled into a chair. "Coffee?" she asked weakly.

Billie was putting the finishing touches on an apple pie. She washed her hands and brought a coffee cup and the coffeepot to the table. Deedee looked at the pot and muttered something indiscernible.

"You'd like me to pour it for you?" Billie guessed.

Deedee continued to stare at the pot. She swayed in her seat and blinked, but she didn't say anything.

Billie chuckled, filled the coffee cup, and put it in Deedee's hands. "When did you get in last night? You look like you've been run over by an eighteen-wheeler."

Deedee drained the cup and slammed it onto the table. "More, please."

Billie refilled the cup and went back to her pie. "Did you have a good time at the embassy?"

"Yeah." Deedee's voice cracked. She drank some coffee and tried it again. "It was great. Everyone stared at my Stargio. You should have come with us. Is Nick mad at me for breaking his window?"

"He didn't say. I stayed to make sure the house was safe until he got home."

"Poor kid. That must have been so boring."

Billie put the pie in the oven. "No. It was nice. We made ice cream and watched a Bogart movie."

Deedee rolled her eyes. "He really does need new material if he hopes to score with you."

"Come again?"

"He only pulls out the Bogart tape in order to get a woman on his sofa. Once that happens, well, he's pretty much assured a good time."

Just what Billie needed to hear. "He didn't succeed."

"That won't stop him from trying again." Deedee made a tsking sound. "Honey, if you're looking for a husband, you need to shop in another bakery. Nick is *slippery*. Women are always after him. And lately, somebody has been leaving him presents. I'm willing to bet my alimony checks Sheridan is sending them."

Billie felt herself frown. "It doesn't make sense. She broke up with him."

Deedee focused on Billie. "Maybe she realized what a stupid mistake she made.

"It's weird. These presents just appear from nowhere. They're always gifts Nick likes. Who else would know him so well?"

Billie had already resolved herself not to get involved in Nick's love life. If Sheridan wanted to send him gifts, that was fine. If they decided to get married, that was their business. She was prepared to be Nick's friend and nothing more.

"Nick doesn't talk about them, of course. Usually they're left on the doorstep at night." Deedee stretched and gave an enormous yawn. "I suppose I should get dressed. Frankie is sending the car around." She held up a lock of red hair. "I need my hair done, and then I'm going to do some shopping, and then dinner with Frankie. What are you doing tonight, honey? You're not going to sit home and do something domestic, are you?"

"Nope. Nick's giving me a riding lesson early this evening."

"*Eeyeuuw.*"

Billie kept one eye on the road leading to Nick's stable and one eye on the apple pie, which occupied the seat next to her. She'd intended the pie to be repayment for the steak and homemade ice cream, but now she worried that it might be categorized with the gifts Sheridan or other women left for him. It was a simple thank-you gift, one she planned to use to establish their new friendship. By doing so, Nick would feel

no obligation toward her. He would not have to feel
guilty about hurting her feelings when he announced
the engagement was back on. And this would be her
last riding lesson.

She'd inadvertently stepped between a man and
woman who still loved one another but had unre-
solved problems. It was up to her to make a graceful
exit so they could work out those problems without
interference.

Billie had resigned herself to maintaining a healthy
distance from Nicholas Kaharchek by the time she
parked her van in the lot by the barn. She was a
happy, well-adjusted mother of two, and the last thing
she needed in her life were problems.

She took a moment to enjoy the small breeze waft-
ing across the green fields. There was a certain free-
dom in knowing she had made a decision that was
healthy for her. At the same time she felt an acute
sense of loss. Nick meant more to her than she'd originally thought. Sheesh, this nobility thing was tough,
and she was already feeling the sting of it.

The clip-clop of hooves made her turn. Nick approached, leading two horses, already saddled. Billie
breathed a sigh of relief to find that Zeke was not
among them. Even though it was her last lesson, she
did not want to end up in the emergency room again.

Nick came to a halt at the sight of her, fresh and
lovely in the late afternoon sun. How could the
woman give him an adrenaline rush one moment, and
then soothe his weary soul the next? he wondered.
He'd spent most of the day scouring the woods for
Max. The kid had, once again, eluded him and his

men, but only after going beneath the hood of Nick's Mercedes and literally dismantling integral parts in ways that only a seasoned mechanic could accomplish. It didn't matter that Max, to Nick's knowledge, had never looked beneath the hood of a car. The genius in him made it possible to do whatever necessary. There was no telling what the boy was up to now, and that's what had Nick worried, but somehow Billie managed to calm his frayed nerves.

He smiled. "Hi."

Billie's breath caught in the back of her throat. She'd never heard anyone instill so much sexuality in a single word. No wonder Sheridan dropped presents on his doorstep. A voice like that could make a woman go nutso. "Hi, yourself," she managed.

Nick motioned to the sleek black horse to his right. "Billie, I'd like you to meet Ryan's Velvet. He's a seven-year-old Arabian gelding and perfectly named. His gait and his personality are as smooth as velvet."

Billie touched her hand to Velvet's smooth muzzle. "He's beautiful."

"He's the reason I went to Upperville yesterday. I bought him for you."

She snapped her head around, facing him fully. *"What?"*

Nick smiled at her reaction. "I promised you a lifetime of free riding lessons. And I promised you no more Zeke. So I thought it prudent to get you an appropriate horse."

"Prudent" wouldn't have been her first word choice. "Extravagant," "insane," "outrageous" seemed closer to the truth. She was no judge of horseflesh, but it was obvious, even to her, that this was a mega-abucks horse. "Nick, I can't possibly—"

"I was hoping for a simple thank-you," he interrupted.

Billie looked at the exquisite four-footed animal standing patiently beside her and then looked at the exquisite two-footed animal standing close in front of her. "He must've cost a fortune." Her brow puckered. "Why on earth would you give me such a gift? You barely know me. This is something you would give a wife or a child, Nick." She met his gaze. "Or a lover." Like Sheridan, she added silently.

Nick was caught off guard by her question. He gave women gifts all the time, especially those with whom he was intimate, but he couldn't admit as much to Billie. Gifts came easily to him because he could afford them, but instead of looking pleased with the horse as he'd hoped she would, Billie looked confused, and maybe a little hurt.

She took a step back. "I can't accept this," she said softly. "This is too much." She thought of the simple pie sitting in her front seat that was meant to establish their friendship, set boundaries. She had spent a lot of time thinking about it, coming to terms with the fact that nothing would ever come of her relationship with Nick. She looked at him.

"Why would you even consider giving me such a gift?" she asked, her thoughts playing havoc in her head. For all she knew he'd spent the previous night with Sheridan. Billie had chosen to back off in order to give him time to work on the relationship and win back the woman he'd claimed had broken his heart.

"I promised you free riding lessons. You need a good horse. I thought—"

"What did you think, Nick?" she demanded, already suspecting the truth. He had no guarantee that Sheridan would reconcile with him, although she seemed hell-bent on it. Was Billie his backup plan, someone he could come to if things didn't work out with the woman he really loved? Someone who would soothe his wounded ego the next time Sheridan flattened it against the stable door? And what did he expect in the meantime? Was she supposed to hang around and wait for him out of sheer gratitude?

Billie had to admit she was not only angry but hurt. If Nick thought he could buy her, he was looking in the wrong direction.

"Listen, I could have bought you a box of stationery or a scarf to show you my thanks for taking Deedee off my hands, but this gift was as meaningful for me to give you as I'd hoped it would be for you to receive."

"A box of stationery would have been more appropriate."

"I know. But I wanted to give you Velvet instead. It would mean a lot to me if you would accept him."

He touched her hand. "Would it help if I told you there are no strings attached?"

Billie took a moment to reconsider. Had she misunderstood Nick's motives? Had he only meant to show his appreciation because she had taken Deedee off his hands so he could turn his attention to Max and now Sheridan? Their worlds were vastly different—a box of stationery was a nice gift to give as far as she was concerned, but a millionaire like Nick could afford to be more generous.

"Nick, I can't possibly accept this horse. I can't afford to board him."

"You can board him here for free."

She wondered how many horses in the stalls belonged to girlfriends, ex- and otherwise. "What about Sheridan?"

He blinked. "What about her?"

"She is, well, she *was* your fiancée."

"Yes, she was. Past tense."

"Nevertheless, I don't want to get into the middle of something unpleasant."

"Sheridan boards her horse here, but she doesn't tell me how to run my business *or* my personal affairs."

"I thought perhaps the two of you would iron out your difficulties and get back together."

Nick couldn't hide his surprise. "That isn't likely to happen. Sheridan and I parted ways months ago."

"It's obvious she wants you back."

"Look, if you really want to discuss this, I will, but the only reason Sheridan would even think of wanting to resume our relationship is because I've backed off, and she loves a good challenge."

"She looks like someone who's accustomed to getting what she wants."

"In most cases, yes, and she's not above using her father's influence to get it. They're very much alike."

Billie was torn. Was it really over for Nick and

Sheridan? At least *he* sounded convinced. But what lengths would the woman go to in order to win him back?

"Nobody has ever given me something this nice," she confessed, gazing at the horse in awe. "I don't know what to say except thank you very much." She turned to him. "In the future, though—"

"You get stationery." He smiled, relieved to have the matter settled. "I thought we'd go out on a trail ride. I need to unwind and you need to make friends with Velvet."

She nodded.

He helped her mount and adjust her stirrups. "We'll just walk tonight. You can give him a loose rein. When you want him to go forward, apply a little pressure like this," he said, positioning her leg against the horse as he'd shown her before with Zeke. He took her hand in his and arranged the double rein between her fingers. "When you want to stop or go slower you apply a little pressure here." He demonstrated a slight tightening of the reins. "Okay?"

"Okay." Billie tried the commands and felt cautiously optimistic when the horse obeyed. She solemnly followed Nick down the wide dirt drive, mesmerized by Velvet's steady rhythm, his long ebony mane and tail flowing to the cadence of his step. Nick pulled his horse up beside Velvet so they could ride side by side, and Billie noticed the tension in his jaw as he stared into the distance. "Tough day?"

He shrugged. "Small domestic problem."

"Want to talk about it?"

"Maybe later. Right now I'm trying to forget."

"You're not being too successful," Billie observed.

"No."

They rode on in silence through the tall grasses of the meadowlands east of the house. Rabbits and pheasant scurried from the intrusion of horses and humans, and a broad-tailed hawk circled overhead, rising and dropping on the evening drafts. Billie tilted her head back to watch him, unaware that she was being watched.

The light reflected off something nearby. Nick spotted Max, but decided it wasn't the best time to go after him. The kid crouched in the crook of a thick-leafed maple that hugged the treeline marking the end of the meadow. He was dressed in long denim shorts and a sloppy T-shirt that read "Save Planet Earth." His baggy socks bunched at the top of his black-and-white high-top sneakers, revealing long skinny legs and scraped knees. His dark hair was too long, slightly unkempt, his bangs falling past his eyebrows where they sometimes got in the way of his wire-framed eyeglasses.

Nick reined in his horse at the top of a hill and drew the boundaries of his property for Billie. They gazed at the sun, fat and red, slipping behind dark clouds and mauve hills. Maybe twenty minutes of twilight left, he thought. Not enough time to get to the barn and send out a patrol. The house was closer, but Nick wasn't sure it was safe. Max would never intentionally hurt anyone, but he was human . . . and humans made mistakes. It was a mistake that Nick worried about.

He sighed and turned his horse toward the barn.

"We'd better be heading back," he told Billie.

Billie glanced at the treeline and then at Nick. He'd seen something he didn't like—the grim look on his face told her as much—but she couldn't imagine what it was, and she had the distinct impression he didn't want to tell her. It was the ornery bit of Irish inherited from her mother's side of the family that made her want to push. "Well?"

Nick looked at her sideways. "Well what?"

"What's out there?"

"Sky, trees, grass . . ."

"And?" Billie prodded.

"And you're pretty nosy," he teased, not wanting to get into a discussion about Max. The kid would bring out the mother and the teacher in Billie, and she'd start talking about the boy needing hugs again. She'd want to reform him, take him under her wing. And Max would make mincemeat out of her. Nick had seen it happen before. Max didn't take kindly to maternal authority, and his methods of rebuffing it could border on the diabolical.

"Not going to tell me, huh?"

"Nope."

Billie looked at him slyly. "There are ways of making a man talk, you know."

Nick grinned. "Sex?"

"Pie."

"Playing hardball again, huh?"

"You don't know the half of it," Billie said. "It's apple. Freshly baked and perfect. Golden flaky crust, just a hint of cinnamon, nice tart apples."

"And if I spill my guts, I get this pie?"

"Yeah."

"And if I don't talk, what then?"

"Well, actually, you get the pie anyway," Billie admitted. "I baked it for you this morning. Sort of a thank-you for the steak and ice cream."

Nick's eyes darkened. "Looks like if you want information you're going to have to find a new bribe. Maybe I should name the terms."

Billie's stomach dipped. "Apple pie is about as high as I'm prepared to go right now."

He shrugged. She had not said no, she was merely putting him off temporarily, especially if she was still concerned about Sheridan. There was a difference, and he had to admit it made the prospect of their mating even more exciting. "Then I'd love some pie." Nick guided their horses toward the stable and dismounted once they reached the entrance. He handed his horse over to the groom who'd taken Arnie's place.

He went to Billie's side. "A little slower this time," he said, waiting for her to swing her leg over Velvet's back. He stepped close, ready to aid her if she needed it. She slid the length of him, and his body responded instantly. "Are you sure you don't want to renegotiate?"

Billie felt her heart accelerate as her body touched his. She took a steadying breath and scooted away. "I'm still counting on the pie. I figure if you mellow on chocolate-chip-cookie fumes, you'll be putty in my hands after you taste my pie."

"Is that what you want?" he said in a sexy whisper, backing her against the partially opened barn door.

"Would you like me to be putty in your hands?" He could only imagine what it would be like having a certain part of himself in her hands.

Playful flirting, Billie thought, but it could easily be turned into something much more serious ... something she wasn't prepared for. "I'd like you to show me how to take care of Velvet."

Nick sighed and eased away from her. While it was definitely physically frustrating, Billie's slow pace was almost refreshing. Most women were easier, but the woman before him presented a challenge. He had known women who couldn't be rushed, not many, but enough to have made him more than capable of planning a strategy that worked, even with the best of them. He realized, even as he thought it, that he was still the same old Nick, the king of cads.

When they left the barn an hour later, Nick walked Billie to her minivan and peered through the window at his pie. "You weren't kidding! You really did bake me a pie."

Billie feigned insult as she opened the door. "Did you doubt me?"

"No. Not for a second."

She handed him the pie and looked around for his car. "Where's your car?" Even in the dark, Billie could see Nick flush under a five o'clock shadow.

"I'd rather not talk about it."

"Seems like there are a lot of things you'd prefer not to talk about today."

Nick sighed and looked longingly at the pie. "What I'd really prefer is to go home with you and eat this pie in your nice sane house."

He was serious, Billie thought, sensing a hint of tired vulnerability in his voice. She gave him a spontaneous hug. It was the sort of hug you'd give to a teddy bear or a toddler, and it brought a smile to Nick's face. "Don't get any ideas," she said. "I just thought a hug might help."

"It did. I needed a hug."

"You can have the pie, too," she said, handing it to him. "And you can eat it in my house. I might even be able to find some second-rate ice cream to go with it."

Nick gratefully sank into the passenger seat, silently acknowledging that Max was wearing him down, that the hostile parting with Arnie had him concerned, and that Sheridan wasn't making things any easier by making demands on him. When her attempt at seduction hadn't worked, nor her ploy to make him feel guilty, she had resorted to threats. Not that he took her seriously. It was only one of the many devices she used to get what she wanted. Her daddy had taught her well. But Nick was determined not to let it ruin his evening with Billie. The pie and the hug had done it. Somehow, while he was lusting after Billie Pearce's delicious body, she had managed to make him feel less tense, and his troubles less bothersome.

Nick remained quiet on the ride to her house, and, as if sensing his need for silence, Billie didn't press for conversation. She parked the minivan and unlocked her front door, taking pleasure in the faint aroma of apple pie that lingered in the still air of the foyer. She and Nick removed their dusty riding boots and padded in stocking feet to the kitchen. Halfway through the pie they gave up slicing it and ate family-style from the pie plate.

"I didn't have dinner," Nick confessed. "I was afraid Max had booby-trapped the refrigerator."

Billie speared a succulent slice of apple. "You're going to have to do something about Max."

"Yeah." Tomorrow, Nick thought. Tonight he was going to do something about Billie Pearce.

Nick pushed away from the pie and stood. "You know what we need to do now? We need to walk the dog."

A surprised Billie followed after Nick as he took the leash from its wall hanger and hooked it onto Buffy's collar. They stepped out into the steamy Virginia night. The air was thick with the smell of freshly cut grass and roses, and light shone from neighbors' windows, emphasizing the cloying blackness of a moonless sky and unlit street. Once again, they were quiet, but Billie was aware of his every move. She caught him looking at her several times.

"What?" she finally said, wondering if she'd smeared apple pie on her face.

"You're beautiful."

Billie suddenly felt flustered. How long had it been since a man had said those words to her? she wondered. And Nick only had to voice them to make her feel that way. It was an odd feeling, considering she'd spent so many years thinking of herself as simply a wife and mother. What had happened to the woman inside of her, that feminine part of her that had once enjoyed long, hot bubble baths and pretty nightgowns that felt good against her skin? Where had that person gone?

"It's nice of you to walk the dog with me," she said, once Buffy had sniffed several bushes and chosen one to squat beside. "I'm used to doing it by myself."

"I felt the need to do something domestic," Nick said, although he knew he was looking for a reason to hang around. He'd walk the dog all night if he had to.

Billie grinned. "I hope this isn't followed by an overwhelming urge to barbecue chicken. We have a barbecuing curfew here."

Nick waited until they'd entered the house to say anything. He closed the door and gathered Billie to him. "I wasn't thinking of following this with a barbecue. I was thinking of following it with bed."

CHAPTER EIGHT

At first Billie thought she'd misunderstood him. But when she gazed fully into his eyes, she saw that he was serious. "Oh."

He lowered his mouth and kissed her, very thoroughly. His tongue slid between her parted lips as his hands moved to her hips, pulling her close. "I was thinking of making love with you," he murmured. "I've been thinking about it a lot lately."

Billie's mind reeled. This was insanity, she thought. A man didn't just announce he was going to make love to a woman. Or did he? The look on Nick's face was dead serious. And Billie had to confess that she liked being in his arms. She could feel the heat seeping into every part of her, sensitizing breasts that ached to be touched and fingertips that were impatient to explore. Lord, Lord, what was happening to her?

It was simple. She felt like making love with Nicholas Kaharchek tonight.

They looked at one another silently. Billie felt connected to him by something that was too difficult to explain, even to herself. She was reminded again of the deep sense of loss she'd felt at the thought of letting him go. Now that he was truly free to explore their relationship fully, she was equally eager.

They held hands as they climbed the stairs.

"This is nice," Billie said once they reached the second floor, and Nick simply held her.

He chuckled and pulled her into the bathroom. "You think it's nice now, just wait." His voice was low; his eyes dark and filled with erotic promise. He tangled his fingers in her silky hair and kissed her with measured passion. "I want to look at you, and touch you and taste you . . . all of you."

He reached for the buttons on her blouse and noted his trembling fingers. The buttons were small and bothersome. He fumbled, but his large fingers made hard work of the task.

"Your first time?" Billie asked, sweeping his hands aside and unbuttoning the blouse. She pulled it off, exposing a pink lace bra.

Nick's eyes widened at the sight of her breasts peeking over the lace. "That is definitely not very motherly looking."

She arched one brow. "What did you expect, Kaharchek, a white cotton nursing bra?"

He dispensed with it immediately and tossed it aside, caressing each perfect breast, rubbing his thumbs across her already aroused nipples.

Billie's lips parted in surprise at the unexpected heat that flared low in her belly. She had never reacted so strongly to a man, but her attraction to Nick Kaharchek was so potent that she felt a change in the very air around them.

They simply stared at one another for a moment.

Nick turned the water on in the shower and adjusted the spray. He removed the rest of Billie's clothes, impatient to see her.

"You take my breath away," he said, stripping off his own clothes and joining her in the shower stall, watching the warm water cascade over her breasts and run in rivulets over her skin.

He soaped her slowly, beginning with her shoulders and down the small of her back.

All teasing stopped as he slipped his soapy fingers between her thighs where he delighted in bringing her to orgasm. Billie clung to him until her trembling ceased.

By the time they lay beside one another on her bed, Nick literally ached for her, but he took his time, kissing her slowly, running his tongue across her breasts, down her stomach, and finally to the very center of her. He tongued her slowly, until she shook and pleaded for him to enter her. Nick paused only a moment. "Damn condom."

Billie arched high when he slipped inside of her, panting as the contractions rolled across her and triggered the beginnings of Nick's release. They moved in perfect unison. Nick whispered her name on a gasp before they shuddered in one another's arms.

Afterward, Nick gathered her close, kissing her, caressing her. Billie lay awake long after Nick's even breathing told her he'd drifted off to sleep. They were lovers, she thought in disbelief, tucked beside his warm body. Nick had loved her well and hard, but somehow they had reached a point beyond the physical, a new level of intimacy that she had never experienced. She had borne two children by another man, and she'd thought at the time that she loved him. But it had been nothing like this. Her own husband had never once touched that part of her that Nick had discovered tonight, deep inside her heart, an emotion that defied words.

She heard the rustle of bushes outside her window, and smiled. No bogeyman tonight, just the wind blowing through the shrubbery. She wouldn't have to lie awake until the wee hours, imagining the worst.

She felt safe in Nick's arms.

Billie took a deep breath and gave a loud satisfied sigh as she looked at the strips of crispy fried bacon draining on paper towels. It was the most incredible morning ever, she thought, whipping four eggs into an omelet. The sky had never been so blue, the sun so sunny, and her body had never felt so . . . mellow. Her entire world seemed to have expanded.

She had it bad.

Nick had awakened her with a kiss that had quickly turned into lovemaking. Billie felt a tiny quiver in her stomach as she recalled the sound of his husky voice as she'd climaxed, and the look in his eyes as he'd emptied himself into her.

Nick was upstairs in the shower, and she was downstairs in the kitchen, unable to stop smiling. "Can you believe it?" she asked Buffy, who immediately thumped her tail in response, all the while eyeing the bacon. "I finally got laid."

Billie looked up in surprise when the front door opened and Deedee sashayed into the kitchen, followed by Frankie and a bronzed hulk who looked as if he might step on his hands if he didn't stand up straight. "Oh, hell," Billie muttered under her breath and put the eggs aside. She checked her watch. Eight-thirty. What was Deedee doing up at eight-thirty? "Isn't it kind of early for you?" Billie asked. "I didn't think you'd be home until this afternoon."

And she had a naked man in her bathroom, she reminded herself.

Deedee took off a pair of diamond earrings and dropped them in a coffee cup on the kitchen counter. "I haven't been to sleep yet. There was a super party at Hammerhead's house, with the most interesting people. And guess what? Ta-daaa," she called out with a flourish aimed at the man standing next to her. "I brought something home for you."

Billie noticed that Deedee had said "something" as opposed to "someone" and thought that was probably significant. "Gee, this is such a surprise," she managed, unable to think of how else to respond.

"Yeah. I knew you'd be excited. This is Carl. He runs a health spa and he's thinking of becoming a wrestler." Deedee rolled her eyes. "Wait until you see his quads! You'll swoon!"

Billie bit her lip. "Probably we should play it safe and keep his quads under wraps. I hate to swoon before breakfast."

Deedee wrinkled her nose at the bowl filled with whipped egg. "Breakfast. Yuck."

Carl jiggled loose change in the pockets of his rumpled cotton workout pants and directed his attention to Billie. "Deedee tells me you're trying to get into shape. I thought we could spend the day working on your body." He winked at her. "And then we could spend the night working on mine."

Billie felt her upper lip curl and was very carefully phrasing a reply when a masculine voice broke in from the hall. "That sounds like a great offer, Carl, but I'm afraid Billie and I have already made plans for the day."

Everyone turned and gaped at Nick, fresh from his shower, hair still damp, resplendent in a royal-blue towel precariously draped over perfect hips.

Deedee narrowed her eyes at her cousin. "What are you doing here?"

"Taking a shower."

Deedee let out a gigantic sigh. "Billie, Billie, Billie," she admonished in her Betty Boop voice. "How many times have I warned you, Nick is *not* for you? He's hazardous to women."

Carl took a step forward. "Should I punch him out?"

Nick casually leaned against the doorjamb, arms

crossed over his chest, his look menacing. "Maybe I'd like to see you try."

Billie rapped a wooden spoon against the countertop to get their attention. "There will be no punching-out in my house!"

Deedee glared at Nick. "Shame on you, taking advantage of a . . . housewife." She turned to Billie. "Honey, this is not a marrying person. He's only after you-know-what. S-E-X."

Billie clapped her hand over her mouth, but she couldn't keep a giggle from escaping. "Uh-oh, too late. I'm afraid he's already had my body."

Carl snorted at Deedee. "I thought you said she was a nice girl. I only date nice girls."

"I understand, Carl," Billie said, trying to sound remorseful, when it was all she could do not to break out into hearty laughter. "Better luck next time."

"Look what you've done," Deedee said to Nick. "You've ruined everything. I'm never going to find a husband for her if you keep this up."

Nick looked at Billie. "So, you're looking for a husband, huh?"

"Well, I—"

"Darn right she's looking for a husband," Deedee snapped. "She's a single mother with two kids to support. Poor girl is barely making ends meet."

"I'm doing okay," Billie said, not wanting the group to think she was on the verge of public assistance. "Really."

Deedee ignored her. "I'm trying to help Billie find a good man, what with my contacts and all, but you're not making things easy popping out of the bathroom half-naked."

Nick padded to the refrigerator and took out a carton of orange juice. "Oh, what the hell, if it's such a big deal, I guess I could make the sacrifice and marry her."

At first Billie was too stunned to reply. Sacrifice? *Sacrifice?* She hitched her chin high. "Excuse me?" she said, her voice rising in pure indignation. Was this the man who had just made mad passionate love to her, the same man who had whispered endearments in her ears the night before and held her while she'd slept? "Did you just say what I thought you said? Did you use the word 'sacrifice'?"

"Oh, puh-lease," Deedee said, tossing Nick a dark look. "Any man in his right mind would jump for joy at the thought of having Billie as his wife. She's smart and beautiful and—"

Billie preened. "Why, thank you, Deedee."

"Her health is excellent," Deedee went on, "except her foot is still that yucky color. And look at her teeth. I'll bet she's never had a cavity in her life. And she's a lady," Deedee added.

"I might be willing to reconsider," Carl interrupted.

Billie crossed her arms over her breasts, suddenly feeling as though she'd just been placed on an auction block. She was growing more annoyed by the moment. Nick was willing to make a sacrifice and Carl had just offered to reconsider. Hell's bells, who did they think they were? She was no slouch, and she wouldn't be treated like one.

She forced a smile. "I appreciate your kind offers,

gentlemen," she said, glancing from one man to another, "but frankly I'm not interested in either of you."

Nick poured himself some juice and chuckled. "And here I was about to suggest a double wedding." He winked at her.

Billie frowned. What was the wink supposed to mean? As if a giant light bulb had suddenly gone off in her head, she all at once realized Nick was trying to get rid of Carl and save her reputation for his having strolled out of her bathroom wearing only a towel.

Lord, but she could be thickheaded at times.

"Oh, Nick," she said, trying to sound breathless. "I didn't realize this was a *real* marriage proposal. And a double wedding, you say? What a wonderful idea!" She closed the distance between them. "I would love to be your wife." She slipped her arms around his waist, stood on tiptoe and kissed him passionately on the lips.

Nick noted the amused look in Billie's eyes and realized she was also playing the game, no doubt to dissuade Carl and convince Deedee to cease fixing her up with potential husbands.

"Are the two of you serious?" Deedee asked, eyes wide as saucers.

Nick draped his arm around Billie. "Absolutely," he said. "I don't know about Billie, but it was love at first sight for me. I'm willing to change my wild ways for her."

Deedee looked from one to the other. "This is weird."

Nick kissed Billie's forehead. "Sweetheart, I'll

make honeymoon plans immediately. Is there any-place special you'd like to go?"

Billie fluttered her lashes. "Oh, darling, it doesn't matter. The only thing that matters is us being to-gether."

"Maybe we shouldn't wait for Deedee's wedding," he said. "Maybe we should get married right away."

"I know waiting is hard, honeykins, but I promised my mother that I'd never marry a man I'd known less than two weeks. I've only known you for five days."

Nick sighed. "Okay. I guess I'll just have to wait."

Carl looked at Deedee. "Does this mean she doesn't want to go out with me?"

There was a look of incredulity on Nick's face and then the beginnings of a smile. "That's okay, Carl. We wouldn't want you to relax your standards."

"Well, I don't know," Billie said. "In less than two weeks I'll be a married woman. Maybe I should sow a few wild oats."

Nick's eyes darkened. "I don't think so. I have plans for your oats."

Deedee kissed Frankie on the cheek. "I'm going to bed. This is all happening too fast for me. I'm ex-hausted."

"I think you make a cute couple," Frankie told Bil-lie and Nick. "I thought that right from the begin-ning." He slung his arm around Carl. "Come on, Carl, let's go to the gym and work out. Maybe we can have one of those great juice drinks you make."

Billie watched them leave and returned to whipping her eggs. She cocked an eyebrow at Nick. "I think we just got engaged. I'm going to leave it to you to get us out of this."

Nick dropped his towel and moved toward her. "What makes you think I want out of it?"

Billie hastily picked up the towel and handed it to him. "Nicholas Kaharchek! Your cousin Deedee is up-stairs!" She wasn't *even* going to ponder his last sentence.

Billie kneeled in her garden and looked at the cluster of ripe fruit hanging from her tomato plant. Every year it was the same. She planted the tiny seedlings in late spring. She kept them watered and weed-free and organically fertilized. And day by day, before her very eyes, tomatoes, beans, and cucumbers grew on her plants. It always left her awestruck.

Nick was more in awe of Billie than of her toma-toes. He stood beside her, admiring the tan on the back of her neck and the sunny highlights in her short tousled hair. What was happening between them? They were locked in a game he couldn't bring himself to end. Neither of them would admit the engagement was a sham, but neither had said it wasn't.

Deedee was thrilled, of course, not only because the thought of a double wedding sounded fun, but because she was glad Nick had come to his senses and decided to settle down with a good woman. He regretted having started the game to begin with, be-cause of the tension it had created between Billie and him. She was obviously looking for a husband, and after the fiasco of being engaged to Sheridan for six months, the word itself left a bad taste in his mouth. Of course, Billie and Sheridan were nothing alike, so he could take comfort in that.

It was no compliment to Billie that knowing the engagement wasn't real brought so much relief to him, but Billie was probably equally relieved.

Truly, he had no idea what Billie wanted or expected from him, only that the last thing in the world he wanted to do was hurt her. She was looking for a husband, or so Deedee had said. It made sense that she would want a stepfather for her children and the security he could provide, but he was not the man she claimed she was looking for, and he would never be that man. All he could offer her was the here and now, based solely on the fact that he found her sexy and fun and intriguing. They enjoyed each other's company, but they were not in love. He knew she cared about him and found him attractive, but she had made it plain what type of man she was looking for, and he didn't fit the bill.

He bent beside her, studying her face, wishing he could read her thoughts. "Aren't you going to pick them?" he asked, as she stared at the tomatoes.

A tear rolled down Billie's cheek. "I planted this garden with my children, and now they aren't here to pick the first tomato. This is so depressing."

Nick pulled her to her feet and held her close. A terrible sadness swept over him because he didn't know these children who were so special to Billie. He wanted to console her, but he had no idea where to begin. Truth was, he didn't understand getting choked up over a tomato. He tried to speak and discovered that her tear had generated an enormous lump in his throat. He stroked her hair. "Can't we let the tomatoes hang around until your kids get home?"

"No. They'll r-r-rot," she sobbed.

Nick leaned his cheek against the top of her head. "Poor Billie," he said, wishing he could do something to make her happy. Which is why he would not bring up the engagement today. No matter how hard he tried to point out the fact he wasn't right for her, she would feel rejected. Even if she had no interest in marrying him either.

Billie pushed away from Nick, took a tissue from the pocket of her shorts, and blew her nose. She hated being pathetic. "It's just a dumb tomato," she said through clenched teeth before ruthlessly ripping it from the vine. "Besides, who cares about a tomato when you're at Disney World?"

Nick gently picked two more ripe tomatoes. "You have nothing to worry about, Billie. Your kids are on a vacation. A vacation is like a slice of birthday cake . . . a nice treat once a year, but not healthy everyday fare. I'm sure your kids are homesick for their vegetable garden . . . and for their mom."

His perception and sensitivity knocked her back a few paces. "Wow. You don't miss much, do you?"

"You were leading with your left." He added a cucumber to his cache of tomatoes. "You know, this is the first time I've ever picked my own salad. I'm thirty-six years old, and I've never had my own vegetable garden. I feel—" He glanced up at the odd sound Billie had made. "Are you all right?"

He was thirty-six! That made her two years older

than him. Billie instinctively felt her face for imaginary wrinkles. She told herself she was overreacting, and then reminded herself of the gray hair she'd found only the week before. What was she thinking? Not only was Nick handsome, rich, intelligent, and in mint condition, he was younger than her! He probably didn't own a pair of sensible shoes or worry about things like crow's-feet or varicose veins. He'd probably never before slept with a woman who had stretch marks across her lower abdomen from being pregnant.

Billie shook her head. What had she been thinking? She'd been living in fantasyland for the past week, that's what. She'd let the infamous smooth-talking Nick Kaharchek convince her she was the most beautiful and desirable woman in the world. She'd forgotten she was simply Billie Pearce, mother of two, who lived a quiet, simple life, kept a tight budget, and seldom made an impulsive decision. And yet, she'd hopped in bed with Nick the first chance she'd had.

"Billie?"

She snapped her head up, having been so deep in thought she'd forgotten that he was beside her. "I'm sorry, I was just thinking—"

"About the kids?" He smiled tenderly. "I understand."

Billie returned his smile, but she knew he would never understand what was going through her mind. Pictures of a younger and stunning Sheridan Flock filled her head. The woman probably wouldn't know what a stretch mark was if it slapped her in the face.

"Maybe we should take the vegetables inside and have some lemonade."

Nick dutifully followed her inside and deposited the tomatoes on the kitchen counter. He drew Billie to him and nuzzled her sun-warmed hair. They'd shared a bedroom for the past four nights, and he liked the easy intimacy it had produced between them. A ripple of heat knotted his stomach when he felt her breasts flatten against him.

"Deedee isn't home," he murmured, "and it's been five hours since I've seen you naked."

"We need to talk."

"Later." He claimed her mouth with a ferocity that surprised even him. The need for her tore at him, stealing his breath, his control, leaving in its wake raw desire. He felt her instantly yield to him, felt her heat hum under his touch. He kissed her deeply, and he could not get enough of her.

Loving Nick may not have been the best decision she'd ever made—losing him was going to break her heart—but she was a woman and people sometimes did things out of simple human need. And she would cherish every single memory, each touch, each kiss. The way his eyes darkened when he made love to her. Each touch had been indelibly imprinted on her body and heart.

Their loving was perfect, and just as Billie thought she could no longer bear his teasing hand and skillful mouth, he filled her with himself. She arched beneath him, wanting to call his name, but found she had no voice. They moved together, staring into each other's eyes for a short moment until they climaxed.

It was the most amazing experience of her life.

She was about to say something just as the phone rang.

Nick watched her answer the call and wondered at the look of disbelief on her face. She hung up, checked the time on the bedside digital clock, and smacked herself in the forehead. "That was my ex-husband. He's in the hospital with a compound fracture of his left leg, and my kids are arriving at Dulles Airport in half an hour!"

They both jumped out of bed and began scrambling into clothes. Nick tugged at the zipper of his Levi's. "Why didn't he call you sooner?"

"Apparently, he was sedated. You get the car out of the garage, and I'll lock up the house."

Forty-five minutes later, Billie introduced Nick to Christie and Joel Pearce. They looked like their mother, he thought. The same silky brown hair, the same slanted hazel eyes and cute little nose. The boy was sturdy and two inches shorter than his long-legged sister. He solemnly shook Nick's hand and with eight-year-old honesty blurted, "You're not my mom's boyfriend, are you?"

Nick ran his hand through his hair. "Um—"

Joel rolled his eyes and looked at his sister. "We leave her alone for two weeks and look what happens."

Christie shifted the weight of the skateboard she carried on her hip and shuffled in her yellow high-top basketball shoes. "Joel, that's not polite. It's not good manners to say things like that out loud." Her eyes grew wary. "This isn't serious, is it?" she whispered to Billie. "Does Dad know about this?"

"Honey, your daddy and I are just friends now," she said, caught off guard by the question. "We're very good friends, but we're free to have other friends, as well." Billie grabbed two suitcases coming off the baggage carrier. "So, did you guys have a good time?" A change of subject was definitely in order. She could always talk with Christie privately if and when the subject came up again.

"It was great. Except when Dad got sun poisoning, and caught himself with a fishhook in the behind, and fell off the pier into shallow water and broke his leg. It was all so totally uncool. Like he just turned into this big klutz or something since the last time we saw him." Christie paused to transfer the skateboard to her other side. "He was really upset over the sun poisoning. You know how he is about his tan."

"Yeah, you should have heard him," Joel added. "He knows a lot of words we're not allowed to say."

Billie sighed and directed them toward the minivan in the parking lot. "I suppose there are all kinds of education." Nevertheless, she was thankful her children had seen the side of their father that made him appear human instead of the superhero he often came off as.

Nick put the suitcases in the back of the minivan and held the passenger-side door for Billie.

"He's driving our car," Joel said. "Boy, this guy moves fast."

Billie bit her lip and whispered under her breath. "I'm really sorry. I think they're a little surprised."

Nick squeezed her knee. "Don't worry about it."

The black limo was parked in the driveway when they reached home. Joel's eyes got wide. "Wow, look at the cool car! Look at the license plate. It says 'THE ASSASSIN.' Awesome!"

"It belongs to a professional wrestler," Billie explained. "Frankie the Assassin."

"Frankie the Assassin! Oh, man." Joel rolled back in his seat. "He's so cool. He's the best!"

Christie was more reserved. "What's he doing at our house?"

"Nick's cousin Deedee is engaged to Frankie. Deedee is living with us until her wedding next Saturday."

"That's so incredible," Joel said. "Frankie the Assassin in our house. I can't wait to see him. You think he'll autograph my forehead?"

Billie stared at her son. "So you're a big fan, huh?"

"The biggest." Joel rushed from the car to the house.

Christie followed her brother but paused halfway across the lawn. "Can I call Molly and Doris and Jody and ask them over to ogle Frankie?"

Billie gave a weak wave. "Of course. I wouldn't want you to have to ogle him alone." She turned to Nick. "Are those *my* children?"

Nick ruffled her hair. "They're happy to be home." He kissed her on the nose and handed her the skateboard from the back seat. "You take this, and I'll get the suitcases."

Deedee and Frankie were sitting at the kitchen table, drinking iced tea, when Joel burst into the kitchen. "*Eeyeuuw,* it's a kid," Deedee said. She wrinkled her nose and squinted at him. "What are you doing here?"

"I'm Joel Pearce. I live here." He saw Frankie and unconsciously took a step backward into his sister.

"Awesome," Christie breathed, not even noticing her little brother, who was smushed against her. "Totally massive."

Billie pried Joel from his sister and introduced them to Frankie and Deedee.

"What a nice surprise," Deedee said. "Did you guys come home for your mom's wedding?"

Joel looked at his mother. "You're getting married?"

Billie felt the color drain from her face. "Actually, Deedee and Frankie are getting married, and—" What was she supposed to say now?

Christie stood motionless with the phone in her hand. "Does Grandma know about this?"

"Nobody knows," Billie said. "I don't even know."

Christie looked shocked. "You're getting married, and you didn't tell Grandma? Boy, the bananas are gonna hit the fan when she finds out about this. Grandma likes to know everything," Christie explained to the group.

"Wait a minute," Deedee said. "Is this the grandma named Mildred? She called while you were out. I told her everything. She said to call her back pronto."

Billie reached out to steady herself on the kitchen counter. "You didn't tell her about the, uh, wedding, did you?"

Deedee winced. "I figured you'd already told her.

I don't think your dad took it so well because there was a lot of yelling in the background."

Coming up beside Billie with the suitcases, Nick heard most of the exchange. He took one look at Billie's face and set the bags down. "You're hyperventilating, honey. Take a deep breath."

It happened suddenly. A few spots floated across Billie's field of vision and then blackness.

Nick caught her before she hit the floor.

CHAPTER NINE

When Billie came around she was lying on her bed. "What happened?"

Nick let out a whoosh of breath, took the wet cloth from Billie's forehead, and wiped his face with it. "Man, I don't think I've ever been so scared in my life. You fainted."

"I didn't! I never faint."

"You hyperventilated, and then you fainted."

She blinked at the anxious group standing behind Nick. "I'm okay now. Could you guys leave me alone with Nick for a few minutes? There's something we have to talk about." Billie watched Joel and Christie and Frankie and Deedee file out of the room and close the door. "So, what are we going to do?"

"Everybody thinks we're getting married," Nick said, brushing a stray lock of hair from Billie's forehead.

"That's ridiculous."

"Is it?" He didn't know *what* to think. Every instinct in his body told him to run like hell, but he couldn't imagine going even one day without seeing her.

Billie pulled herself up to a sitting position. "For starters, you've never asked me to marry you. I certainly am not going to marry a man who's never even proposed. And even if you did propose, I don't know if I'd say yes. I hardly know you."

Nick grinned and raised his eyebrows.

"Well, maybe I know you pretty well in some ways. But what about my children? You can't just spring this sort of thing on a kid. And there are other things to think about . . . like the fact I'm thirty-eight years old. Old enough to be, well, your older sister."

"You must have hit your head when you fell. I certainly don't think of you as my sister, and I hardly think a couple of years' difference in our ages makes it an issue."

"I don't have a dress. And besides, I think I have an appointment to have my teeth cleaned next Saturday. If I cancel that appointment I won't get another one until October. You know how dentists are."

Nick put the wet cloth back on her forehead. "Maybe you should lie down for a while. You're sort of . . . um, babbling."

"I am not babbling. I'm having a nervous breakdown. There's a difference."

Nick sighed. "Do you *want* me to ask you to marry me?"

"I don't know what I want. Everything is happening so fast I can't catch my breath."

He knew the feeling well, but he wouldn't risk losing her.

"I think we would make a good team."

"Team?"

"You're looking for security, and I'm looking for—" He paused, trying to think of what it was exactly he had found in Billie Pearce that had made such a difference in his life. There were so many things that made her special.

"Sex?"

He looked at her. "Sex has a lot to do with it, yes."

"Get out."

"What?"

She pointed. "I am not about to prostitute myself for any man."

"Sex isn't the only reason, Billie. I like your cookies, too."

"Don't you have someplace you need to be?"

Nick banged his head against the wall. "What would it take to convince you?" When she didn't answer, he planted his hands on his waist and regarded her. "I care about you, dammit. I care what happens to you and your children. I can provide a good home, a stable home." At her look of incredulity, he went on. "Well, once I find Max, and I *do* intend to find him. Today. I don't care if I have to hire the National

Guard, I'm going to find the kid and bring him to his senses."

Billie stared at the ceiling above her bed. He cared about her, but he hadn't mentioned love. "I need time alone."

"Are you waiting for me to tell you I love you?" he asked, feeling as though she were expecting him to go out on an emotional limb when she had never once given him any indication of her own feelings. The words had never come easy for him, and he didn't want to say them unless he was certain.

"I most certainly am not waiting for you to tell me that," she lied. "I don't expect either of us to have fallen in love this quickly. What we have here is a serious case of lust, nothing more."

Nick felt his shoulders sag. Lust? Is that all Billie felt for him? He had felt that way about a lot of women, none of whom he had considered spending his life with. Even with Sheridan his emotions had been different from how he felt about Billie. Billie Pearce, whether she knew it or not, had been giving him large doses of his own medicine.

Nevertheless, he had no intention of letting her go. "Just let me say this," he began. "I'm a man accustomed to getting what I want, and I want you. I don't care what it takes to have you. If you want to be properly courted, okay. I will wine and dine you and, hell, whatever it takes, but in the end, I'm going to have you, even if it means, um, you know." He had trouble saying the word. "Marriage."

He stepped close and kissed her on the nose.

"Don't worry about the kids. I'm great with kids."
Even as he said it, Nick wondered if it were true. The
closest he'd ever come to dealing with a kid was Max,
and he didn't seem any closer to mending the relationship than he had been two weeks ago.

Billie felt the panic rise from her chest. "I can't
discuss this right now."

"We have to at some point." Yet, he didn't feel any
more prepared for the discussion than she did. Wanting her and marrying her were two different things.
And there were children involved. Not to mention a
dog and a cat. Hell, it felt as though he were taking
on an entire city. If only they could have a trial run.
But he knew she would punch him in the face if he
suggested they live together.

"I need time to think," she said. "Why don't you
come to dinner Sunday? We can talk some more
then."

"Okay," he said. "Right now, I need to get home
and see if there's been a Max sighting."

Billie looked at the dining room table and decided it
was satisfactory. Lace tablecloth, good china, pretty
candlesticks, and her mother's linen napkins folded
just so. She straightened a fork and a crystal goblet
and took a step backward.

Joel stood beside her in the neat slacks and starched
cotton shirt he'd worn to church. It was obvious he
wanted to get into his play clothes. "You think this
guy's worth all this fuss?" he asked, tugging at his
collar.

"It's not just for Nick. It's Sunday, and I thought it would be good to have a nice family dinner."

"Are you going to marry him?"

"It's too soon to think about marriage."

"Then how come you haven't called Grandma back?"

"I did call her back. I left a message, remember?" Billie had taken the coward's way out and called that morning when she knew her parents would be attending the early church services. She'd left a message that the marriage thing was a misunderstanding and she would call them in a few days. Knowing what penny-pinchers her parents were, she suspected they'd wait for her call instead of putting additional charges on their phone.

She had never felt so stressed. She cared deeply about Nick, but she wasn't going to let that sway her. She had no intention of following in the footsteps of Deedee and engaging in an endless procession of short-term marriages. This next marriage was for keeps. Husband number two was going to be reliable, mature, and monogamous, and he wouldn't come with a lot of baggage, including an ex-fiancée who obviously wanted him back.

"I guess Nick isn't so bad," Joel said after a moment, "but Frankie would have been better. Is Frankie coming to dinner?"

Billie tried to imagine Nick in flannel boxer shorts and couldn't. "Frankie and Deedee are gone for the day," she said. "Nick is the only one I invited."

Christie passed by the dining room on her way outdoors. "I invited Lisa Marie to dinner. Is that okay?

She's going to scope out Nick for us. She's had lots of practice, since her mom has been married several times."

"Wonderful. Only next time I'd appreciate it if you'd ask in advance." Billie went to the kitchen to get another plate. "Anything else I should know?"

"Buffy threw up on the couch. I think it's because she ate Deedee's eyelash. Buffy probably thought it was a spider."

Joel wrinkled his nose and curled his upper lip. "Gross!"

"We only have about a million spiders running around this house," Christie complained. "It's so disgusting. I'm almost embarrassed to invite my friends over."

Billie shuddered. She knew Christie was exaggerating, but she had found a spider crawling in the bathtub that morning. She had beat it to death for about ten minutes with the broom before she was convinced it was dead. Once she'd rinsed it down the drain, she scrubbed the entire tub with bleach. She made a mental note to call Raoul. If he no longer wanted to handle her pest-control problems because he thought she was ruining her life, she would hire someone else.

So many things to worry about, she thought, grabbing a rag and heading into the living room.

Nick pulled his battered pickup into the driveway and studied the two girls sitting on the lawn. Neither of them looked impressed with his mode of transportation.

Lisa Marie wrinkled her nose. "What's that smell?"

"It's either Nick or the truck," Christie said. "It smells like . . . something rude."

Lisa Marie pretended to gag. "Oh, it's nasty!"

Nick almost chuckled at the looks on their faces. "Good afternoon, ladies," he said as he walked to the door.

"Wow," Lisa Marie said, her gaze following him. "Nice body."

"Is that good?" Christie asked.

Lisa Marie shrugged. "My mom's second husband was a hunk. A real studster. Spent all day in front of the mirror, combing his hair."

"I don't think Nick does that. I've never seen him comb his hair."

"Of course not. You don't find these things out until *after* the wedding. They're always on their good behavior beforehand. As far as we know, this Nick could be marrying your mother for her money."

"I don't think she has that much," Christie whispered.

"Yes, but Nick doesn't know that," Lisa Marie whispered in return. "He might be hoping for a new truck."

Both girls pressed their lips into grim lines.

Billie opened the door with a can of air freshener in her hand.

"I brought some fertilizer for your garden," Nick said, looking at the can. "But I guess you already know that."

Billie grinned. "This is for Buffy. She threw up on the couch."

Nick took a step back and looked at Billie. She was wearing a jeans skirt that came to just above her knees, showing off long slim tanned legs and dainty feet in red flats. She wore a matching red tank top that tucked into the skirt and molded to her high round breasts. If you took away the tiny laugh lines at the corners of her eyes she wouldn't look a day over sixteen, Nick decided. He grabbed her at the waist and pulled her to him for a possessive hello kiss. "I didn't want to disappoint the girls," he explained when he set her free.

Billie looked over his shoulder at Christie and Lisa Marie. They seemed frozen in time, their mouths hanging open, eyes wide. "They appear to be properly impressed."

Nick followed her into the kitchen and pinned her to the counter. "How about you? Are *you* impressed?" he asked, running his warm hand the length of her arm, nibbling on the sensitive area just below her ear.

His touch stirred memories of more intimate encounters, causing her heart to beat faster and her breasts to grow heavy. She felt his hand drop to her hip and begin to explore the contours of one buttock. She raised her arms to encircle his neck and tilted her head back for a kiss.

"Yuck," Joel said from the kitchen table. "Is this going to get mushy?"

Nick and Billie jumped apart. "I didn't see him sitting there!" Nick whispered. "I'm not used to looking for little people."

Billie swallowed. "No, it's definitely not going to get mushy. We were just discussing the chicken, weren't we?"

Nick smiled at Joel, but the boy glanced away. Billie's kids didn't particularly like him. Not that he blamed them. They'd come home to find a new man in their mother's life and talk of a wedding. He needed to find a way to get to know them better so they could all feel more comfortable.

Billie stuffed her hands into mitten-type potholders. "Yessir, the chicken . . . we were wondering if it was done." She hauled the chicken out of the oven and stuck it with a giant fork. "Yup, this sucker's done, all right." She looked at Nick and shuddered at the desire she found in his dark eyes. "Let's eat," she announced a little breathlessly, deciding this was going to be one long meal.

Lisa Marie selected a piece of white meat and turned her attention to Nick. "So, do you have a job?"

Nick thought about it for a minute, surprised to discover that he didn't actually have a job. He gave a few riding lessons, he bought and trained horses, and he owned the newspaper. None of those things seemed to be in the "job" category. A job sounded stuffy and obligatory to him. And while all his activities were in the black, thanks to sound financial management, he didn't really need the income from any of them. "Not what you'd call a real job."

Lisa Marie and Christie exchanged glances.

Nick leaned forward and smiled at Lisa Marie. "I could give you a full financial disclosure, if that would help."

"Are you solvent?" she asked.

"Excuse me," Billie said, deciding Lisa Marie had interrogated him enough.

"Absolutely," Nick said.

"No debts?"

"I put a case of dog food on my charge card yesterday."

Joel looked interested. "You have dogs?"

"A whole herd of them."

"Boy, could I see them sometime?"

Nick helped himself to mashed potatoes. "You bet. In fact, we could all go to my house after supper and take them for a walk in the woods."

Joel turned to his mother. "Could we do that?"

Lisa Marie still looked skeptical. "About your truck—"

Nick took a sip of water. "The one in the driveway?"

"Why does it smell so bad?"

Nick tilted back in his chair and laughed. "Because it's partially filled with fertilizer. Composted manure from my horses."

Lisa Marie and Christie exchanged glances again. "You have horses?" they said in unison.

"A whole herd of them."

"Oh, wow, horses," Joel said, jumping up in his chair. "That's so neat." He accidentally tipped his milk over and everyone scrambled to avoid the flood. "Oh, gross, it's in the peas," he said. "I'm not eating milk peas."

Nick contributed his napkin to the blotting effort and decided this was infinitely different from eating alone at his place. Even when Fong was at home, meals were usually quiet affairs dispensed with be-hind a competing newspaper. And lately, when he had a dinner date it became a sparring match for the main event. This meal was . . . on fire!

In his rush to help clean up the milk, Joel had knocked over a candlestick and ignited the paper nap-kin lining the wicker basket of dinner rolls, which in turn set fire to a sprig of baby's breath in Billie's dried-flower arrangement. All at once, the whole thing lit up.

Nick felt himself knocked aside and stood dumb-founded as Billie trained a fire extinguisher on the table.

There was a full minute of utter silence as everyone stared at the foam-covered mess. A stunned Nick was the first to break it. "Maybe we should go out for burgers."

Billie looked dazed. "Burgers?"

"Can we get greasy, salty French fries?" Joel asked. "And thick shakes? The kind you suck your guts out when you try to drink them through a straw?"

"Yeah," Nick said, "we can get all those things. And afterward, we can go back to my house and all go on a trail ride." He paused, suspecting it would be quite an ordeal saddling five horses, teaching the kids the fundamentals, and then trying to keep everybody together.

"We don't have to ride in your truck, do we?" Christie said.

Nick looked at Billie. "I think your mom will lend us her minivan."

"Everyone needs to change clothes," Billie said

dully, as her children raced up the stairs in unbridled excitement, even Christie and Lisa Marie, who tried so hard to forget they were still kids. Billie stared at her ruined dinner. She had worked so hard to see that everything was perfect. "What a mess."

Nick put an arm around her. "It was a wonderful dinner, honey. I'm sorry your meal got ruined. I'll help clean up when we get back." He looked around. Cleaning up would be no small task. "Does this sort of thing happen often?"

"We have a lot of milk spills. We usually only have a fire once or twice a year." Billie sighed. "You don't have to take us for burgers. I'd understand if you wanted to leave now."

"Not a chance. I'm going to put Lisa Marie on Zeke."

Billie chuckled as she hurried upstairs to change.

An hour later Nick watched his novice horsemen move their mounts into the outdoor ring. He gave them a fifteen-minute lesson and led them down the dusty drive to the fields bordering his house. The grass was tall and sunburned, sprinkled with hardy blue cornflowers and purple thistle. A hint of a breeze stirred the tall weeds and grazed the horses and riders. They followed a narrow path where the brush had been beaten into submission by previous horses carrying riders on evening trail rides throughout the spring and summer.

Since Billie was the only other semi-experienced rider, Nick had put her and Velvet last in line. She looked ahead at her children and her lover and thought her heart would burst. Even if they didn't get married, she would always love Nick for calmly sitting through what was possibly the worst dinner of the century, for scarfing down burgers and fries while Lisa Marie continued to grill him about his health habits, and because he was now pointing out a whippoorwill to Joel who was fascinated.

She watched the heads of her children bobbing before her on their ponies and breathed a long sigh of contentment. It was nice to have them home. She felt at peace with the world. She only wished she could feel more secure in her relationship with Nick.

The sound of a muted boom startled the horses and riders alike. Nick quickly dismounted and got the situation under control, calming the animals as a shaken Billie watched in amazement the small puff of black smoke rise from the trees bordering Nick's house.

Nick uttered an expletive and mounted his horse. "Max."

Everyone strained to see beyond the trees, but the only thing visible was a strange little cloud that slowly traveled with the wind and dissipated piece by piece.

Noting that the children were safe, Billie nudged Velvet over to Nick. "You think he blew up something?"

He turned his horse off the path and headed for the house. "I guess I'd better investigate."

So much for peace and tranquillity, Billie thought as she ordered the kids to stay close.

They approached from the back of the house and saw no apparent damage. The acrid smell of gunpowder permeated the air, and a gray fog hung low to the ground. "Looks like a smoke bomb," Nick said.

"Why would he set off a smoke bomb?"

Nick clenched his teeth. "Bait."

"Ohmigod, what do you think he has in mind?"

That was when they saw it—the white sack sitting in the middle of the patio. A whistle blew and a portable tape recorder kicked in. "Attention. Attention. If you want to be heard, then you have to make a loud noise."

Nick whirled around and sent the horses running away from the sack. "Head for the stable," he yelled, knowing the horses would eagerly comply.

"Ten, nine, eight . . ." the recorder counted. There was an enormous *barooom,* and the white sack exploded.

Christie pulled her horse to a halt and wrinkled her nose. "Holy Toledo, what is that smell?"

Nick shifted in his saddle. "I think it was a stink bomb."

"You know what it smells like?" Joel giggled. "It smells like a giant—"

"Joel Pearce," Billie warned, "please watch your language. We know what it smells like. All of you dismount now." She wasn't about to take a chance on another scare that might cause one of the children to be thrown from a horse.

"I'll probably smell like this for the rest of the summer," Lisa Marie said, once a groom had taken the reins from several horses and led them inside the stable. "It's probably in my hair. I'll have to shave my head. Can you imagine me, the most popular girl at school, with no hair?"

Billie stroked Velvet's neck and tried to calm him. *"Max!"* she shouted. "I know you're out there, you irresponsible, self-centered, spoiled brat. I want you front and center right this minute. I demand an apology for putting my children at risk."

"Yeah, you little twerp," Christie yelled, "if I get my hands on you, you'll be dog meat." She turned to her mother. "Who's Max?"

"Irresponsible?" an indignant voice answered from a large azalea bush. "Irresponsible? I'm not irresponsible. He's the one who's irresponsible!" Max emerged from the bush and pointed at Nick. "He won't take a stand. He won't lift a finger to save millions of innocent birds."

Billie handed her reins to the groom and stomped over to Max. "Listen to me, you juvenile delinquent. You don't just go around destroying other people's property because you have a differing opinion. You could have frightened these horses, and my children could have been thrown off and injured." She had to pause to catch her breath. "And who do you think you are anyway to dictate what Nick should do with his paper? We respect people's rights in this country. For crying out loud, Max, grow up!" She hadn't realized she was shouting.

Max squinted at Billie. "Who *are* you?"

"Billie Pearce. And these are my two children, Joel and Christie, and Christie's friend Lisa Marie."

"My hair is ruined, thanks to you," Lisa Marie said.

"My mom teaches sixth grade," Joel said when Max's gaze fell on him.

Max rolled his eyes. "I would have figured her for a prison guard at San Quentin."

Nick put a firm hand on Max's arm. "I'd like to speak with you in private," he said between clenched teeth. "In the house."

"Man, he's gonna get it now," Joel said.

Billie felt a stab of compassion for Max when he returned. He looked so small next to Nick. Not to mention confused.

"I'm sorry," he said to Billie. "I was rude."

"Yes, you were. Why did you come out of the bushes just now? I thought you were in hiding."

Max tipped his baseball cap farther back on his head. "I've run out of money and candy bars." Max plunged his hands into the pockets of long denim shorts and stared at the toes of his high-top sneakers.

Billie shook her head sadly. He was just a kid. And he couldn't be as bad as all that if he cared passionately about a bunch of ducks and snipes. "So," Billie said to Max, "have you had supper?"

He pulled four candy wrappers out of his pocket. "I've been living on field rations."

Billie grimaced. "No wonder you're not thinking clearly. How about if we go inside, and I whip up some food for you?" She looked at Nick. "Is that all right? Can you watch my kids?"

Nick shrugged, but his eyes hardened when he turned to Max. "No funny stuff. I mean it."

"Max and I will be just fine," Billie replied, pointing toward the house authoritatively. "Let's go." She started walking and he followed.

"Seems to me there were some hamburger patties in the freezer," Billie said to Max once they walked through the front door of the house. "You like hamburgers?"

"If you do them on the grill."

She shot him a look. "As long as you behave yourself."

A few minutes later, Billie placed the patties on the indoor grill and handed Max the recipe for homemade chocolate ice cream. "You're in charge of dessert."

"I can't cook."

"You're about to learn." She dragged the ice-cream maker to the front of the counter and plugged it in. "You make the ice cream while I fix a salad."

Max surveyed the ingredients lined up before him and began measuring. "This is like chemistry," he said.

"Do you like chemistry?"

He nodded. "I have my own laboratory at home. I set one up on Nick's property, but it's pretty simple compared to my other one."

"Don't you have anything better to do than make bombs?"

Max licked a splot of chocolate sauce off his finger. "No. I'm on vacation. Actually, I don't have anything better to do ever. I go to college, but I don't need a job because I'm so rich. It all seems kind of pointless."

Billie looked at him, nonplussed. "That's ridiculous. You have a chance to do all kinds of wonderful things. What about the birds? If you're so interested in them, you could be a naturalist or an ornithologist."

"I'd rather be a rock star. They get all the girls."

Billie set a bowl of salad in front of him. "You like girls?"

Max ate a radish. "Yeah, but it's a little limiting being four years younger and six inches shorter than all the girls you go to school with."

"Don't you know any girls your own age?"

"I don't know *anybody* my age."

Billie checked on the ice cream. "Must be lonely."

He shrugged. "I'm used to it." He poured ketchup and mustard on the hamburger Billie handed him, added a few pickle slices, and chomped into it.

Nick, Joel, Christie, and Lisa Marie came in just as Max was finishing his third hamburger.

Christie's eyes were shining. "Nick said next time we come we can brush the horses before we ride them, and he's going to teach me how to jump, and he says I need a pony-club-approved hat."

Joel rubbed his eyes and yawned. "I'm tired."

Billie scooped out the fresh-made ice cream. "Too tired for dessert?"

"I made it," Max said. "I made it all by myself."

Christie looked at him suspiciously. "Will it blow up or smell bad?"

"I've decided to go into retirement on the bomb stuff. It was getting boring."

"I've got more important things for Max to do," Billie said.

He looked at her. "You do?"

She smiled sweetly. "If you're such a genius, I figure you could fix a number of things in my house. To sort of make up for scaring me and risking bodily injury to my children."

Max squirmed in his seat. "Okay."

"I'll see you at eight A.M. sharp."

"How will I get there?"

"You're smart enough to figure it out."

Nick tried to hide his amusement as he watched Max's shoulders sag. Max had just met his match, and it would probably do him a world of good.

Nick ate his ice cream in silence, watching Billie, her children, and Max. A ready-made family, he reminded himself. A little different from what he'd imagined getting involved in. Kids were noisy, demanding, and took up a lot of time. It would mean a lot more responsibility than he presently had.

Was he up to it?

Billie glanced over at Nick, and from the look on his face she knew instantly what he was thinking. He was reminding himself she was a package deal. She came with children and pets, doctors and dentists and vet bills. There were school clothes to buy, shoes that needed to be replaced several times a year, birthdays to remember, holidays to shop for. There were small and large dramas in raising children, sacrifices and responsibilities that could shake even the most devoted parent.

It was one thing for Nick to want her in his bed but another thing to involve himself with a woman and her entire family. If he was smart he would git out while the gittin' was good, as her father used to say. Perhaps he was considering just that. His gaze found hers, and their eyes held for a long minute before Billie resumed cleaning the counter.

CHAPTER TEN

Billie returned home to find the house two doors down surrounded by police cars with flashing blue lights. Joel, Christie, and Lisa Marie bounded up from their seats, craning their necks to try to get a look at what was going on.

"Go straight inside," Billie said as soon as she parked in her driveway. The kids argued, but she was firm. They did as she ordered, but peered out the windows as Billie crossed the street and spoke with a young policeman.

"We had a break-in," the officer said. "About an hour ago. Seems the owners are on vacation."

"Yes," Billie said. "The Sherringtons took an Alaskan cruise. I don't expect them back for a few more days. Do you have any idea who did it?"

He shook his head. "Doesn't look as though anything was taken. Someone tried to pry open the back window and set off the alarm. Needless to say, they didn't hang around."

"Thank goodness. The Sherringtons are such nice people."

"I understand there was another minor burglary in the neighborhood not long ago. Have you seen anything out of the ordinary recently? Kids loitering about? Anybody suspicious-looking?"

She hesitated, wondering if she should tell him of the strange noises she'd heard outside her bedroom window. Had she simply been going through a period of paranoia with her children away?

"Anything you can tell me will help, ma'am," the man said, as though reading her mind.

Billie smiled. "I know it's just my imagination," she said, "but from time to time I hear rustling sounds outside my bedroom window. I'm sure it's nothing. This neighborhood has always been so safe."

"We suspect kids setting off alarms as pranks," he said, "but it never hurts to be cautious. I'll check around your house before I leave."

Billie spotted a set of headlights and saw Raoul's truck pull up in front of the house. "You might want to talk to that gentleman," she said, pointing. "Mr. Hernandez keeps an eye out when people go out of town. I know he's collecting the Sherringtons' mail and newspapers."

The officer thanked her and headed in Raoul's direction. Billie sighed and started toward her house. She had always felt so safe there. Perhaps it *was* time she purchased an alarm system.

Christie and Joel hit her with a dozen questions the moment she stepped inside the house. "Everything's okay," she assured them and explained what the police suspected. "Where's Lisa Marie?"

"She's calling her mom to come get her," Christie said. "She's scared to stay here, what with the burglary and the spiders. I dread going back to school and having the other kids tease me about all the bugs in our house and my mom marrying a man who's almost a stranger. I mean, what do we really know about Nick and his crazy cousins?"

"It's *so* cool," Joel said. "I can't *wait* to tell my friends."

Lisa Marie came into the living room. "My mom's on the way. I'm allergic to insect bites. Nothing personal, you understand."

Billie nodded. "Don't forget your clothes," she said.

Ten minutes later, Lisa Marie's mother picked her up. Billie assured the woman everything was okay, but she didn't look convinced as she hurried down the walk with her daughter in tow.

Billie sent Joel and Christie upstairs for showers and put on a pot of coffee. She was getting ready to pour a cup when the doorbell rang. She let Raoul in.

"The Sherringtons are going to be upset over this," he said. "I was supposed to be watching the house."

"You can't be there twenty-four hours a day."

"I could have prevented it if I hadn't fallen asleep on the sofa watching TV."

He looked so downtrodden that Billie felt sorry for him. "Come in and have a cup of coffee with me."

He started inside and paused. "Is that crazy woman here?"

Billie chuckled. "No, Deedee is out. Probably won't get in until the wee hours."

Raoul closed the door behind her and followed her into the kitchen, taking his usual place at the table. He remained quiet as Billie prepared their coffee. "Any luck with the German roaches?" she asked, taking a chair across from him.

He shrugged. "I'm still working on it. How's your place?"

"We've seen a few more spiders. Deedee shrieks every time she sees one, and I think Christie is considering running away."

He looked tired and worn. "I must be losing my touch."

"I'm sorry to complain, but it's getting out of hand."

"I'm going to try something stronger. You'll have to put your animals outside and leave the house for a few hours once I spray." He paused. "Have you heard any more noises at night?"

"A couple of times. I told the officer. He's going to look around before he leaves."

"You're not the only one hearing things at night," Raoul said. "I ran into Mrs. Cartwright at the grocery store, and she complained about it. Said her dog went crazy barking last Tuesday night. She called the police, but they didn't find anything. Of course, the police insist it's just kids messing around and since nothing is ever missing they don't take it seriously. I think there's more to it."

Billie shivered. "What do you mean?"

"I haven't figured it out yet, but I plan to spend the night in my truck tonight so I can keep an eye on things."

"Don't you think that's going beyond the call of duty? You have a family at home."

"These people count on me."

Billie opened her mouth to respond but was interrupted when the front door opened and slammed shut. "Men!" Deedee screeched at the top of her voice.

The door opened and slammed again. "Lady," Frankie shouted, "you are a fruitcake! The nuttiest of them all."

"Oh, yeah? Well, you don't exactly have both oars in the water either, mister. I never want to see you again. The wedding is off."

"That suits me just fine because no way am I going to sleep on French provincial furniture. It's for sissies. Wrestlers need big leather stuff."

Billie raced from the kitchen with Raoul on her heels. "What's going on here?"

"We're having a fight," Deedee said. "Mr. Big Shot here flirted with some slut right in front of me."

"She's not a slut, and I didn't flirt with her. She simply asked me to write something on her forehead. People do it all the time."

Deedee crossed her arms over ample breasts. "Your telephone number?"

"I can explain that if you'd shut up long enough."

"You were looking at her boobs."

"Was not."

"Was, too."

"Excuse me!" Billie said, glancing up to find Christie and Joel watching the whole exchange from the top of the stairs. "I would appreciate it if you'd take this fight elsewhere. My children are in residence." She tossed Joel and Christie a stern look. "Bedtime," she announced.

"Aw, Mom!" Both kids disappeared into their rooms.

"I'm sorry," Deedee said, tears welling in her eyes. "I'm not used to a man, especially my fiancé, trying to pick up a woman in my presence. Most men usually can't take their eyes off me."

"I wasn't flirting," Frankie told Billie. "The woman came stumbling up to me—I think she was drunk—and she asked me to sign her forehead."

"She asked for his phone number, and he gave it to her."

"I was surprised," Frankie said, "but I realized my mistake as soon as I started, so I wrote down Nick's number instead."

Deedee glanced at him in shock. "You gave her Nick's phone number?" All at once, she laughed. "Boy, he's going to be mad as hell when some strange woman calls in the middle of the night."

"Maybe not," Raoul said.

Billie shot him a dark look. "You stay out of this."

"You really gave her Nick's phone number, Frankie?" Deedee asked in a little-girl voice.

"I tried to tell you in the limo, but you wouldn't stop yelling at me long enough to listen. I didn't realize you were the jealous type. I mean, a woman with your looks. What do you have to be jealous about?"

"Oh, Frankie, what a sweet thing to say."

He stepped closer. "Does this mean you're not mad at me anymore?"

She paused. "I don't know. That statement about the French provincial furniture cut me pretty deep."

"I love French provincial furniture, baby. I was just saying that to get back at you for calling me a low-life scumbag, womanizing useless piece of meat."

"Why, I never—"

"I know you didn't mean it." Frankie reached for her, and Deedee went willingly into his arms.

They kissed deeply. Billie and Raoul exchanged looks.

"I love fighting with you," Deedee said as soon as they broke the kiss. "It means we get to make up. Come with me." They started for the stairs.

"Hold it right there," Billie said. "Once again, let me remind you there are children in the house."

"Oh, yeah," Deedee said.

"We can make up in the limo," Frankie suggested. "I'll have the chauffeur take a walk. A long walk."

Deedee beamed. "Good idea."

They hurried out the front door without another word.

Billie and Raoul exchanged looks. "Would you care for more coffee?" she asked as if the entire incident had never occurred.

"No, I need to plan my stakeout. Call me when it's

convenient for me to come in with the heavy-duty spray." He started for the door and turned. "You know, this used to be a nice quiet neighborhood before the riffraff moved in."

"Excuse me?" Billie said, taking offense.

He let himself out and closed the door behind him.

Much later, when Joel and Christie were asleep, Billie lay alone in her bed and stared at the ceiling. She still felt the sting of embarrassment that Raoul had witnessed the craziness going on in her life. He had called her friends riffraff. Worse, her children had come home to an entirely different life from the one they'd left to go on vacation, and she wondered what her son and daughter must think. Not only that, Billie was too embarrassed and confused to call her parents because they would start asking questions about her wedding plans, and she had no answers.

She had no idea where the relationship with Nick was going. Oh, he wanted her all right, that much was clear. But he had never once told her he loved her or if he was merely looking for her to keep his bed warm. He thought they'd make a good team. *A good team!* He'd offered security for her children, but he hadn't given any indication that he wanted to take an active role in their lives.

And how about her? Did she love him enough to let go of all her doubts and try to build a future with him despite the odds? The double marriage might have started out as a joke, but it wasn't anything to joke about at the moment because neither of them knew whether to call it off or go along with it.

She would have to deal with Max and Deedee on a regular basis if she married Nick, Billie reminded herself. They were both basically nice people, but she wasn't sure she'd like having her children exposed to them over long periods of time. They weren't her idea of perfect role models. From what she could tell, they drifted in and out of Nick's life as if he ran a halfway house for wayward cousins. It left her to wonder who else periodically occupied bedrooms in the comfy mansion. And there was Fong, the mystery man who had raised Nick. What on earth would they do with Fong?

That left Sheridan. Would she be willing to back off or would she continue to haunt them? Despite what Nick had said about the relationship being over, Billie couldn't imagine a woman like Sheridan Flock—a woman accustomed to getting her way—simply disappearing into the woodwork.

Billie didn't need problems. She had tried to protect her children to the best of her ability, giving them the love and security and strong sense of family that wasn't always easy to do when their father played only a part-time role in their lives. She'd tried to make their home a stable one, passing on the teachings she'd received as a child in hopes of turning them into two well-adjusted and productive adults. As far as she was concerned, raising a child was the single most important task there was.

What kind of life could she hope to offer them if she became more involved with Nick? Or eventually married him?

Billie stretched in her bed and absently ran her hand over the untouched pillow next to her. It was shocking how quickly she had become used to having a man in her bed—when it was the right man. She could close her eyes and recall the way Nick looked in sleep. She thought about the way the sheets rustled as he turned toward her, and the protective arm that kept her snug against him while she slept.

She thought about their lovemaking, and as always, her stomach fluttered. Perhaps she was pretty hot stuff after all. She owed her children the best, she told herself. But what about her? Did she not deserve the best, as well? Even if it meant change?

It did not strike her as being odd that she was not one who enjoyed change. It had to do with the divorce. It was the reason she'd struggled to keep the house. The upheaval following the breakup of her marriage had convinced Billie that everything else in their lives must remain perfectly intact. Her children would continue to live in the same house, attend the same school, enjoy the same friends, and so on. She had not even changed the shelf paper in her cabinets, and she'd balked when Christie wanted to redecorate her room.

Four years was a long time to resist change.

It was scary because Billie could not imagine loving another man as she did Nick. He was easy to talk to, and easy to love. He made her feel sexy, and he made her laugh. She thought about the way he'd stood in shocked silence when the dinner fire had been extinguished, and then offered in a matter-of-fact tone to take everybody out for burgers. It had been awful, but Billie loved him even more for remaining calm in the midst of a disaster. He was a man she could live with for a very long time, but only if they were both willing to make changes and take risks.

It was her last thought before she drifted off.

Billie had not been asleep long when she heard the noise. Her eyes popped open, and she stared into darkness. Even though her mind was dulled from sleep, she knew something wasn't right.

She had been dreaming that someone had come into her room. She had literally felt a presence standing over her, watching her while she slept. Then a noise so light that she might have imagined it, the sound of a footstep.

She sat up. "Christie? Joel?"

There was no answer. She reached for the lamp beside her bed, found the switch, and turned it on. Light flooded her room. She was alone. There was no sign that anyone had been there, but she sensed it. It was as though the air had shifted. She smelled something nice. Perfume?

Her bedroom door was closed. Odd, because she always left it open in case one of the kids needed her during the night. A night-light in the hall made it easy for them to reach her room. The light gave off a soft glow so that if she got up during the night, her room was not cloaked in darkness as it had been when she'd awakened only seconds before.

Had she closed the door tonight without thinking?

Billie whipped the covers aside and hurried down

the hall to her children's bedrooms, flipping on the light as she went. She almost tripped over a football entering Joel's room, but she found the boy sleeping peacefully in his bed. Christie was tucked beneath her cover as well. Buffy raised her head and wagged her tail at the sight of Billie.

Some watchdog, Billie thought, knowing that the animal would sleep through a demolition team.

Next, Billie checked Deedee's room. She had heard the woman come in shortly after she'd gone to bed. She found Deedee in her bed, eye mask in place.

Billie went through the house, turning on lights, checking closets. She looked in the garage. Everything seemed to be in place. She checked the back door and found it locked, then moved to the front door.

The door was unlocked, even the dead bolt that Billie always locked because Deedee had keys for both locks. She had to choke back anger. Deedee had obviously forgotten to lock up when she came in. The thought that the woman had been so thoughtless annoyed the hell out of her, and she was tempted to go upstairs and wake her. Deedee might be an airhead at times, but there was no excuse for leaving the door unlocked, especially since the neighborhood had been plagued with break-ins.

Deedee had to go.

CHAPTER ELEVEN

Billie awoke at six the next morning, tired and groggy after lying awake half the night listening for sounds. She climbed from bed and headed straight for Dee-dee's room. The woman was sound asleep and probably wouldn't wake till noon, if she were left alone.

Billie had no intention of doing so.

She tapped Deedee on the shoulder several times before pulling the mask from her eyes. "Wake up, Deedee," she said.

The woman moaned. "This had better be good."

Billie planted her hands on her hips. "You left the front door unlocked last night."

Deedee yawned and sat up. "What are you talking about?"

Billie didn't want to tell her about the noise that had awakened her during the night and risk having her tell the children. "I woke up last night and found the door unlocked."

Deedee looked offended. "I'm not an idiot," she said. "I always lock the door, as well as the dead bolt. Besides, I used the back door last night because I didn't want to wake anyone. And guess what? I found *it* unlocked."

Billie gaped at her. "Are you sure?"

"Yes, I'm sure. I was surprised because I know what a stickler you are about locking up before bedtime."

Billie tried to think back. She was certain she had locked the doors. "Tell me something. Did you come into my room last night?"

"No, why?"

"Are you sure? Maybe you had too much to drink and ended up in the wrong room."

"I seldom drink anything except diet tonic with a slice of lime. What's going on?"

"I must be getting paranoid," Billie said. "I had a bad dream last night, that's all." Even as she said it she wondered how it was possible when she had distinctly smelled a woman's perfume. Had that been part of her dream as well?

"I'm sorry for accusing you," she said, leaving the room. She went downstairs and poured a cup of coffee. She paced the kitchen. Her eyes caught the key rack beside the door and she froze. The spare keys that she always kept on hand were gone. A chill raced down her back.

She told herself to calm down. There had to be a reasonable explanation. Had one of the kids lost their keys and taken the extra ones? Or could Deedee or Frankie have taken it?

She hurried upstairs to Christie's room. The girl opened her eyes. "What?"

"Do you have your house keys?"

"Of course I do. Why?"

"Someone took the spare set off the key rack."

"Don't look at me. Ask Joel."

Billie found the boy sleeping soundly. She hated to wake him, but she had to know what was going on. "Joel?"

"Yeah?"

She went through the same spiel she had with Christie.

"My keys are in my book bag," he said. "They're in the side pocket."

Billie found the keys. "Go back to sleep, honey."

She thought about waking Deedee again to see if she'd taken the spare set and decided it could wait. She didn't want to wake her again. With the hours she kept, the poor woman needed her sleep.

Billie bumped into Christie on her way downstairs. The girl was headed for the bathroom.

"I'm going out for a walk," Billie said, hoping the fresh air would clear her head. Her foot was too sore for her usual morning jog, but she could walk and think and maybe lower her stress level over the missing keys. "I'll be back in half an hour."

Christie looked skeptical. "Why would you walk when we have a perfectly good minivan?"

"For the exercise. Usually, I jog."

"At your age? Did you check it out with a doctor first?"

Billie rolled her eyes. "For goodness' sake, I'm only thirty-eight."

"You're no spring chicken, Mom, and you're the perfect candidate for shin splints."

Some people were really good at taking the wind out of one's sails, Billie thought. "Yes, but the exercise helps my rheumatism and arthritis so I just have to take my chances. Thanks for your concern."

Billie returned to her room. She no longer smelled the scent. She must've dreamed it. She slipped into her slinky black running shorts and dropped a cutoff T-shirt over her head. She laced up her running shoes. The swelling in her foot had gone down, and it wasn't as sore, but her skin was still tinged a light purple. She let herself out the front door a few minutes later.

It was a beautiful morning; sun shining, blue skies, birds singing. Billie stretched, took a deep breath, and started down the driveway, taking care with her foot. No matter what, she wanted to get out and enjoy the day.

She wondered if she should call the police.

Of course, they would probably assume someone in the house had forgotten to lock up before going to bed. Was it possible she had forgotten? It wasn't like she didn't have a lot on her mind these days. Maybe she *had* forgotten. She would hold off notifying the authorities and calling in a locksmith for now. Tonight she'd make a point to check the windows and see that they were securely locked, and she would double-check the doors before going to bed. And she'd hunt for the missing keys. They'd probably turn up—after all, in a house as hectic as hers, her kids and their friends coming in and out all the time, she was accustomed to items being misplaced on a regular basis.

Billie pushed these worries aside and thought of Nick. She had no idea what she was going to do about him. All she knew for certain was that she loved him.

Thirty minutes later, Billie returned home and smiled to find Nick's truck in the driveway. She opened the front door and gave a sigh of pleasure at the aroma of coffee brewing. Only Nick would think of doing something so thoughtful. She paused. He was having a conversation with the dog.

"Just one more piece of muffin," he said to Buffy, "as long as you don't cough up a fur ball like the cat did."

Billie entered the kitchen. "The cat coughed up a fur ball?"

Nick smiled when he saw her. "I thought the dang thing was having a seizure. Don't worry, I cleaned it up." He studied the slim woman standing in front of him, and the grin got broader. She was a sight to behold, and his heart seemed to beat faster just looking at her, cheeks flushed pink under her tan, the hair around her face curled in damp ringlets. She wore the standard fare in running shorts, but Nick thought they looked incredibly sexy on her, as did the cutoff T-shirt that displayed a tantalizing swath of midriff.

"Cat got your tongue?" Billie asked when he didn't answer.

His smile suddenly became wolfish and his eyes heavy-lidded as his hands reached out for her. "I like looking at you. I definitely like this little shirt."

All the tiredness of her sleepless night disappeared. Billie wondered if she should tell Nick about her fears of the night before but decided against it. Nick had enough problems of his own at the moment. He reached for her, and she forgot about all her worries, even the missing keys.

It seemed right that he should be in her kitchen making coffee.

"I made breakfast," Nick said.

"Oh, yeah?"

Nick opened the door to the microwave, releasing the sweet, homey smell of cinnamon buns. He took the coffeepot to the table and filled two mugs, and Billie brought the buns.

"What are you doing here?" Billie asked. "Did you come over just to make me breakfast?"

Nick sipped his coffee. "Max needed a ride. I caught him going down the driveway on an old go-cart he rebuilt last night using parts from my car engine."

"The Mercedes? You're kidding. Please tell me you're kidding."

Nick shook his head. "He was going to drive over here on the go-cart, but I told him he would get pulled off the road by the first cop who saw him. Just because Max's IQ is out of sight doesn't mean he always thinks things through. He just found your name in the phone book and decided to head over."

"What are you going to do about your car?" she asked, unable to believe the boy had actually taken parts from beneath the hood of a brand-new Mercedes 550 SL.

"Oh, he's going to fix it or I'm sending him home. I've had enough of his nonsense." He paused. "Besides, how can I take my girl on a date if I don't have a car?"

Billie suddenly thought of her minivan sitting out front, unprotected. "Where is he now?"

"In the garage pouring gas and oil in your lawn mower. You must've scared the bejesus out of him, because he plans to mow your grass before he starts on his other chores."

"The lawn mower doesn't work."

She'd barely gotten the words out of her mouth before she heard the engine of her antique lawn mower roar to life.

Nick grinned. "It does now." He paused and studied her face. "I adore you, Billie Pearce."

She stopped chewing. "Yeah?"

He nodded. "So, do you think we should get married? For real?"

She couldn't hide her surprise. "What brought that on?"

"Fear of losing the best thing in my life."

She was touched by his sincerity. "That's very sweet, Nick." Sweet, but not enough. You didn't marry a person because you feared losing them. You married out of love, plain and simple.

"It makes sense when you think about it. We're together most of the time anyway."

His reasons probably sounded good in his own ears, but for Billie it wasn't enough. "I've never just jumped into anything," she confessed. "I've always taken my time and thought things over carefully."

Nick saw the unease in her eyes. "Do you trust me, Billie?"

Oddly, enough, she did trust him, although there was a time she'd thought she would never trust another man as long as she lived. "Yes."

"There's your answer." He stroked her cheek. "We'll be good together."

Billie felt her throat fill with emotion. She turned away so he couldn't see how close to tears she was. He simply couldn't bring himself to say the words. "I need more time."

"We don't have much time if we're going to be in Deedee and Frankie's wedding."

"Is that what you want? A double wedding?"

He shrugged. "It's a little unconventional, but it might be fun."

Fun. Nick thought it sounded fun. Billie didn't respond.

Four feet thumped on the stairs and Christie and Joel burst into the kitchen. "I told you I smelled fresh rolls down here!" Joel shouted triumphantly to Christie. "I could smell it all the way in my bedroom. Wow, what is it?" He looked at the plate of steaming buns. "Cinnamon rolls! I knew it!" He became more subdued. "Are they for *all* of us?"

Nick held the plate out to him. "Absolutely."

Joel held the bun in one hand and opened the refrigerator door with the other, reaching for orange juice. The heavy glass bottle slipped through his fingers and smashed on the floor. "Oh, crumb!" he shouted.

"Gross," Christie shrieked. "I've got orange juice on my feet. I'm going to be all sticky, and it's probably going to attract more spiders. Why can't you watch what you're doing?"

"Don't move," Billie said, "or you'll cut your feet."

Nick noted the red flush on the boy's face as he picked him up and set him at a safe distance. "It's okay," he said, putting Christie down next to him. "I spilled a half-gallon of milk this morning."

"You did?" Joel looked relieved.

Billie suspected it was a lie, but she appreciated Nick doing what he could to make Joel feel better. The boy seemed to be going through a clumsy stage, and it was all she could do to remain patient with him. She began picking up glass, even as the orange juice spread across the vinyl floor.

Joel looked at his bun. "It's all soggy."

Nick patted him on the head. "We have lots more." He tiptoed around the juice and glass and grabbed a wad of paper towels. He wet them in warm water and handed them to Christie and Joel who immediately began wiping their feet. "What's this I hear about spiders?"

"We're having a small problem with them," Billie said, "but my pest control man is working on it."

Deedee staggered into the kitchen. "What's all the yelling about?"

"A little accident," Nick said. "No big deal."

"I can't live in a house that has accidents before noon. What are all you people doing up, anyway? It's indecent to be up at this hour. And who is the idiot that just came by my bedroom window with a lawn mower?"

"Max is cutting the grass," Nick said.

Deedee's eyes widened. "Max is on the premises? No wonder I feel a migraine coming on."

Billie reached out with her broom. "Watch out for the glass, Deedee."

"*Eeyeuuw,* why is there orange juice on the floor?"

"Do you want some coffee or a cinnamon bun?" Nick asked, trying to get Deedee's mind off the spilled juice and save Joel further embarrassment.

"Ohmigod. You mean that's what you people are doing? You're *eating*? How can you possibly put anything in your mouth at this hour?" She gave an involuntary shiver. "I'm going back to bed. I can feel bags forming under my eyes." She looked at herself in the hall mirror and groaned. "I do have bags under my eyes!"

Joel helped himself to a new bun. "What does she do all night? And how come there was so much yelling after I went to bed last night?"

"She and Frankie had a fight," Christie said, having cleaned her feet and dispensed with the paper towel. "Something about French provincial furniture."

"It was just a silly disagreement," Billie said, intent on getting up even the tiniest sliver of glass. "They made up right away."

Nick stood with his hands in the pockets of his

Levi's. "This is all my fault. I never should have forced her on you, but I was afraid to leave her in my house with crazy Max blowing up the geraniums. Now that Max has calmed down I can move Deedee back with me."

Billie wet her mop and began cleaning the orange juice. She continued to avoid looking at him. "I really don't mind her staying here for the rest of the week."

"We'll see." Nick looked at his watch. "I have a ten o'clock meeting at the newspaper office, and I need to go home and change. Do you think you'll be okay with Max around?"

"Don't worry, I can handle Max. I'm going to keep him so busy he won't have time to get into trouble."

Nick looked doubtful. "You don't have any gunpowder in the house, right?" He grinned at the look she shot him. "Just kidding. Have him call the barn when you're ready to send him home. One of the stable hands will come get him. Oh, and by the way, I dumped the fertilizer on your garden while you were out. You might want to look at it. I'm not known for my green thumb."

Billie followed him to the front door. "Thank you for breakfast and for the fertilizer."

He kissed her on the tip of her nose. "Any time. I'm going to be busy today and tonight, but tomorrow is free, and I have the whole day planned. I'll pick you and the kids up at seven-thirty A.M. Wear shorts."

"Where are we going?"

"It's a surprise. Someplace romantic." He started for the truck, only to make a quick detour and say something to Max, obviously in a stern voice, because the boy nodded soberly. Billie stood there with a smile frozen to her face as Nick pulled away. She sighed. What to do, what to do? Finally, she motioned for Max. He cut off the lawn mower, wiped sweat from his face, and came her way.

"Have you had breakfast?" Billie asked. When he shook his head no, she opened the door wider. "Take a break and join us."

Max followed Billie inside where Joel and Christie were on their second cinnamon buns. Christie looked startled to see him.

"Are you armed and dangerous?"

Max looked at her. "I have a Swiss Army knife in my pocket."

"Keep it there," Billie said, and then pointed to a short hallway off the kitchen that led to the garage. "There's a small bathroom off the hall. Wash up, and I'll fix your plate."

Max did as she said. When he returned, Billie was setting a plate with two buns on it. "What would you like to drink?"

"Black coffee is fine."

"Aren't you a little young for coffee?" she asked.

"I've been drinking it since I was three years old. Our cook used to sneak it to me."

"Coffee it is." Billie poured him a cup and brought it to the table, then joined him and her children. "I didn't expect you to mow the grass, Max, but I appreciate it."

"I figured it was the least I could do. Besides, Nick laid down the law to me last night. One more screw-up, and he sends me home."

"You don't sound thrilled about it."

"I hate that place. It's like a mausoleum. The servants are old and crotchety."

"What about your parents?"

"They're never around, and when they are it's one social gathering after another. I'm expected to attend, of course. In my tux," he added grimly. "I'm not big on socializing."

"Imagine that," Christie said.

Billie shot her daughter a don't-be-rude look. "How are you at repairing toilets?"

"I've never done it, but I'm sure I could learn." He tried the coffee, put it down, and stood. "Mind if I grab an ice cube?"

"Help yourself."

Max opened the freezer. "Your ice bin is empty."

"Oh, the ice maker doesn't work. Get the ice from one of the trays."

He popped a cube from a tray, dropped it in his coffee, and rejoined them. "What's wrong with the ice maker?"

"I bought the refrigerator used a couple of years ago. The previous owner said the ice maker never worked properly, even though the manufacturer tried to fix it several times. Finally, it just died."

"I'll have a look at it."

Billie opened her mouth to tell him it wasn't necessary, then decided against it. If the boy wanted to tinker with the ice maker, fine. At least it would keep him busy and out of trouble.

"So tell me a little about yourself, Max," she said. "Where do you go to college?"

"Right now I'm at MIT. I got kicked out of my last school because I made a big, um, fuss about the science lab using mice for experimentation."

"Oh, gross!" Christie said and slid her chair from the table.

"My sentiments exactly," Max said. "I'm an animal rights activist. Mice have feelings, too. I threw out half of Deedee's cosmetics for that very reason."

Billie chuckled. "I would have paid money to see that."

"So, did you bomb the school after they kicked you out?" Joel asked.

Max shook his head. "I took a more mature approach. I rewired the building. You should have seen the commotion it created. The computer lab was closed for a week. Naturally I was expelled. Again," he added.

"I think it's good to have causes that are important," Billie said.

"My parents don't agree. I managed to organize a boycott against a major cosmetic manufacturer, although it took an entire summer to do it. They lost millions, but in the end they agreed to stop experimenting with animals."

Billie couldn't hide her astonishment. "*You* did that? I remember that. It was in all the newspapers. Why, your parents should be proud."

Max shrugged. "Nah. They don't like the fact they have to bail me out of jail a lot because I manage to get myself into trouble quite often over my, um, causes."

"What's it like in jail?" Joel asked, eyes bright with interest.

Max started to say something, glanced at Billie, then shifted in his seat. "It's bad, Joel. Believe me, you don't want to go there."

Billie smiled at Max for not encouraging her son. "I'm sorry you were locked up for what you did," she said, "but I, for one, am proud to see young people taking a stand against injustice of any kind. Perhaps if you came up with a more diplomatic way of handling the situations . . ."

"Like how?"

She shrugged. "You could write letters to congressmen and senators. Or post flyers or have people sign petitions. You have the right as an American citizen to protest, but there are certain procedures to follow that will keep you out of jail."

Max pondered it. "Instead of going off half-cocked? That's how Nick puts it. He says I'm too impulsive and that's why I get into trouble."

"It all depends on *how* you go about it."

"Do you think there's any way to save the marshlands?"

"I honestly don't know, Max. It sounds like a done deal."

"A lot of people are unhappy about it. I've cut out dozens of letters from the editorial page."

"Perhaps you should get together with some of the people who wrote them and discuss a solution."

He perked up. "I could form a committee."

"Yes, you could."

He stood so quickly he almost toppled over his

chair. "That's it! If you want to be heard you *do* have to make a lot of noise, and if you get enough people together you can make a lot of noise."

"Even more noise than the small bombs you've been setting off," Billie said.

"Where's the toilet?"

"I beg your pardon?"

"I need to get working on the toilet. I think better when I'm busy."

"At the top of the stairs," Billie said. He raced toward the stairs, almost knocking Deedee over as she cleared them. "Max, what on earth are you doing here?" she demanded, grabbing the boy by his shirt.

"Going to the toilet."

"You keep your grubby hands off my makeup, little brother, you got that? You so much as go near my bedroom, and I'll have Frankie hammer you into the ground."

"You need to get a life, sis."

"I *do* have a life. Frankie treats me like a queen."

Max grinned. "Now he needs to find you a castle far, far away."

"And someone needs to throw you into a loony bin, kid."

Max pulled free and hurried up the stairs, chuckling to himself as though he found his big sister amusing.

CHAPTER TWELVE

At precisely seven-thirty in the morning Nick rumbled down Billie's street in a rented motor home, trying to keep the smile from spreading across his face. He felt a little foolish, but the truth was, he'd always wanted to drive one. If he liked it, he might even buy it. He spied Billie's driveway and slowed. They were waiting for him.

Billie didn't know what she'd expected, but it wasn't this. She tipped her head back and laughed at the sight of her handsome, suave polo player/newspaper owner and lover trying to negotiate a big, gas-guzzling motor home into her driveway. She shook her head. With Nick Kaharchek you never knew what to expect.

Joel and Christie catapulted themselves off the front step with a shriek of excitement.

Joel was the first inside. "It's got a bathroom. Oh, neat!"

Christie climbed into the bunk above the cab. "Mom, look at this! You can sleep up here and it has a big window and it's so cozy and comfy."

"It has a refrigerator and there's food in it," Joel said, wide-eyed. "There are grapes and peaches and juice in here. And cupcakes and yogurts and lots of other stuff. Man, this is great!"

Nick leaned close to Billie. "It's also got a bedroom in back with a queen-sized bed. What do you think?"

"I think Joel's right. It's great. Are we going camping?" She had not planned to be gone overnight. Both animals were out of the house and Raoul was coming in to spray. She hoped Deedee would remember to leave as well so the fumes would not make her ill.

"Nope. This is a day trip—in style. Actually, a friend of mine sells these. Ever since I expressed an interest in buying one he's tried to get me to take one out for a day or two. What do you think?"

"It's very nice." Nice didn't come close to describing it. Billie couldn't imagine what it would be like to simply buy something because she wanted it; she'd always had to budget carefully or put things on a layaway plan. She had taught her children to budget and save their allowances for special items they wanted because she felt it was important for them to know the value of money.

"You look pensive," Nick said, glancing over at her. "You don't like the motor home, do you?"

"It feels—" She paused. "Extravagant. Just like when you purchased Velvet for me."

"I can afford it, Billie," he said gently. "Surely you know I'm not hurting for money."

"I know that, Nick, but I worry what my children will make of it. I try very hard not to spoil them."

He nodded. "I understand. But you have to realize that while I play hard, I also work hard. The newspaper was struggling before I took it over."

"I know there's been a vast improvement."

"Circulation doubled within three years. And it has continued to grow enormously. I take the newspaper very seriously. Giving polo lessons is just a hobby of mine."

"I'm not trying to criticize you, Nick. I just don't want my children to think they can have everything their little hearts desire simply because you can afford it."

"Point taken. But I hope you'll let me do special things for them once in a while, like today, for instance."

Billie nodded. "I think it's sweet of you to include Christie and Joel in fun things."

They drove on in silence. Billie had no idea where they were going; she was just comfortable being with Nick and her kids, who were watching a program on TV in back.

"How'd Max do yesterday?" Nick asked.

"He repaired my toilet and two electrical outlets." She chuckled. "Only problem, every time I turn on the lamp in the living room, the garage door opens. He assures me he can fix it when he comes back tomorrow to work on the ice maker."

"He's coming back?"

"Yes. I think he likes being around us."

"Probably. He's never really had a normal family."

This time Billie laughed out loud. "Nobody said our family was normal."

Three hours later Billie looked up in amazement at the entrance to Virginia's largest amusement park, Kings Dominion. "I thought you said we were going someplace romantic."

"This is romantic," Nick told her. "It's got an Eiffel Tower. I know because I read the brochure." He bought four tickets and led them through the gate. "What do we do first? I guess we should go on a roller coaster, or maybe we need ice cream . . . Oh, wow! Look at these ugly hats!"

"Gross," Christie said.

By the time they got to the first roller coaster, they'd eaten ice cream, pizza, and funnel cakes, and were wearing Foreign Legion–type hats that sported the park logo. Nick looked up at the high-tech roller coaster and swallowed. "These things safe?"

"Yeah, they're so cool," Christie said. "This is the best, but we have to sit in the first seat. The first seat is the coolest. And then we have to go on the pirate ship. The one that goes upside down."

"Yeah," Joel said, "the pirate ship is great. We were on that last year and three people got sick all over everything."

"Maybe I shouldn't have had that second funnel cake," Nick said to Billie.

She put her arm around him. "You'll be fine. Haven't you ever been to an amusement park?"

"Not since I was nine. And that was Seaside Heights, New Jersey. I went on the whip and the merry-go-round."

"Uh-oh, maybe we shouldn't start him off on this one," Christie said. "This is a world-class coaster."

A set of cars zoomed on the rail high above them, leaving Nick with a vision of screaming, terrified faces.

"I don't want to sit with Nick," Joel said. "I don't want him blowing chunks on me."

"I'm not going to throw up," Nick told him. "I'm a polo player. Polo players are tough. You joining us?" he asked Billie.

"I think I'll sit this one out. But you go ahead, big brave guy."

He tossed her a sheepish smile as he followed the kids to the line of people waiting to get on the roller coaster.

Joel turned around to observe Nick when the ride was over. "Did you like it?"

"Yeah."

"Did you get sick?"

"Nope." Nick thought Joel looked disappointed. "I was too scared to get sick."

"Me, too," Joel said. But as the three of them descended the steps to where Billie waited, Nick walked over to a fence and pretended to throw up on the other side.

Billie chuckled and shook her head sadly.

"Oh, gross," Christie said, hurrying toward her mother. She covered her face with both hands. "This is so embarrassing. I hope I don't run into anyone I know."

Joel laughed so hard he had to grab Nick's belt to keep from falling to the ground.

Late in the afternoon they discovered the water rides and got soaked.

"Oh, gross," Nick said. "My shoes squish when I walk."

He looked so cute, standing there dripping wet, eating a corn dog, that Billie didn't have the heart to tell him he was beginning to sound like her children.

The sun went down, and the lights came on in the park—tiny twinkling white dots in all the trees, lining all the shops. The fountains were glorious in a bright display of color, and the rides seemed magical in the dark. They rode the elevator to the top of the Eiffel Tower and looked down at what appeared to be a fairyland.

"You were right," Billie murmured to Nick. "This is romantic. Especially for family people."

Nick put his hand on Joel's head. "Are you tired?"

"Nope. This is great."

"Good. Because I have something to ask all of you. I know we haven't known each other for very long, but sometimes that doesn't matter. Sometimes you meet people that you like right away, and in a very short time it seems as if you've known them all your life. I feel like that about you guys."

"Are you going to get mushy?" Christie asked, frowning.

"Yep." He took Billie's hand and looked into her eyes. "If I spent the rest of my life searching, I'd never find anyone like you." He looked down at Joel and Christie. "Except maybe for you two." He rubbed his thumb across the tender flesh of Billie's palm. "Will you guys marry me?"

Billie froze. She hadn't even seen it coming. She looked at her children.

"I guess so," Joel said. "I wanted Mom to marry a wrestler, but she said she isn't into wrestlers, so I guess you'll be okay. You're pretty fun to be around."

"Yeah, we'll marry you," Christie said. "If you promise not to do disgusting things like you did earlier. I can't have my friends seeing stuff like that, you know?"

Nick nodded soberly. "I'll try to be discreet."

Billie was the last to answer. She loved him without reservation, and she'd had a wonderful day. And this was a romantic proposal, just as she'd requested. Why was she hesitating? She knew very well the reason.

He had never mentioned the word "love."

He thought a double wedding would be fun, but he had not promised to love her for the rest of her life.

He was having fun right now, like a big kid, but he hadn't discussed with her the responsibilities involved in taking on a family.

"Mom?" Christie prodded. "Aren't you going to answer Nick?"

Nick watched her as he waited. She wasn't com-

pletely sure. She was a woman who made careful de-
cisions, and she felt a strong commitment to her
children. He respected those qualities. If she didn't
say yes tonight, he'd court her for as long as it took
to get the right answer.

Billie held her breath and bit her lip. "Um . . ."

"I'm getting tired now, Mom," Joel said, rubbing
his eyes and yawning. "I want to go home."

"Yes," Billie said. "I think—"

"Mom said *yes*," Christie shouted. "Do I get to be
in the wedding? Can I wear a gown?"

Nick moved fast. He knew Billie had said yes to
Joel's question and not to his, but he took advantage
of the situation and slid a two-carat diamond on her
finger. He grinned and winked at her and said, "Got-
cha."

Joel hooted and Christie giggled. Billie felt her
knees go weak. "I guess you do."

"You tricked me," Billie said when they were driving
home and the children were asleep in their bunks.

"I thought you needed some help with the decision."

"I'm sorry I'm so skittish about every little thing,
but marriage is not to be taken lightly. It's not just
our future that's at stake . . . it's my children's as well,
and you don't want to make any mistakes that might
cause them pain."

Nick took his eyes from the road for a moment and
glanced at her. "We'll be fine, Billie. I promise."

It was late when they finally arrived home. The

place was dark as Nick carried a soundly sleeping Joel inside and up the stairs to his bedroom. Deedee was out and probably wouldn't arrive home until all hours. As Billie checked to make sure the back door was locked, she wondered how the girl managed to keep going night after night. Christie mumbled a quick good-night and went to her own room while Billie managed to get Joel in his pajamas.

Nick paused at the door to Billie's room. "How about me? Do I get tucked into bed?"

"You get tucked into your RV and sent home."

He wrapped his arms around her and gently pulled her close to him. "It's lonely in my home."

"Nonsense. You have Max, and he needs attention."

Nick closed his eyes and groaned. "I know. I plan to try harder."

Billie saw the look of yearning in his eyes as he kissed her good-night, and she would have liked to invite him to share her bed. He felt good next to her. He was strong and possessive, in a flattering way.

Nick wasn't surprised Billie was sending him home. "I guess you have to be careful when you mess with a mother."

Billie moved so that she was perfectly molded to every part of his body. "We have to uphold our virtue and dignity."

Nick's breath hitched in his throat at the slight pressure caused by her thigh sliding between his. "You're teasing me."

"I'm just getting even with you for tricking me."

He chuckled. "You would have said yes eventually." He leaned close and whispered against her mouth. "I like the way you get even." His hands cupped her buttocks and he kissed her hot and hard to prove his point.

Billie felt the heat rush through her. She swayed and clutched his shirt, waiting for the sensation to pass.

"Good thing my bedroom isn't close to the others," he said. "We'll be able to make all the noise we want."

Billie's eyes fluttered open. She hadn't thought about houses. She liked Nick's house, but this house was hers. There it was, that question of change, made more difficult by the fact Nick seemed to be taking their engagement lightly. She suddenly thought of the doorjamb in her kitchen where she had recorded her children's height, and the garden she loved.

Nick held her at arm's length. "What's wrong?"

She yawned. "Life is very complicated."

"Yes."

"Sometimes it's overwhelming."

"Getting engaged is a big deal." He noted the fatigue in her eyes. "I think you're just overtired." He turned down the bed linens. "Get into something comfy, and I'll give you a good-night backrub. You'll be so relaxed you'll melt into the mattress."

"You promise this won't be a stimulating back-rub?"

Nick selected a Redskins jersey-type nightshirt from a drawer and draped it over her shoulder. "My magic fingers are prepared to give a legitimate massage. How your body reacts to that massage is your problem."

Billie stepped into her bathroom to change. She experienced a feeling of unease at the thought of going to bed. She'd lain awake for hours the previous night listening to every sound. Perhaps a backrub was just what she needed. She crawled onto the bed and stretched out on her stomach.

Nick grabbed one foot and started to work on it.

"What are you doing?" Billie asked.

"Massaging your foot."

"I've never had my foot massaged. In fact, now that I think of it, I've never had anything massaged. I've never . . . oh! Oh dear, that feels good." His thumb was making little circles on her arch. Billie groaned in satisfaction when his hands moved to her calves, squeezing, stroking, kneading. His thumbs strayed up the inside of her thigh and retreated, leaving in their wake the beginnings of an erotic ache deep within her.

"The most important part of a massage is the neck and shoulders," he said, straddling her, gently pulling at her tired muscles.

He should do this for a living, Billie thought lazily. His hands were strong and talented, easing away tension, smoothing out all the kinks and knots. He rubbed his thumbs over the nape of her neck, and a delightful warmth trickled along her spine. Heat radiated from the pads of his fingertips to every part of her body, fueling barely latent desire. His hands were doing legitimate massage things, but he was sitting astride her, and the massage she was getting on her backside was disturbingly sensual.

Billie swallowed and tried to keep her breathing normal. His hands moved along her shoulder blades, then traveled the length of her back and swept up under her nightshirt. Billie gasped and buried her face in the pillow. She was on fire. His fingers firmly pressed against the sides of her breasts, tugging at them slightly as he caressed her back. The need was building in her with each passing second. She wanted him—desperately. The heck with dignity and virtue. The heck with the kids.

She lifted her head and watched Nick move from the bed. "Where are you going?"

"Home. The backrub is over. Are you sufficiently relaxed?"

"Relaxed?" she croaked. *"Relaxed?"*

He put his finger to his lips. "Shhh. You'll wake the children."

It suddenly occurred to her that she'd been had. He'd been toying with her. "You tease!" she whispered. "You knew exactly what you were doing!"

"I wanted to make sure you'd dream about me tonight." He kissed her lightly, made for the door, and shut off the light.

"Nick?"

"Yeah?"

"Would you please make sure you turn the lock on the front doorknob before you leave? Deedee will lock the dead bolt when she gets home."

"Of course." He tiptoed down the stairs. The last

thing Billie heard was the sound of the motor home rumbling down her street.

Joel sat at the kitchen table and wrinkled his nose at the bowl of smelly brown mush Billie had placed in front of him. "What is this?"

"Lunch," Billie said, staring at her new engagement ring. It was beautiful. It was absolutely perfect. And the sight of it made her stomach upset.

Joel poked at the malodorous mound with his fork. "Yuck. It looks like dog food."

Billie looked up and blinked. "What?"

"You gave me dog food for lunch."

"That's ridiculous. Why would I do a thing like that?" She bit her lip when she saw the bowl sitting in front of Joel. "What happened to your peanut-butter-and-jelly sandwich?"

Joel turned in his seat and looked at Buffy finishing off a crust of bread.

"Oh, great," Billie muttered through clenched teeth, putting the dog food back into the refrigerator and getting out the peanut butter and jelly again. She was turning into a basket case. She couldn't eat or sleep, and she was feeding dog food to her children. And it was all Nicholas Kaharchek's fault. "Nick and his damn thumbs."

Joel took the sandwich Billie handed him. "What's wrong with Nick's thumbs?"

"Nothing's wrong with Nick's thumbs. I didn't mean to say that. I was thinking out loud."

"Boy, Mom, you sure have gotten weird."

"I have a lot on my mind."

"Oh, yeah," Joel said between bites, "Deedee called this morning while you were out in the garden, and she said you guys were going shopping today. She said you needed to get a wedding dress."

Billie felt her fingertips go numb. She was hyperventilating again. She grabbed a brown paper lunch bag from the pantry so she could breathe into it, but paused when she found the set of keys she'd been searching for. Relief flooded her, although she couldn't imagine why the keys were in her pantry to begin with, but in her house anything was possible. She wasn't going to hyperventilate after all, she told herself as she returned the keys to the rack. She was going to be okay.

Besides, she wasn't the nervous type. She was good, solid Billie Pearce. She was the person who stayed calm in emergencies. She was the rock in her family. She didn't go all to pieces over every little thing.

"Oh, and Grandma called. Dad told her you were getting married to a man you'd only known two weeks, and she sounded pretty upset."

Billie had to literally choke back the anger. How dare her ex-husband call her parents about her wedding! "How did your dad find out?"

"Christie must've told him. Anyway, Grandma said you either call her or she's catching the next flight here."

To hell with being the rock, Billie thought. She put the bag to her mouth and began to breathe into it.

Deedee opened the front door and went directly to the kitchen. If she thought it strange to find Billie with a bag over her face, she was courteous enough not to mention it. "Are you ready to go shopping?"

"No!" came her muffled reply. Billie removed the bag and took a moment to compose herself. "I can't go shopping."

Deedee poured herself a cup of coffee. "What about a wedding dress? I thought you needed to buy a wedding dress."

"Well, I thought I'd just wear something from my closet. No sense spending all that money on a dress you'll only wear once."

Deedee looked at her as if she were deranged. "Honey, you're getting married. You can't walk down the aisle in running shorts."

"I guess that's true, but I can't go today because . . . I don't have a baby-sitter. I can't leave the children home alone."

"Max can watch us," Joel said. "I like Max."

As if on cue, the doorbell rang. Joel raced toward it and let Max in. The teenager carried a box of metal objects and copper tubing. "How's it going?"

Billie reached behind her for another brown paper bag.

"Billie needs a baby-sitter today," Deedee announced to her brother, "and we thought you'd be perfect for the job."

Max shrugged. "Sure. I can fix the ice maker in my spare time." He glanced at Joel. "You want to play some chess? Want to learn the quadratic formula or discuss quantum theory?" He was smiling.

Joel looked at Max. "I know how to play checkers."

"We can start there and work our way toward bigger and better things."

Deedee put her arm around Billie and nudged her toward the front door. "Let's go."

"I have some unpleasant business to attend to first," she said. "I have to call my parents."

Deedee shook her head sadly. "It was bound to happen sooner or later."

Billie went into her bedroom, picked up the telephone and dialed. She spent most of the next hour on the telephone with her mother discussing Nick and their wedding plans. As for her dad, she just told him the truth. She loved Nick. By the time she got off, she had convinced her parents she wasn't crazy, only impulsive.

Deedee frowned when Billie came downstairs. "You don't look so good. In fact, your face is kind of green. Are your parents upset?"

"Actually, they're taking it better than I thought."

"Then what's the problem?"

"They plan to attend the wedding."

"Well, of course they do."

"You don't understand, Deedee. I have a very large family. Brothers and sisters, aunts and uncles, and about a million cousins. My mother plans to have them all chip in and charter a bus."

"A bus? Gee, how many people are coming?"

Billie sighed. "Probably somewhere between sixty and seventy-five."

"Ohmigod!"

"I need to lie down for a moment," Billie said. "I'll shop later." Billie started for the stairs, just as the doorbell rang, only to be followed by a loud pounding. "What in the world?"

She hurried to the front door with Deedee right behind her and found Nick on the other side, a menacing look on his face. "Where is he? Where's Max?"

"He just went upstairs with Joel to play checkers. What's going on?"

Nick started for the stairs. "I'm going to kill him with my bare hands. Then I'm going to press charges and have him locked up until he's an old man."

"I think he means it," Deedee said.

Billie grabbed his sleeve. "Hold on, what happened?"

"Someone from the newspaper office called early this morning. A new guy, supposedly. I didn't recognize his voice. Said there was an emergency. I got there and discovered everything was fine, but I hung around and looked over today's paper. It was a setup, Billie. When I got home, I found three fire trucks, a rescue squad, and two ambulances in my driveway. Max blew up my car!"

CHAPTER THIRTEEN

"Wait!" Billie said as Nick started for the stairs once more. "Stop right there."

"You should let him kill Max," Deedee said. "At least for what the little creep did to all my makeup."

Nick came to a halt. "Don't try to stop me, Billie," he said, gritting his teeth. "I've put up with as much from that kid as I plan to. He's dangerous. He needs to be behind bars."

"Do you *know* that Max did it? Were there any witnesses?"

"None of the stable hands saw anything and nobody was at the house, but it happened shortly after

Max caught a ride over here with Mrs. Duffy, who was on her way to the grocery store."

"Just calm down. I'll get Max. Deedee, you pour Nick a cup of coffee and try to talk some sense into him." She realized, even as she said it, how ludicrous that sounded.

"Come on, Nick," Deedee said. "Together we'll figure out where to bury the body."

Billie shot Deedee a dark look as she started up the stairs. "That's not funny."

Billie heard loud music coming from the other side of Joel's door. She had to knock twice before her son called out to her to come in. She found Max and Joel sitting cross-legged on the floor, already intent on a game of checkers. She wondered how someone like Max could feel challenged with a kid's game, then wondered if Max had ever really been a kid.

"Max, could you come downstairs a moment?" she said, trying to make herself heard over the music. "Nick needs to speak with you."

He looked up. "What'd I do this time?"

"I'd rather you talk to him about that." Joel started to get up as well. "And you need to stay in your room until I call you," she said to her son. "This is private business." Joel opened his mouth as if to argue, but the look on her face obviously told him it was best to do as she said.

Max followed Billie downstairs and into the kitchen. Nick bolted from the stool and grabbed the boy by his collar. "By the time I finish with you,

you're going to wish you'd never been born." Max's eyes widened.

"Hold it!" Billie ordered. "Take your hands off him right this minute. I'll not have any violence in this house."

"What's going on?" Max demanded, jerking away from Nick.

"Don't act like you don't know what this is about," Nick almost spat. "My Mercedes has been blown to hell and back. The explosion shattered half the windows in the house."

"Oh, man!" Max blinked several times behind his glasses. "Was anybody hurt?"

"Why should you care? According to the bomb squad, that bomb was timed to go off an hour after it was activated. You were long gone by then."

Billie had never seen Nick so upset. The veins stood out in his forehead, his jaw was hard as concrete. "Nick, please," she cried. She saw that her children had come to the top of the stairs and were listening to the entire exchange. There was little she could do. If she walked away from Nick in his rage, he might hurt Max.

"Why are you trying to protect him?" Nick demanded.

Billie looked at Max. "Did you blow up Nick's car? Tell me the truth."

"Hell, no, I didn't blow it up."

Nick almost snarled a response. "You expect me to believe that?"

Deedee stepped in. "Max has done some pretty

dumb things, but he's never blown up a car." She looked at her brother. "Have you?"

"Of course not." He looked at Nick. "All I did was take a few things from under the hood to try and get your attention. I'm not stupid enough to blow up a brand-new Mercedes. Jeez."

Nick didn't believe him. "If you didn't do it, who did?"

"How should I know? Maybe somebody who doesn't like what you put in the newspaper. Maybe it was Sheridan. She hangs around all the time anyway. Didn't she buy you that car as an engagement present? Maybe she decided she no longer wanted you to have it."

Nick wondered how Max knew so much about his personal life. "It's over between Sheridan and me."

"So why is she still leaving you gifts?" Deedee said.

Nick flashed her a look of impatience. "Max is the one leaving those gifts," he said. "Your brother leaves me a gift and a cryptic note right before he sticks it to me. Why is that, Max?"

The boy blushed. "Because I feel guilty. I don't like causing you problems, but I don't know how else to get your attention."

"Well, you got it this time, kiddo, only I didn't get a gift beforehand. How come? Didn't you feel guilty sticking a time bomb beneath the hood of a sixty-thousand-dollar car? Or were you trying to get even with me for threatening to send you home?"

"Oh, man," Joel said. "Sixty thousand dollars for a car. Awesome."

Billie frowned. "I asked you to stay in your room," she said, much louder than she'd meant. She wanted to know why Sheridan was spending so much time at Nick's when he claimed it was over between them. Billie was wearing his engagement ring, they were talking about getting married in a matter of days. Her parents had probably already put a deposit on the tour bus. What the hell was going on?

Christie and Joel, obviously suspecting that their mother meant business, hurried to their bedrooms and closed the doors.

Max sank into the nearest chair and wiped his brow. "Look, Nick, I know you don't have any reason to believe me, but I swear I didn't touch your car."

Nick realized there was no way he was going to get Max to own up to it, and the longer he stood there the angrier he got. He needed to cool off. He headed for the back door, stepped out, and closed it behind him.

Billie saw the color had drained from Max's face. The kid looked as though he would be ill. "Stay put," she said. "I'm going to see if I can talk to Nick."

She stepped outside and found Nick sitting on her back step. She sat down beside him. "Are you okay?"

He shrugged. "I will be."

"I believe Max."

Nick looked at her. "He suckered you in, didn't he?"

"No. Max isn't a violent person, Nick. The bombs he set off were made from flour and other household ingredients. Kid stuff, really, just to get your attention.

The bomb you described was obviously put there by a professional."

"Do you really think Max couldn't put together a real bomb if he wanted?"

"Of course he could, but that's not his MO, so to speak."

"What?"

"Modus operandi. I watch a few cop shows now and then. After Joel and Christie go to bed, that is," she added quickly. "Max is an environmentalist, and an animal rights activist, among other things. He believes in protecting life. Why would he do something that might end up killing someone?"

Nick pondered it. "Back to my original question. If Max didn't do it, who did?"

"Probably the person who called and said there was an emergency at the newspaper office. Did you recognize his voice?"

"No, but it's easy for someone to disguise their voice." He shrugged. "It doesn't matter if I believe Max or not. The police are going to question the Duffys, the security guards, and the stable hands." Nick paused. "Shit."

"What?"

"Arnie Bates. The stable hand I fired. He was pretty pissed."

"Would he do something like this?"

"I don't know. He's spent time in prison. I hired him because nobody else would."

"Oh, jeez."

Nick looked at her. "Everybody deserves a second chance, Billie."

"Where is he now?"

Nick shrugged. "Nobody knows. The police are looking for him for parole violation."

"Oh, jeez."

"Why do you keep saying that?"

"Because you keep insisting on surrounding yourself with strange people."

Nick sighed. "I completely forgot about Arnie. I was so sure Max was behind this, I didn't think."

"Why was Arnie Bates in prison?"

"Arson."

They looked at one another. "Oh, jeez," Billie said.

Nick raked his hands through his hair. "I don't know what to do."

Billie sighed. "Okay, here's the deal. We need to keep Max out of sight until the investigation is over. He can stay here."

"Are you out of your mind? We don't know that he *didn't* do it."

"Max is innocent. If I didn't believe that with all my heart I would never allow him in the same house with my children."

Nick shook his head emphatically. "I can't do that to you. I'm not going to risk it."

Billie hitched her chin a fraction. "I'm not asking your permission."

His jaw dropped. Finally, he closed his mouth and tried to think. "Damned if I know what to do."

"You need to go home and help with the investigation. If the police ask, tell them that, as far as you know, Max could be anywhere. In the meantime, all we can do is hope they find Arnie Bates before—"

She paused. "Before anything else happens."

A sudden chill crept up Billie's spine. "You could be in big danger, Nick. Did Arnie Bates know your car wasn't drivable?" When he merely shrugged, she went on. "If he didn't know the car was out of commission, then he intentionally made the call, knowing you'd jump into your car and head straight for the newspaper office. That changes everything. We're not dealing with simple destruction of property, we're talking attempted murder."

"Oh, jeez," he said.

"You have to stay here, too."

Once again, Nick shook his head. "No way. If I'm the target, I'm not moving in under the same roof with you and the kids."

"But—"

"I'll hire more security." He stood. "I have to go home and change. I've got a meeting I can't cancel. I'm telling you right now I don't like the idea of Max staying here."

Billie covered her ears. She couldn't deal with more at the moment. "It's settled. I don't have time to argue because I have to go out and buy a damn wedding dress."

He looked amazed. "You still want to go through with it after all this?"

"My parents are renting a damn bus so that all my damn relatives can attend my damn wedding," she said, her voice rising as a wave of panic suddenly rushed over her. "I have a lot of kinfolk. They're expecting a wedding, dammit!"

She was near the brink. "Okay, okay," Nick said,

taking her hand in his. "Just calm down. Everything is going to be okay. Trust me."

"I'm having a real problem with that right now."

"Because of Sheridan," he stated flatly. "I can't tell her to stay away when she boards her horse on my property."

"Can't or won't?"

He looked at Billie long and hard. "I have to go, okay?" He left without another word.

"Okay, listen up," Billie said, once she reentered the kitchen. "Max will be staying here for a couple of days."

"You're kidding, right?" Deedee replied.

"He's not a suspect. I can't go into it right now because I have to run out and buy a wedding dress. Deedee, I want you and Max to baby-sit."

"You're kidding, right?" Deedee repeated.

"I don't mind baby-sitting," Max said. "Do you have cable TV? There's a sci-fi movie coming on in an hour. That'll give me time to repair the ice maker. I think I have everything I need."

"Yes, I have cable," Billie said. "By the way, you can sleep on the twin bed in Joel's room. We'll need Nick to bring you a few things."

"What if Max blows us to kingdom come?" Christie said.

"Max is not responsible for blowing up Nick's car," Billie said. "That was the work of a professional. I would not have insisted he stay if I didn't believe he was one hundred percent innocent."

Max looked touched. "You're the only one who believes me," he said.

"I believe you," Joel said.

Max looked at Deedee.

"I suppose I do, too," she said. "You've done some weird things, but I can't imagine you blowing up an automobile."

Everyone looked at Christie. Finally, she shrugged. "If Mom believes him, I believe him."

"Nick believes you, too," Billie told Max. "He's just upset right now. You just need to lay low while the police investigate."

"Do they suspect me?"

"Among others."

Christie's eyes grew wide. "Does this mean we're harboring a fugitive?"

"It depends on how you look at it," Billie replied.

"Awesome," Joel said.

Billie looked from her son to her daughter. "Nobody is to know about this, you understand? Absolutely nobody. If word leaks out, I'm going to ground you both until you're eighteen."

"Okay, I won't tell Grandma or Dad if they call," Christie said. "I won't even tell Lisa Marie."

Joel pretended to zip his lips.

Billie sighed. "Thank you." She grabbed her purse and headed for the front door. "I won't be gone long."

"Am I supposed to cook or anything?" Deedee asked anxiously. "Because I don't know how."

"I'll pick up a pizza on the way back."

Billie was out the door in a matter of minutes. There was a little dress shop in Leesburg that would have something suitable. If she hurried she could be back in an hour. Anyone else would have said she was insane to leave her children with a kid who was suspected of blowing up a car, but that was nothing compared to buying a wedding dress when the bride-to-be suspected her future husband still had the hots for his ex-fiancée. *That* was insane. Billie was convinced as to Max's innocence, but she was clueless as to what Nick was thinking.

Yet, he'd asked her to trust him, and despite all the craziness surrounding them, she did.

On her way into Leesburg she passed the large brick building that housed Nick's newspaper. She stopped for a light, and stared at the structure, feeling a strange sense of pride. It was a good paper. Despite the fact Nick had managed to pick up so many new subscribers, he'd intentionally kept it from growing too large, so he could personally maintain quality and stay responsive to the needs of Loudoun County. She understood about the paper now. It was something real to Nick. Something that made an important contribution to his community.

While she was waiting for the light a new navy blue BMW sports car pulled out of the newspaper parking lot and took its place in line. Traffic began to move, cars changed lanes, and Billie found herself behind the sports car, staring at the back of a familiar head. It was Nick!

Nick accelerated slightly and checked his rearview mirror, his eyes growing wide as they locked with Billie's. His attention returned to the road in time to see the car in front of him stop for another light.

Billie's reflexes weren't as quick as Nick's. By the time she applied the brakes she'd shortened his car by six inches. She uttered an expletive and got out to inspect the damage. "Nice car," she said. "Is it new?"

He looked at it incredulously. "Yes, as a matter of fact, it is."

She felt the color drain from her face. "I'm really sorry, Nick. I was just so surprised to see you in front of me."

He arched one brow. "If you wanted to get my attention, you could have beeped your horn."

"I didn't do this on purpose," she said, feeling on the verge of tears. The poor man would, no doubt, be reduced once again to riding in a pickup truck filled with manure while he waited for repairs to his brand-new car. And here she thought things couldn't get any worse.

"It's okay, Billie," he said gently. "The important thing is nobody was hurt." He ruffled her hair. "The cars both look drivable. They're just a little . . . crumpled." He glanced at the traffic jam they were creating. "Let's pull into that parking lot across the street."

Billie followed him to a space and parked her car. "You know what this means? This means they'll raise my insurance rates," she said.

A small, pleased smile played across his mouth. "That should bother me more than you, since I'm the one who's going to be paying your premiums. *If* you want to give up teaching for a while and stay home with the kids, of course. Money isn't going to be a big issue anymore."

Billie felt her heart skip a beat. This man was going

to be her husband. Dear Lord, she didn't even know him. She knew a polo instructor and a casual sort of guy who wore moccasins, but she didn't know the man before her now in a charcoal-gray suit and flattering tie. Nicholas Kaharchek in a suit was . . . devastating. The crisp white shirt made his skin seem darker, and it somehow left her feeling intimidated.

This Nick carried with him a sense of power that was subtly contained by the perfectly cut suit. Yet she read the seductive messages he was sending her in his brown eyes, and her blood seemed to flow faster in her veins. The fact that she had already slept with him, that he knew every millimeter of her body, only added to her discomfort.

"How's everything back at the house?" Nick asked.

"Fine, just fine. Max and Deedee are baby-sitting."

"Now, there's a pair. Are you still sure you want to offer him sanctuary for a couple of days?"

Billie stared at him, tongue-tied. Finally, she nodded.

"You didn't hit your head when you ran into my car, did you?"

Her answer was breathless. "No. I'm fine. I have to go shopping."

He continued to look at her, memorizing her face, the sheen of her hair. The memory would serve him well during long board meetings. He found it more and more difficult to keep his mind on his work because of her. He wanted to touch her, to take her in his arms and kiss her until she was panting and feverishly moaning his name. And he wanted to do this in a parking lot, in broad daylight, in downtown Leesburg. He was losing it, he decided. He was turning into a crazed sex maniac.

"Oh, yeah, the wedding dress. Didn't want to let it go till the last minute, huh? I kind of like those running shorts you're wearing."

Billie was beginning to relax. He was teasing her, and he sounded like the Nick she knew. She'd just been thrown for a minute by the suit. It was really dumb to get into such a state over a suit, right? Wrong. He wore power and authority as comfortably as he wore his custom-tailored clothes, and the expensive trappings of civilization served to enhance rather than minimize the force of his virility. She felt swept away. Her life was like a package, floating downstream while she ran helplessly along the bank, trying to keep up. She looked down at the ring on her finger and began to hyperventilate again.

"I need a bag," she gasped. "I'm nervous. I'm hysterical. I'm going to faint. I almost never faint."

Nick grasped her shoulders and roughly pulled her to him for a kiss that would be considered a wee bit passionate on the respectable streets of Leesburg. "Feel better?" he asked once he released her.

Billie swayed toward him. "Mmmmm."

She looked much better, Nick thought, pleased with himself. The color was back in her cheeks and the panic in her eyes had turned to hazy desire. "I have a meeting with my lawyer in ten minutes. I should be done around four. Can you stay in town for dinner?"

Billie's only consolation was that his voice sounded as ragged as her breathing. She shook her head no and struggled to collect her thoughts. She was supposed to be shopping for something. What was it? Oh, yeah, she remembered, a wedding dress. "I don't want to stay in town too long," she managed.

He looked disappointed, but he nodded his head as if he understood. "Probably a good idea," he said, remembering that his place was crawling with cops who were as eager to find Max as they were Arnie Bates. "Maybe we can catch up with one another later."

By the time Billie reached the dress store, she was having second thoughts, not only about the wedding but about Max as well. What if she was wrong about him? He was undoubtedly a genius, but he was still a sixteen-year-old boy whose intellect had outgrown his level of maturity by leaps and bounds. What if he'd been so mad at Nick at the thought of being sent home to his parents that he'd lost control?

Billie considered herself a pretty good judge of character—heaven knows she'd dealt with enough children and parents over the years that she felt she really knew people—but she had never dealt with someone like Max.

"May I help you?" a middle-aged woman asked once Billie stepped into the dress shop, setting off a tiny bell over the door. Billie blinked at the sight of her. She wore more makeup than Deedee.

"I need a wedding dress fast."

"For your daughter?"

Billie blinked. "My daughter is ten years old. It's for me."

"Oh, I'm sorry. My mistake. I've lost my glasses, and, well, you must be tired, dear."

Billie's self-esteem dropped lower than a gopher hole. Had she not needed a dress so badly she would have turned around and left the shop. "Yes, I am tired, but—"

"You should try under-eye concealer. Takes years off your looks."

Did she look *that* bad? Billie wondered. Perhaps Nick's family and the noises in and out of her house had taken a bigger toll on her than she'd imagined. "Gee, maybe I should."

"So you're getting married, huh?" the woman said, putting on her glasses. "Oooh, *nice* ring." She held Billie's hand up so she could get a closer look. "Diamond looks genuine, but I'd take it to a jeweler if I were you. They make those fake diamonds today that resemble the real thing. You wouldn't believe how many jewelers can't tell the difference."

Billie smiled tightly. "I'm going out on a limb here, but I'm willing to bet this diamond is the real thing."

"Yes, well, it's certainly not zircon."

Billie had to bite her tongue. "I'm really in a big hurry."

The woman tapped her red lips with an index finger that was perfectly manicured. "Why don't we look over here on this rack? We have some lovely designs suited for women your age."

This time Billie gaped. "Excuse me, what happened to the other woman who used to own the shop?"

"She moved to North Dakota, hon. I'm the new owner, Emma Glebe. Now, this dress would look nice on you."

"What kind of work did you do before?"

"I was an IRS auditor."

"Oh, yes? Well, I'm sure you're going to bring in tons of customers. You have a certain way about you."

The woman beamed. "That's what all my friends say. Now, about this dress—"

Billie looked at it. The outfit resembled draperies one would find in a grandmother's house. "I prefer something simple. Unassuming."

"Yes, less *is* more," Emma said, flipping through the racks.

"You're checking through the wrong size," Billie said, noting she was looking in the fourteens. "I'm a ten."

"Of course you are."

Billie shook her head and walked over to the rack that held her size. She flipped through the dresses and pulled out a simple cream-colored linen suit.

"Oh, that would look lovely on you, dear," Emma said, "and I have a hat that would set it off nicely."

"Sounds good. Just toss it in a bag, and I'll be on my way."

"Aren't you going to try it on?"

"Like I said, I'm in a big hurry. No time to lose, wedding is on Saturday." She reached into her purse for her checkbook.

"Oh, I see. One of *those* kinds of weddings." Emma raised both hands to mimic a shotgun.

Billie didn't bother to correct her as she wrote out the check and raced from the store.

Billie made it home in record time. Frankie's limo waited out front. She sighed. Would her house ever return to normal? she wondered. She walked through the front door and found Max, Joel, and Christie watching TV.

She sagged against the front door in relief, and then was immediately ashamed for doubting Max to begin with. He didn't look much older than her children, his eyes fixed on the program that seemed to be about the spirit world. Just what Joel and Christie needed to watch.

"Where's the pizza, Mom?" Joel asked.

Billie sighed. She'd been in such a hurry to get back that she'd completely forgotten to stop and pick up one. "I'll call and get one delivered. Where are Deedee and Frankie?" she asked, hoping the two weren't up in Deedee's bedroom humping one another like wild rabbits while her children were in the house.

Joel put a finger to his lips. "Shhh!"

"Looking at the garden," Christie said, eyes glued to the set.

Looking at the garden? Billie thought. That's weird. She dialed the number for the pizza parlor and ordered. She pulled a twenty-dollar bill from her purse, laid it on the table, and walked out the back door. She found Frankie and Deedee kneeling beside her tomato plants as if they'd never before seen one.

"What's up, guys?" she said.

"Frankie and I are thinking about buying a farm and growing our own vegetables," Deedee said. "We're getting tired of the limelight."

"When I retire," Frankie said, "but that won't be for a while."

Billie knew there was about as much chance of the

two becoming farmers as there was of her playing in a polo tournament. "Somehow, I just can't see you as a farm wife," she told Deedee.

"I want to learn to bake my own bread and sew my own clothes," she said, flashing Billie a smile.

Frankie nodded. "We're going to have cows and horses and chickens. It'll be cool milking my first cow."

Billie nodded. "Only problem, Deedee doesn't like stepping in *stuff*. You know how particular she is about her shoes."

Deedee suddenly took on a look of pure horror. "She's right, Frankie, honey. I can't bear the thought of stepping in, well, you know."

He seemed to ponder it. "I forgot about that. Perhaps we should retire someplace like Scottsdale, Arizona, instead."

"Or the West Coast," Deedee said. She looked at Billie. "We have to think about our future now that we're getting married. Have you and Nick discussed plans?"

"Right now I'm just trying to get through one day at a time."

"Poor Billie, we've all been such a burden on you. But don't think for one minute that Frankie and I don't plan to return the favor. You and Nick have to promise to come visit us when we get settled into our new home. Wherever it is." She suddenly brightened. "Oh, did you get a dress?"

Billie nodded. "I'll show it to you, later." She excused herself and went inside. The TV program was obviously over. Max and Joel were checking out the ice maker, Christie had the stereo blaring in her room. Billie grabbed the plastic bag that Emma had slipped over her suit to protect it, and carried it upstairs, debating whether to put the bag over her face.

Billie closed her door and locked it, then slipped the bag off her suit.

As she gazed at it, she thought back to her first wedding. There had been enough pomp and ceremony in that one to last her a lifetime. She'd worn the traditional white gown with yards and yards of froth trailing from a cap of satin and pearls securely fastened to her head with an army of bobby pins. Her parents had gone all out with a band and a caterer. The bills for the wedding had probably lasted longer than the marriage itself, she thought ruefully.

Now she was tagging along on Deedee's wedding, which from all indications would be a monumental carnival. The guest list included senators, ambassadors, and a gaggle of wrestlers. Add to that a busload of very conservative farmers and shopkeepers from Lancaster, Pennsylvania. Maybe she should round it out by inviting last year's sixth-grade class, Billie thought, feeling a little hysterical.

She slipped into the suit and looked at herself in the mirror. The suit was flattering, what her mother would refer to as understated elegance. It was form-fitting, emphasizing her trim figure. The hemline fell just above her knees. Her legs might not be as long and as slender as Deedee's, but she prided herself in the fact they were toned and shapely.

The doorbell rang, calling Billie from her room in her dress. She let Raoul in. He stopped in his tracks and whistled. "Where are you off to, Princess Grace?"

Billie cringed as she heard Deedee's shriek of pleasure from the stairs. "Is that the dress?" she said. "Oh, you're going to make a beautiful bride."

Raoul looked at Billie in pure astonishment. "You're getting married?"

"On Saturday," Deedee said. "We're having a double wedding. Isn't that way cool?"

"Yes, way cool," Raoul said. He looked at Billie. "Is it true?"

"Yes."

"But—" Raoul paused. "You just met him."

"It was love at first sight," Frankie said, coming up behind Raoul. He introduced himself and the two men shook hands.

Deedee smiled at Raoul. "I know you're Billie's friend and all, and we'd love to invite you to the wedding, but it's going to be a small, intimate gathering. Family and politicians only."

Billie saw the hurt in Raoul's eyes. "I wanted to tell you, but—"

He held up a hand. "Hey, I'm happy for you, kiddo. You deserve a good man. How many times have I told you that?"

Which was true. He had even tried fixing her up with a couple of men he thought were good catches and would treat her right. "Oh, Raoul, that's so sweet," she said.

The doorbell rang. The delivery man handed over the large pizza Billie had ordered, and she went for the money. She paid him and carried the pizza to the kitchen table. Raoul followed.

"I suppose me and the missus need to cough up a good wedding present. Won't be easy, seein' as how you're marrying a man who has everything. Maybe I'll give you and the groom free pest-control service for a year."

"We're not accepting gifts," she said, noting that Max had pushed the refrigerator away from the wall and was standing behind it.

"What's he doing?"

"Trying to repair the ice maker."

Raoul laughed. "Good luck."

"Oh, it's working all right," Max said. "I'm just making a few minor adjustments."

"You fixed it?" Raoul looked surprised.

Max beamed. "As far as I can tell."

Joel peeked out from behind the refrigerator. "He fixed the toilet, too."

Raoul nodded. "Looks like you've got yourself one hell of a repairman," he told Billie. He glanced at his wristwatch. "Well, I came by to see if that new industrial spray I used the other day helped."

Billie hesitated. "I have found a few dead spiders," she said, "but it didn't kill all of them."

"She's right about that," Deedee said. "I keep finding them in my shoes. Alive and kicking." She shuddered. "I can't live in a house with spiders."

"Try not to think of it, sweetie," Frankie said, as he led her out the front door.

Raoul was quiet as he set his container of bug spray on the floor and began checking inside the kitchen cabinets for pests. "I think I may have killed most of the adult insects," he said, "but no telling how many eggs are in the house. I'll have to come back in a couple of weeks, once they've hatched."

Billie simply nodded.

The kids were eating their pizza in front of the TV. Billie had no appetite. Instead, she offered Raoul a cup of coffee. She wanted to tell him about her weird experience the other night and see what he thought.

He accepted her offer of coffee and sat at the table. "I needed to chat with you anyway," Raoul said, keeping his voice low. "I didn't want to tell you this in front of the others because I knew it would upset them."

Billie noted the concern on his face. "What is it?"

"There's been another break-in."

Billie felt the hairs on the back of her neck stand up. "When did it happen? Whose house was it?"

"The Callahan place, a couple of streets over. It had to have happened some time during the night because I sprayed yesterday and everything looked fine. You know, Mr. Callahan is the one with German roaches? I go in twice a week to spray because they've gotten inside the walls. Anyway, his mother is in the hospital, and he asked me to look after the place while hc's gone. And so I could keep working on the roach problem. He left me a key. When I went in this morning, the place was a mess, drawers pulled out, papers strewn everywhere. I immediately called the police. I tell you, this whole neighborhood is going whacko."

"What do the police say?"

"They still think it's teenagers, but I noticed things missing this time, and I pointed them out, like the coin collection Mr. Callahan has hanging on his wall. You get to know a house after a while. No telling what it was worth, but it was Mr. C's pride and joy." He shook his head sadly. "The wife was going to come over and help me pick up the mess so poor Mr. Callahan didn't have to see it, but the police don't want anything touched."

Billie decided against mentioning her own troubles and having Raoul worry more. "Thank you for telling me," she said. "I'll take extra precautions."

Billie zapped the television with the remote and sank lower in the couch. It was ten-thirty. The children were in bed. The laundry was done. The kitchen was clean. And she hadn't heard from Nick. They were getting married in three days, and she didn't even rate a phone call after supper. She changed the channels. She had a choice of watching home repairs, learning to cook borscht, or buying a product guaranteed to clean driveways. She frowned, thinking of that awful oil spot that she'd tried to get up for months. She always made sure to park her minivan there to hide it.

Maybe Nick had changed his mind, she thought. Maybe he didn't want to marry a woman with kids, a cocker spaniel too lazy to bark when the doorbell rang, and a cat that had a tendency to cough up hairballs. Or maybe he was annoyed at her for rear-ending his new car.

She felt her old doubts return. Marriage was for a long time, she reminded herself, and in Nick's case she wanted it to be permanent. She should feel more positive about it. Marriage wasn't something you did on a whim and hoped for the best. You didn't get married because your family had chartered a bus and planned to bring the entire town of Lancaster, Pennsylvania.

Yet, there were times she felt very positive about marrying Nick. She certainly loved him enough. They simply had not been able to date and get to know one another like most couples because of the madness around them. Then there were times she worried they were rushing into things. Perhaps she was just overreacting to the side of Nick she had never seen before, the newspaper magnate in the hand-tailored suit. That man seemed to have little in common with the Nick who'd raided her refrigerator and cookie jar, who rode roller coasters with her children and made love to her until she thought she'd go right off the deep end. She had definitely been thrown off balance by this new facet of his personality.

Or maybe she was still worried after learning that Sheridan was spending so much time at Nick's place. Did Nick honestly believe the woman wanted to be around her horse that much? Was he blind to the fact that Sheridan wanted him back, or was Nick encouraging her to spend as much time at the stables as she liked in order to sift through his feelings for her? Billie didn't like it.

"Isn't this the most boring Wednesday night you've ever had to endure?" Deedee said, joining Billie in the living room.

"I was watching television."

"Television isn't any fun. You don't get dressed up when you watch television. And nobody sees you."

Deedee was wearing a poison-green jumpsuit with her name stitched across the back in rhinestones. She would be noticed no matter what she was doing, Billie thought, even watching television. "I was sort of expecting Nick."

"Forget it. Nick is out for the night. Frankie's manager decided to throw a bachelor party for the two of them."

Billie thought it odd that Nick hadn't mentioned it that afternoon. "What are they doing at this bachelor party?"

Deedee shrugged. "The usual. Drinking, ogling girls who come out of cakes, acting stupid."

Billie couldn't imagine Nick acting stupid, and from what she could tell, he drank very little. "Will there really be a girl coming out of a cake?"

Deedee rolled her eyes. "You better believe it. Not to mention half-naked cocktail waitresses. That's Frankie's favorite part. He wouldn't miss the chance to watch some woman twirl tassels at the end of her ta-tas."

Billie thought about that for a minute. "How do they keep those tassels on?"

"It's a special glue."

"Eeyeuuw."

"Have you ever seen a tassel twirler?" Deedee asked. "It's an art form. Or so they say."

"No, and I don't especially like the idea of Nick seeing it, either."

Deedee shrugged. "It's a guy thing."

"It doesn't bother you that your fiancé is ogling some woman with tassels on her, uh, ta-tas?"

"Oh, well, boys will be boys. Tradition, you know? Nothing we can do about it."

"That's where you're wrong."

"I don't think I like the sound of this."

Nick sat in his office and wondered how long the party in the other room would last. He'd had a friendly drink with the guys, and then slipped off. Obviously, they were so busy gawking at the topless girl serving drinks that they hadn't noticed. Not that he hadn't attended his share of bachelor parties in the past and done just as much hooting and hollering and slipping bills into G-strings. But that was in his younger days. He'd feel kind of dumb doing it now.

Besides, he had other things to worry about, namely Arnie Bates and Max. Billie swore Max was innocent of blowing up his car, but the police were convinced Arnie had left town, so who else could have done it? If Nick had enemies, he didn't know about it. He made a point to try to get along with everybody. Max had suggested it could be a disgruntled newspaper subscriber, someone like Max, who thought Nick should take a stand against the incoming developers. The thought that an old girlfriend might be responsible was ludicrous. Even as angry as Sheridan was, and she was pretty angry after the row they'd had earlier about her taking away her horse, she would prefer embarrassing him in some way in front of their mutual friends. That's why she had sent a trailer for her horse. She would, no doubt, start a rumor that Nick's stable, as well as his riding school, were inadequate. She had no idea how hurt he had been, how devastated that their relationship had ended so badly. He had felt the loss very deeply.

Other than Arnie, none of his employees seemed unhappy. He had a reputation for being overly generous with them, not only where their pay was concerned, and he always commented favorably when they went out of their way to do a good job. He saw that they had a turkey at Thanksgiving, and the ham he gave at Christmas always came with a healthy bonus check, depending on how long they'd been with him.

He'd made a mistake hiring Arnie Bates. He'd let the man con him into believing he really wanted to change. He'd let the fact that Arnie's wife was pregnant color his thinking. Arnie probably wasn't even married.

With Arnie out of the picture, it didn't help that Max was supposedly "missing," as well. It made him look guilty to the police and took their minds off anyone else who may have planted the bomb, including Arnie.

Thank God Max *had* removed essential engine parts from the Mercedes. If Nick had driven the car with that bomb in it, well, he would have been at ground zero for the explosion.

He continued to sit there and wonder who wanted him six feet under.

CHAPTER FOURTEEN

An hour later Billie was sneaking up to Nick's house, commando-style, with Deedee on her heels, insisting that they were doing the right thing in denying the male "traditional rite of passage."

Billie motioned for Deedee to be quiet and directed her to a first-floor window.

"Holy cow," Billie said, "they're all dressed in tux-edos."

"Yeah, Frankie's a classy guy. He wouldn't give a second-rate party."

"Someone's wearing a gorilla suit."

"That's Frankie's best friend, a wrestler. They call

him 'Killer.' He always wears a gorilla suit. It's his thing."

"Uh-huh."

"And see the guy wearing a garter belt on his head? That's Frankie's manager, Bucky."

"He looks classy."

"Yeah. He's got style."

"Oh, my Lord, would you check out the boobs on the woman serving drinks?"

"They're not real, honey. Nobody that skinny has breasts that size."

"I don't see any cake girls. We should scout around and look in the kitchen windows."

"I have a better idea," Deedee whispered. "Why don't we go home? I don't feel comfortable looking in windows."

Billie looked at her. "Is this the same woman who broke into Nick's house and set off the alarms, almost getting me arrested?"

"That was different. It involved jewelry."

Billie rolled her eyes and pulled Deedee by the hand. She very carefully crept around the corner and peeked through a door that led to an oversized laundry room. "Bingo! It's the cake girl!"

Deedee's curiosity obviously won out. "Let me see. Oh, my! I would give every single Donna Karan gown I own for that kind of muscle tone. I may have to start working out." She shuddered.

"I want to get a better look."

"Billie, don't!" Too late. Billie was already knocking on the door.

The door opened, and a drop-dead gorgeous blonde smiled wearily at them. "I wasn't expecting *two* of you."

Bille and Deedee exchanged looks. "I beg your pardon?" Billie said.

"When I called the agency they told me they couldn't find another dancer to replace me, but I'm too sick to work this gig, and none of the others will do it because they'd rather make money pushing drinks." She paused and sneezed, automatically reaching in the front of her G-string for a tissue. "I've got a temperature of a hundred and one. I need to go home and go to bed."

"Do you belong to a gym?" Deedee asked.

Billie simply stared at the woman. "I don't think—"

"Where's your costume? Oh, never mind, I always carry a spare in case a guy spills his drink on me, which is often what happens." She handed Deedee a cloth bag. "You'll find everything you need in here. What's your name, honey?"

"I'm Deedee Holt, and this is my friend Billie Pearce."

"I'm Gloria." She slipped into tight denim shorts and pulled a tight T-shirt over her head. "Call the agency in the morning and leave your phone number so I can arrange to pick up my stuff." She stepped into flip-flops and walked out the door.

"Boy, you've done it now," Deedee accused Billie, holding up the bag as evidence. "Those guys are expecting a half-naked woman to jump out of a cake.

They're going to be mad enough to spit teeth when they find out the cake is empty."

"It wasn't my fault," Billie objected.

"You should have told her why we were here. Gloria will probably lose her job."

"I'm sure the agency will understand when she tells them she's sick."

"Not when Frankie's boss, Bucky, calls and complains. I heard he spent a fortune on this party. They expect a girl to jump out of a cake. Gloria is history. Take it from someone who knows."

Billie looked at her. "You used to jump out of cakes?"

"Damn right. How do you think I met Frankie?"

"I thought you were an ex-model."

"There are all kinds of models, honey."

"Then you can jump out of the cake in Gloria's place."

"No way. Frankie made me swear to give up the business when we became engaged. He'll call off the wedding." She shook her head. "Those guys are going to be furious. They're probably in there slobbering all over the place waiting for the big shebang."

Billie tried to imagine Nick standing in the other room waiting to see a partially clothed woman jump out of a stupid cake, and her temper began to rise. This was a part of Nick she'd never met before—Nick the womanizer. Why on earth would he be interested in such things when he was marrying her? Probably for the same reason his ex-girlfriend was still hanging around. And she was only hours from marrying him!

It was time she got acquainted with the *real* Nick Kaharchek.

"I'll jump out of the damn cake," Billie said, snatching the bag from her.

Deedee's mouth dropped open. "You!"

"What's wrong with me?" Billie thought of Emma in the clothing store. Why were people always making her feel older than she was? She had a good body, dammit, and she was a damn good person. If people couldn't see for themselves, they needed to look closer.

Perhaps it was time everybody got acquainted with the *real* Billie Pearce.

"Well, I just never thought of you as someone who'd do that sort of thing," Deedee said. She reached into Gloria's bag and pulled out two tassels and a G-string. The two exchanged looks.

"Holy crap," Billie said.

Someone banged on the door, causing both women to jump. A man opened it and peered in at them. "What's taking so long?" he demanded. "We're ready to bring out the cake."

Deedee gave him her most beguiling smile. "Give us five minutes."

The man grinned. "Sure, honey." He closed the door again.

Billie began stepping out of her clothes. "I can't believe I'm doing this," she said. "If something happens to me, please don't ever let my children or my mother find out."

Deedee drew an imaginary X across her left breast. "Nick is going to be so surprised."

Billie gritted her teeth. "I'm counting on it."

*   *   *

Nick was still sitting at his desk when he heard the band break into a new song, and a thunderous roar of applause go through the crowd of men on the other side of the door. Just what he needed, a room full of rowdy men who would probably spill beer and liquor all over his furniture and carpet. He left his office to investigate. What he saw stopped him dead in his tracks.

Nick blinked several times as the woman who'd just torn through the cake started a bawdy bump-and-grind routine. Was he seeing things? Was that his fiancée, Billie Pearce, standing up there in front of a room of intoxicated men thrusting her hips and— He swallowed hard. Damned if she wasn't wearing tassels. He could see them through her sheer t-shirt. And doing a pretty good job of goading the crowd, from what he could see.

Where the hell had she learned to dance like that?

What had happened to the sweet, demure sixth-grade teacher he had fallen like a ton of bricks for?

Why wasn't she home baking cookies and helping the kids with their homework?

All at once, several men rushed up to Billie with money, and she paused long enough to stuff the bills into her G-string before going back into her sexy number. Nick felt the blood rush to his head. Adrenaline gushed through his veins. Just what the hell did she think she was doing?

*   *   *

Billie tried to swallow back her panic. She'd forgotten her little pep talk the minute they'd rolled her out in the cake. What in heaven's name was she doing, standing there in almost no clothes while a roomful of men ogled her and called out suggestions that would have earned them a slap on the jaw had the situation been different? Was this how Nick's friends talked to women? Was this how *Nick* talked to women? The thought that she might be marrying a man who saw women in such a light sent a wave of fury through her.

She tried to keep time to the music as she scanned the crowd for Nick, but it was all she could do to concentrate on the band with her heart thumping wildly in her chest. Please God, don't let a tassel fall off, she prayed. The backs of her eyes stung, but the absolute last thing she needed to do was start crying. She would cry a river later. Right now she had to concentrate on keeping a smile plastered to her face while shaking her booty, as Deedee had demonstrated before she'd climbed into the cake.

All at once she saw him, standing at the back of the crowd, gawking. He was mad as hell, that much was clear.

He started toward her. Billie saw the feral look in his eyes, noted the menacing scowl on his face, and she wished she could duck back into the cake and disappear.

"What time do you quit for the night, baby?" a man said, handing her a hundred-dollar bill.

"The lady is finished for the night," Nick said, trying to keep his voice low. "Get down, Billie."

Billie hitched her chin high and met his gaze head-on. "You obviously expected a show tonight, big guy, and I'm here to oblige you."

"You have no business here," he said. "Get down before I drag you down."

The man with the hundred-dollar bill looked at Nick. "Hey, Kaharchek, I'm trying to do business here, do you mind?"

Nick glared at him. "You need to sober up, Harry. I do not permit this kind of business in my home."

"Oh, yeah?" Billie said. "Then how come you hired these women in the first place, Mr. Kaharchek?" Instead of waiting for him to answer, she turned her back to the crowd and wiggled her fanny. The men went wild.

Nick saw red. He reached for Billie. He grabbed her wrist, and she tried to yank it free. She lost her balance. He saw the fear in her eyes as she began to topple. She tried to catch herself, overcorrected, and fell in the opposite direction. She hit the table beside the cake and slid through dishes of smoked salmon, lox and bagels, and a cold shrimp platter. She cried out as she slammed into an ice sculpture of a naked woman. The sculpture toppled over and crashed onto the floor.

Billie heard the raucous laughter as she tried to raise herself from the table. Strong arms pulled her up. She almost flinched at the sight of Nick's handsome face masked in anger. Without a word, he threw her over his shoulders and carried her upstairs while the men below whistled and shouted obscene remarks.

Nick burst through his bedroom door and dumped

Billie on his bed like a side of beef. "Just what in the hell did you think you were doing down there?" he demanded.

Billie shook her head, trying to clear her thoughts. She was covered with food. She plucked a shrimp from her G-string and looked up at Nick. She had never seen him so mad. She steeled herself.

"I was giving you what you wanted," she said.

"What I wanted?" he repeated in disbelief. "Do you think I want the woman I love strutting her stuff in front of a room full of strangers? Have you lost your mind?"

Billie stared at him. He'd said it. He'd said he loved her!

He stalked to his closet, pulled out a bathrobe, and tossed it at her. "Get dressed."

Billie jumped from the bed and snatched the robe. "You're just like every other man," she accused. "It's okay for you to attend wild parties and maul women, but you expect your future wife to sit home and knit sweaters. That's called double standards, Nick."

His eyes almost glittered with fury. "I'm not your ex-husband."

Billie sat in her dark living room waiting for her hair to dry. Deedee had checked on her several times before going to bed, but Billie had not been in the mood for conversation. She had made a fool of herself.

Not only that, she would never get the smell of fish out of her hair.

Billie sniffed. She would not cry. She was a woman

of morals, and she expected the man she planned to marry to have them, as well.

Billie got up and made her way through the dark house to the kitchen. She needed water. She switched on the light over the stove, and the kitchen lit up softly. Billie turned for the refrigerator and opened the freezer.

Ice cubes spilled out like an avalanche. She tried to catch them in her hands, but the cubes continued to fall, literally hundreds of them, hitting the floor and sliding in all directions.

Hell's bells, she'd never seen so much ice in her life! It clattered on the floor like giant hail. She looked up and jumped when she found Max standing there, a sheepish look on his face.

"I fixed the ice maker like you asked," he said. He sniffed. "What's that smell?"

"It's a long story."

He nodded. It took twenty minutes for the two of them to sweep up the ice and mop the floor. Billie forgot all about being thirsty.

"Boy, when you repair something, you really go all out," she told the boy.

He looked embarrassed. "I guess I need to make some more minor adjustments. At least the garage door doesn't go up every time you turn on the lamp in the living room." He gave her an odd look. "Have you been crying?"

Billie shrugged. "Nick and I had a disagreement earlier."

"Are you still getting married?"

"Probably not."

Max looked down at the floor. "I haven't exactly made things any easier for you."

Billie put her hand on his shoulder. Sometimes he seemed so young. "Everything will be okay." She gazed past him and froze. The dead bolt on her door was unlocked. "Max?"

"Yeah?"

"Did you go out while I was showering?"

"No. I only got up because I heard someone down here. Why do you ask?"

"The door is unlocked."

He turned. "Maybe Joel or Christie?"

Billie shook her head. "I've drilled it into their heads how important it is to keep the doors locked, even during the day. I can't imagine them forgetting."

Max walked over to the door and flipped the dead bolt into a locked position. He checked the doorknob and locked it as well. "Are you okay?"

Billie sank into one of the chairs. Max sat in the chair opposite her. "I think someone came into this house the other night." Max just stared at her as she told him what had happened. "I could have been dreaming someone was in my room, but it felt so real, and I smelled perfume. Not only that, I never close my bedroom door or turn off the night-light in the hall."

"That's weird."

" 'Scary' is a better word."

"Have you told Nick?"

She shook her head. "I didn't want to add to his worries, especially now, what with someone blowing up his car."

Max hung his head. "I think he still believes I did it."

"Maybe in the beginning, but I bet now he's considering other options."

"Maybe. By the way, I killed five or six spiders tonight, not to mention a couple of roaches."

Billie's unease worsened. "What kind of roaches?"

"Small ones. German roaches."

Billie told him about the infestation problem in the neighborhood and Raoul's concern about the bugs. "Everybody's having problems. And we've had all these break-ins, two in the past couple of nights."

"Do any of the kids in this neighborhood work in grocery stores, specifically in the produce section?"

"I've no idea. Why?"

"If someone is bringing in bugs, which sounds kind of crazy to me, that's one place I can think of that they could be getting them." He shook his head. "And I thought I was strange."

"Why would somebody do something like that?"

"Who knows? I'm going to start sleeping on the sofa," Max said. "I wake up at the slightest sound. If someone tries to unlock either door or manages to get inside the house, I'll know."

"I don't want the others to find out."

"I'll just say Joel's twin bed isn't long enough for me. Which is the truth. My feet hang off."

"Why didn't you say something?"

"Hey, I've slept in the woods at Nick's. A bed is like heaven to me. But that's the best excuse I can think of at the moment."

"Thanks," Billie said. "I'll rest easier knowing

you're out here." Unless Max was not innocent as he claimed to be, she thought, then chided herself for being so paranoid. But it wasn't like she could call the police. She was harboring their main suspect. She prepared herself for another sleepless night.

Flowers began arriving the next morning at nine o'clock sharp, roses in every imaginable color, along with large pots of daffodils and daisies, Billie's favorite. The small card attached contained an apology from Nick.

"I don't know what Nick did to make you angry," Max said, "but I think whatever it was, he's really sorry for it."

"Oh, my goodness!" Deedee exclaimed when she came down shortly before lunch. "Are all these for me?"

Christie gave her a smug look. "No, they're for my mom."

Deedee's smile faded. "Frankie's never done anything like this for me. Maybe I shouldn't marry him after all."

"Sounds good to me," Billie muttered. "Then I won't have to feel guilty backing out at the last minute."

"Mom!" Joel looked indignant. "You *have* to marry Nick. You promised him you would."

"Joel's right," Christie said. "Besides, Nick is cool. Even Lisa Marie agrees, and she's not easy to please, believe me."

"You guys just think he's cool because he has horses," Billie said.

Both of her children looked at her. "You're wrong, Mom," Christie said. "Nick cares about Joel and me. Lisa Marie said all her mom's boyfriends acted like they cared about her in the beginning 'cause they wanted to butter her up so her mom would marry them. But Nick is different. You can tell he loves all of us."

Joel nodded in agreement. "I just hope he doesn't send any more flowers because this house is starting to smell."

"That's your mother's hair you smell," Deedee said. "But I have to hand it to you kids. You're really deep."

"I didn't want to say anything to hurt your feelings, Mom," Christie said, "but how come your hair smells like fish?"

Billie shrugged. "I dove into a plate of salmon last night."

Christie rolled her eyes. "How come you can never get a straight answer from anyone around here?"

"Sometimes you're better off not knowing every little detail," Deedee said.

Billie looked at Max. He smiled, and she marveled at how much he resembled Nick.

"Nick's a good guy, even if he does sometimes lose his temper with me," Max said, "but you're the one who has to live with him the rest of your life."

"Thanks, Max," she said. "For everything." She felt guilty now for suspecting him the night before.

He smiled. "Since you're feeling so grateful, would you mind taking me to the library when it's convenient? I've been making plans in my spare time on what to do about the marshland problem."

"Uh-oh," Deedee said. "I smell trouble."

Billie ignored her. "Oh, yeah?"

Max nodded. "I'm going to contact the people who've complained in the editorial section about the developers, and I'm going to form a committee of volunteers."

"And?"

"I'm going to fight it, but I'm going to do it legally with flyers and peaceful protests. In the meantime, I need volunteers out there banding and counting birds so we can have some accurate statistics."

Deedee almost choked on her coffee. "Is this my brother talking?"

"I've turned over a new leaf," Max said proudly. "If you want to be heard, you have to make sense to people. Blowing up pots of geraniums just makes you look stupid."

Billie checked her wristwatch. "Tell you what, I'll grab a quick shower, wash my hair again, and then I'll drive you to the library."

When Billie returned after having driven Max to the library, she found Nick's car, dent and all, in the driveway. Her stomach seemed to do a little flip-flop as she walked to the front door.

He was sitting on the sofa looking at a comic book with Joel. Deedee sat at the kitchen table doing her nails. He brightened at the sight of Billie. "Hi."

"Hi, yourself," she said.

Deedee held up a hand and blew her nails. "Christie went over to Lisa Marie's. I hope that's okay."

Billie nodded.

Deedee looked from Billie to Nick to Joel. "Uh, Joel, how would you like to make a dollar?"

The boy glanced up quickly. "Doing what?"

"I lost my tweezers, which means I can't pluck my eyebrows."

"Pluck your eyebrows?" he said, wrinkling his nose distastefully. "Why would you want to do something like that?"

Deedee stood. "You want to make a buck or not?"

Joel stood as well. "Okay, I'll look for them." He followed Deedee upstairs.

Billie allowed her gaze to meet Nick's. "Why don't we go out back?" He nodded and followed her through the back door. Finally, she faced him. Silently.

"I didn't sleep last night," he said.

"Why am I not surprised?"

"It's not what you think. The party ended shortly after you left."

Billie grimaced.

"I didn't plan the party, Billie. It was a surprise. I wasn't even in the room when they rolled in the cake. The only reason I came in was because I heard all the racket and wondered what was going on. I've never been the jealous type before," he said, "but when I saw you standing up there wearing next to nothing, and all those men whistling and making lewd comments, I flipped out."

"It was me! I acted like a moron."

"Actually you looked pretty good," Nick said.

Billie chewed on her lip.

"What?" Nick asked. "There's something else bothering you. I can tell."

"I know it's stupid," Billie said, "but I'm still feeling weird about Sheridan."

"She and I grew up together. Our families were close. Neither of us had brothers or sisters, and we were practically neighbors. Sheridan was pretty much a tomboy in those days, if you can believe it; we did everything together. We pulled a helluva lot of pranks. Our fathers were rich and important; I guess we did it partly to embarrass them and maybe get their attention. Both of us stayed in trouble in and out of school."

"Nick—"

"Hear me out, please. Sheridan was my best friend, and I was hers. We dated other people, compared notes, but it never interfered with our friendship. Then a couple of years ago her mother died, and we grew even closer. She and I weren't serious about anyone else at the time, and—

"It just happened, I don't know how, but it did. We began seeing one another. Sheridan was still grieving, and I felt I should be there as her friend. Our parents seemed so happy about it. I think it was their dream for us to marry, so I asked her. It was the biggest mistake of our lives when we became engaged. We were perfect pals, buddies, but we weren't cut out to be lovers, so I broke it off."

"You said *she* called off the engagement."

He rolled his eyes. "She made me say that. You

know, her pride and all. It would be unthinkable to suggest that a man would call it quits with her."

Billie tried to digest it. "So if it's over between the two of you, why is Sheridan still following you around?"

Nick sighed. "Nobody has ever said no to her. *Ever.* As much as I care about her, the bottom line is Sheridan has always gotten exactly what she's wanted. Her father has pulled strings, called in favors, you name it, in order to see that his daughter is happy. It only got worse after her mother died. Sheridan is all he has left."

"I understand he's a retired general," Billie said, "and very powerful. What would he do if his daughter *didn't* get what she wanted?"

Nick met her questioning gaze. "Lord only knows."

Billie was silent for a moment. "I don't know, Nick. My life was pretty normal before I met you. No bombs, no ditsy redheads, no insanely jealous ex-fiancées. I would never have considered doing what I did last night. I just hope my students never find out."

"Why'd you do it?"

"I didn't like the thought of you looking at another woman. I figured that if you were going to look at a scantily clad woman at all, you were going to look at me. It was very immature of me to react as I did. Especially for someone who craves normalcy in her life."

"But if you crave normalcy above all else, life might become boring. Haven't you ever done anything even remotely kooky before you met me?"

Billie pondered it. "My sister and I once put a dead chicken in Edna Kuntz's mailbox."

"You have a sister?"

Billie suddenly realized she had told him very little about her growing-up years. How could the two of them have created such a bond without knowing one another's history?

"There are four of us. My sister Mary is a year older than me, my sister Margaret is two years younger, and I have a little brother, Richard. They're all married, and all have children, and I'm sure they'll all be on the wedding bus."

"Which one mailed the chicken with you?"

"Margaret. She was in the third grade, and she had this terrible teacher named Edna Kuntz. Everyone hated this woman. Margaret used to come home crying all the time because Mrs. Kuntz was so mean. On the last day of school I thought Margaret deserved to get even, so I defrosted one of my mom's soup chickens and that night we stuffed it in Edna Kuntz's mailbox. The mailman, Sonny Moyer, hated Mrs. Kuntz, too, so when he delivered the mail the next day and found the chicken in her mailbox he shoved her phone bill into the chicken's . . . opening. By the time old Edna went to get her mail the temperature was ninety-two and there were five dogs hanging around the mailbox."

Nick chuckled in approval. "You underestimate yourself. Not even Deedee could top that one."

An afternoon breeze ruffled his hair and Billie had to stop herself from reaching out and brushing the curl from his forehead. It was peaceful and comfortable—

the way Billie imagined a good marriage would be, the way she had hoped she and Nick could be. But how could she hope for such peace when they felt so passionate about one another? Not that passion was a bad thing. She expected ups and downs, hills and valleys, but she wanted some smooth-running moments, as well. "Do you really love me?" she asked.

He touched her cheek. "Those words don't come easy for me. I didn't hear them often when I was growing up. I don't think I truly understood the meaning until I met you.

"I see the love on your face when you look at your children, and I ache deep inside because I've spent so many years without it. You radiate with love, Billie. It's because of you that I was able to find it."

She was so touched she feared she might cry. He'd finally said the words. All their obstacles seemed small and insignificant when he looked at her that way. "Oh, Nick. I will do everything in my power to make you feel loved for the rest of your life."

He reached for her hand and put it to his mouth. Slowly and thoughtfully, he kissed her fingertips. "Billie, we need to have a serious talk. This has been sort of an unorthodox courtship. I know you're wearing my ring, but I also know you were . . . nudged into accepting my proposal. If you have any doubts . . ." He stopped for a minute to make sure his voice wouldn't waver, wondering what he would do if she decided not to marry him, if she thought it was happening too fast. He'd known her for such a short time, but he couldn't imagine life without her. "We don't

need to get married this Saturday if you feel pres-
sured."

Billie smiled tenderly. For some reason, she no
longer felt rushed. At the moment, she felt as if time
were moving very slowly and Saturday would never
come. Marriage was a state of mind, she decided, not
a piece of paper. She already felt married to Nick, and
the ceremony on Saturday would probably mean more
to her friends and family.

"Saturday will be fine."

CHAPTER FIFTEEN

"It's nerves," Deedee said. "You just haven't gotten married enough."

Billie squinted into her foyer mirror and watched her left eye twitch. "Nerves," she repeated. "I'm going to be okay because I'm marrying a wonderful man and everything's going to be, well, wonderful. His parents, his manservant, his grandmother . . . they're all coming tomorrow and I'm going to meet them, and it's going to be, uh, wonderful. And then everyone in the world, with the exception of those living in third world countries, is going to arrive on a chartered bus and that's going to be wonderful, too. It's all going to be absolutely wonderful."

If only her damn eye would stop twitching.

"Just be thankful you and I didn't have to arrange it all," Deedee said. "Nick's secretary is a jewel for doing all the work and sending out last-minute invitations. Believe me, there's a lot to attend to."

"And Deedee should know," Frankie said.

Deedee nodded. "It's going to be okay, honey."

Billie wanted to believe it. She really did. But she had this premonition of disaster. She checked her watch and looked out the front window. "Nick was supposed to be here hours ago. You don't suppose he's been in a car accident?"

"Nick is busy," Deedee said. She looked over her shoulder at Frankie. "That's why we thought we'd take you to dinner or something. Isn't that right, Frankie?"

"Yeah, Nick is busy."

Billie looked first at Deedee and then at Frankie. "What's Nick busy doing?"

"Things," Deedee said. "He had things to do."

Frankie averted his gaze. "Probably tied up at the newspaper office."

Billie pressed a fingertip lightly over her left eyelid and hoped she wasn't forced to do the same thing walking down the aisle. "Both of you are keeping something from me. I want answers. Now."

"Nick swore me to secrecy," Deedee said.

Billie crossed her arms. "I refuse to have secrets between Nick and me."

Deedee hesitated. "You'll have to promise not to rush over there. He's dealing with a lot right now."

Billie felt a sense of dread wash over her. "What has happened?"

Deedee looked at Frankie, who shrugged as though he had no idea what to do. "Someone torched the stable," she said.

Billie's heart gave a jerk. "What!"

"It happened late this afternoon, after the stable hands went home. Nick was taking a shower, getting ready to come over here. Luckily, there are smoke alarms in the stables that connect to the house, and Nick heard them go off."

"Is he—?"

"He's perfectly fine, honey." Deedee patted Billie's hand. "A couple of the horses had to be treated by the vet for smoke inhalation, but the others are okay."

"I should call him."

"Nick was pretty shaken over the whole thing. He asked us to keep you busy so he could, well, regroup. We were supposed to tell you he had a problem at the newspaper."

"Seems neither of us is good at lying," Frankie said.

Billie's eye began to twitch double-time, and her heartbeat accelerated. Max had returned to Nick's early that afternoon, saying he needed to get busy on his computer so he could design the necessary flyers for the marshland project. "Does Nick suspect Max?"

Deedee shrugged. "I don't know what Nick is thinking right now, except he's probably relieved those dumb horses are okay. The police are there." Deedee chewed her lower lip. "So, do you want to go out to dinner, or what?"

Billie shook her head. "No, thanks. I appreciate the thought, but I think I'd like to be alone."

Deedee and Frankie looked at one another, and Deedee shrugged. "At least we tried," she said.

At eight o'clock Christie and Joel came in from outside and found Billie sitting at the kitchen table. "How's your eye?" Christie asked.

"The twitching isn't as bad."

"Why are you just sitting at the table?"

"I'm resting. Just resting."

"Are you resting up for your marriage night?" Joel asked. "I hear it's exhausting."

Billie looked at him. "Where did you hear that?"

"Television."

She frowned. "Figures."

"Well," Joel persisted. "*Is* it exhausting?"

"I think the wedding and all the preparations beforehand are what's exhausting. By the time you leave for the honeymoon, all you want to do is rest."

"Is that why newlywed couples spend most of their time in bed?"

Billie arched one brow. "What shows have you been watching?"

"Some daytime shows with a lot of kissing."

"I think you need to stick to the Disney Channel, kiddo." Billie decided a change of subject was in order. She heaved herself to her feet. "How about we go to the video store and rent a movie? One where there's not a lot of, uh, kissing. We can grab some food on the way back and throw sleeping bags on the floor in front of the television set like we used to do."

"Can we make popcorn?" Joel asked.

"Sure. I'll even put real butter on it." Her children looked pleased. Billie wondered if Nick, who'd traveled all over the world, had dined at the most exclusive restaurants and seen all the best plays, would find as much pleasure as she did in the simple things.

The three of them piled into Billie's minivan a few minutes later. Already, Christie and Joel were arguing over which movie to rent. Billie didn't care what they watched as long as they were together. She longed for that feeling of normalcy.

Besides, spending time with her kids might take her mind off Nick's latest disaster.

At ten-thirty Billie sat alone in the living room and listened to the sounds of her house. The children were asleep. She had tucked them in and gazed down at them, feeling her heart swell with love. Sometimes she wished she could stop time and just enjoy these precious moments. The sigh Christie gave before she turned over and closed her eyes. Buffy sprawled across the foot of her bed, thumping her tail as Billie backed from the room. The wet kiss Joel gave her as she tucked him in, the cat curled on the pillow beside him.

Billie wondered what it would be like to carry Nick's baby, how he'd react the first time he saw the child they'd created together. She knew in her heart that he would make a wonderful father.

She jumped when the ice maker dumped more ice

in the bin, a sound she was not used to hearing. It had not stopped making ice since Max had repaired it. She had already begun bagging it up and sending it to neighbors. She shook her head. For an ice maker that had never worked, it was certainly making up for lost time.

She stretched. She was getting married tomorrow. If the groom made it to the wedding in one piece, she reminded herself. She looked at her watch for the hundredth time in the past half hour and pressed her lips together in annoyance because Nick had not called. Her eye had resumed its twitching. Truly, she was more worried than anything. Nick had certainly suffered his share of problems lately.

Billie perked at the sound of a car pulling into her driveway. The headlights shone through her front windows and then blinked out. A car door slammed. Her heart began pounding in her throat when she looked out the window and spied Nick's car.

Get a grip, she ordered herself. He was going to be upset as it was, without her doing more fretting over the situation. Billie threw open the door just as Nick raised his hand to knock. He wore simple jeans and a T-shirt, and his hair was damp from a recent shower. "Are you okay?" Billie asked, stepping aside so he could come in.

He noted the worry in her eyes. "Deedee told you."

"I forced her."

"The stable is gone, but the horses are okay. The police have been questioning my employees most of the evening."

"What about Max?"

"Him, too." Nick gave a weary sigh. "I may as well tell you he's a suspect, even though nobody saw anything. They can't find hide nor hair of Arnie Bates, so they're just looking for someone to pin this on. I had to do a lot of talking to keep them from hauling Max in."

"Where is he now?"

"Out in the car. We decided to get something to eat."

"Max isn't responsible, Nick. You have to believe that." She paused before asking the next question. "What about Sheridan?"

Nick gave her an odd look. "Sheridan loves horses. She would never put innocent animals at risk." Nick felt a sudden chill. Sheridan had removed her horse from his stable, she'd said, on the advice of her father, who thought it time they made a clean break. Although the general accompanied his daughter to all her horse shows and proudly displayed her many trophies and ribbons, he was not a horse lover.

"We have police protection, at least for the next few days," Nick said, deciding to keep his thoughts to himself. It was ludicrous to think Sheridan or her father would get involved in something as serious as arson. "There will also be plainclothes detectives at the wedding tomorrow. Security will be tight." He frowned. "What's wrong with your eye?"

"Nothing, really. I'm just tired and hysterical. I think I'm having a nervous breakdown, but I'm not sure."

He bent over and kissed the tip of her nose. "It's just pre-wedding jitters."

Like hell, Billie thought. Their lives were suddenly falling apart around them. Someone had been tampering with her locks, possibly breaking into her house while she slept, spiders were breeding in her closets at breakneck speed, an infestation of German roaches was a possible threat, and Nick's life was in danger. The police were watching his house and obviously felt it necessary to attend their wedding because they were concerned about his safety.

Other than that everything was fine.

"Perhaps we should hold off on the wedding," she said.

He looked disturbed. "Is that what you want?"

She no longer knew *what* she wanted.

"I'm scared, Nick," she confessed. "It seems silly to hold a wedding with all that's going on."

"To me it seems silly to let someone think they can toy with our lives and our happiness. I'm sure, what with all the security, we'll be safe, so stop worrying."

"I don't like worrying any more than you do," she said. "I've always tried to be strong and optimistic about life. I was always the rock in my family. The one who managed to stay cool during emergencies."

He saw her eye twitch again and felt bad for her. They were to be married tomorrow, and he had wanted this night to be special for both of them. "Maybe your body is tired of being the rock," he said. "Maybe it's taking a well-deserved vacation now that there's going to be another rock in the family." Nick pressed his thumbs into the base of her neck and rubbed away the tension.

"I just had a thought," Billie said. "I know it's going to sound crazy, but could any of this be related to Frankie?"

"In what way?"

"It's just a thought, but what if a crazed fan knows he's about to be married to your cousin? Maybe that person doesn't know Deedee is presently living here. Frankie certainly wouldn't be the first famous person who was stalked."

"I think we should let the police worry about it," Nick said, trying to keep his own concern hidden from her. He had spent most of the evening wondering who could be holding such a grudge against him. Had Arnie Bates resented his firing enough to kill over it? Was it possible, as Max had suggested, that one of his readers was striking out over the fact that Nick hadn't publicly opposed the marshland project in his newspaper? The police had even questioned the Duffys and the high school boys Nick had hired to help with the horses, asking what they thought of Nick as an employer. It seemed everybody was a suspect, including Nick's polo students. Even Nick was trying to come up with possibilities. Who hated him that much?

All he knew for sure was that he loved the woman before him, and he was going to make her his wife the next day, come hell or high water. He had hired enough security so that the Pope would feel safe attending the wedding, but he wasn't about to let some nutcase spoil his and Billie's big day.

"Like I said, security is going to be tight tomorrow, so we have nothing to worry about." He paused. "I don't want to upset you, but I've got a couple of men watching the house tonight."

Billie felt the back of her neck prickle. "Do you think that's necessary?"

"No, but I'm doing it anyway." He took her hands and raised them to his mouth for a kiss. "I know everything seems all screwed up right now, Billie, but try not to lose sight of the fact that I love you deeply, and I want to spend the rest of my life with you."

"Nick, I'm scared for you."

"My place is crawling with cops, babe. Nobody gets in without a damn good reason for being there."

Joel shuffled from his room to the top of the stairs and stood rubbing his eyes. "What's going on?"

Billie glanced at her son and smiled. He looked so innocent standing there. Her determination to protect her children became stronger. She was glad Nick had someone watching the house. "Nick and I were just talking, honey. Is something wrong?"

"I had a bad dream. Would you tuck me in, Mom?"

Nick and Billie exchanged looks, and she was certain he knew what she'd been thinking. "Go ahead," he said, giving her a quick kiss. "I just stopped by to let you know everything is okay." He squeezed her hand. "I'll see you in the morning."

Billie locked the door behind him and followed Joel upstairs. She would see him in the morning.

She prayed he was right.

Billie paced the bedroom Deedee had slept in during her stay at Nick's as Deedee touched up her nails. It was a beautiful day for a wedding. The caterers had arrived at the crack of dawn to set up the tents and canopies that stood out stark white against the brilliant blue sky and billowed with the warm breeze that persistently flowed over the hills and meadows. Padded chairs had been arranged for the ceremony and reception; flowers and white satin bows adorned everything; the grass had been cut into a perfect green carpet.

Billie looked out the window at the circular drive where valets were parking luxury cars and directing the chauffeured limos to a separate area.

Nick certainly had his share of rich friends. Not that Nick was exactly impoverished, she reminded herself. Still, he seemed unaffected by it all. He didn't brag or put on airs, nor was he the flashy type. And while he was accustomed to nice things, he didn't seem to take them for granted. He liked hot dogs and ice-cream cones and chocolate-chip cookies; he wore goofy-looking hats, rode roller coasters with her children, and seemed to be well adjusted despite the power and wealth he'd inherited.

He was just Nick.

Christie ran across the lawn, the frilly skirt to her gown flying high above her knees, hair ribbons streaming behind her. Two other girls ran with her. They stopped short at the sight of Snakeman emerging from his Porsche, his boa constrictor draped around his neck. The girls screamed and ran toward the house, just as a man in a dark suit headed toward Snakeman. A detective, no doubt. The place was crawling with plainclothes detectives and uniformed security guards. The valet was a retired policeman, as were a couple of those helping the caterers.

Billie wondered how many weddings included wrestlers with snakes, not to mention plainclothes detectives and security checks at the front door.

"This is going to be some wedding," Billie said, unable to hide her annoyance. "Snakeman just arrived with his favorite pet and scared my daughter and a couple of other girls half to death." She shook her head sadly. "This isn't a wedding, this is a carnival." Billie thought one of the girls looked vaguely familiar, but she couldn't place her. "I hate when I can't remember where I've seen people," she mused aloud.

"Did you say something?" Deedee put the cap on her fingernail polish and joined her at the window.

"That little girl with the dark hair standing next to Christie. I've seen her before, but I can't remember where."

"Oh, that's little Julie Favor. She lives down the street. Her parents are friends with Nick. You've probably seen Julie riding her bicycle during one of your visits here."

"I don't know," Billie said. "There's something odd about her."

"Odd about Julie?" Deedee shook her head. "Honey, would you relax and try to enjoy yourself? This is your wedding day." Deedee sighed. "I love weddings. My second wedding was in St. Patrick's Cathedral in New York, and I got to walk down this huge long aisle. That was the best. My dress for that one cost more than Nick's new car."

Billie tossed a look at Deedee. The dress she'd chosen to wear to her latest wedding was a tea-length pink organza dress that made her hair seem outrageously red. It was Edwardian-style with a dropped waist and trimmed with long dangling crystal beads that tinkled when she walked. Her headpiece was a big pink pouf with a long train. It was held in place by a pink organza sweatband, which was also trimmed with the dangling crystal beads. She looked like a heroine from a silent movie, Billie decided. All she needed was Snidely Whiplash tying her to a train track.

It would never occur to the woman that a wedding was not a good place for a boa constrictor *or* dangling crystal beads.

The sound of air brakes caught Billie's attention, and she gasped at the sight of a huge maroon-and-gold tour bus. The bus doors opened and Billie's father was the first to emerge. He stopped, looked at the house, and took a picture of it. Billie's mother followed, then her Aunt Kate, her Uncle Henry, and her sister Margaret's two kids, who took off at a run. They seemed very remote down on the lawn. They looked like tourists.

"Is that your family?" Deedee asked.

"Yeah."

"They look nice. I bet you're excited to see them."

Billie gave her a weak grin. "Excited" wasn't exactly the right word. Billie had reached the numb stage. She sat down on a window seat and immediately stood, because she didn't want to wrinkle her suit, which she was sure Deedee found boring compared to her own getup. She looked in the mirror and adjusted the hat covering her brown hair. Organ music wafted through the closed bedroom door, and Billie felt her stomach flutter. There was a knock at the door and Christie burst in with Billie's mother and father in tow.

"Grandma and Grandpa are here!" Christie said, cheeks flushed from running in the heat.

Billie hugged her mother and father and felt the tears spring to her eyes. They weren't remote anymore. They were here, and she hadn't seen them in a long time. She introduced them to Deedee. If her parents thought the woman looked strange in her dress, they didn't say anything.

Her father scraped a tear from Billie's cheek with his thumb. "You're not supposed to be crying," he said gruffly, although his voice suddenly choked with emotion. "You're supposed to be happy."

"You'll ruin your makeup," Deedee warned.

Billie ignored her. "Oh, Daddy."

Finally, she turned to her mother's outstretched arms. They hugged. "We had to pass through a metal detector," the woman said to Billie, "then some man actually ran a wand between my legs, and me wearing a dress. I thought your Aunt Flora would faint."

"There are a number of celebrities here," Billie said, hoping to put her parents at ease about the tight security. "Not to mention a few politicians. That's why there are so many policemen."

"I'm glad I brought this camera," her father said. He suddenly became serious as he put his index finger beneath Billie's chin and raised it so she was looking him directly in the eyes. "Do you love Nick? Do you really love him?"

"Yes, Daddy." She was sure of that. In fact, it was the only thing she was certain of at the moment. Everything else felt weird and unreal, as though she were walking through a fog and trying desperately to see through it. So many questions, so few answers.

Billie's father nodded his approval. "That's all I need to hear. Like I told your mother, sometimes love hits you fast and hard, and sometimes it just eases along like a lazy river when you least expect it."

"Wow, that's deep," Deedee said.

"Oh, now, look what you've gone and done," her mother said. "I've got tears in my eyes." She grabbed her husband's hand. "Let's go before I start bawling." She smiled tremulously at Billie. "We'll see you downstairs, honey."

Billie tried to remain calm as the wedding party moved to the solarium. It had been agreed that Christie would serve as maid of honor for both brides, and that Billie would follow Deedee to the outdoor altar.

Billie tried to organize her thoughts as the first chords of the wedding march reached her ears. In her own mind she had already accepted the vows, but this was the day when her parents and her children would accept her as Mrs. Kaharchek.

All at once, there was a commotion. A lovely blonde broke through the small crowd waiting to go in and stood before Billie. Her denim shorts bordered on indecent, and two pert nipples stood at attention, barely veiled by her thin tank top.

"Omigod!" Deedee said.

"Remember me?"

Billie blinked. "Gloria?"

"Yes. Not only was I fired over the fiasco you caused here the other night at the bachelor party, but you didn't return my G-string and tassels as you promised. Do you have any idea what they cost?"

"Who is this woman?" Billie's father demanded. "And what's this nonsense about a G-string?"

"What's a G-string?" Christie asked.

"You're too young to know," her grandfather said sharply, still eyeing Billie, obviously waiting for an explanation.

"It's a long story, Daddy." Billie looked at Gloria. "I'm sort of in the middle of something right now, and I don't have my purse on me. Would it be okay if I paid you for them later?"

The music changed.

"Mom!" Christie hissed. "We're supposed to go out now."

"I'm not leaving till I get my money," Gloria said. "One hundred bucks."

"One hundred dollars!" Deedee cried. "That's highway robbery."

Gloria shrugged. "Take it or leave it."

"Mom, they're waiting!" Christie said. "Everybody is staring at us."

"Get lost," Deedee told the woman.

Gloria stuck her tongue out at her. "Okay, fifty bucks, and I'm outta here."

"Oh, for Pete's sake," Billie's father said, reaching into his back pocket. He pulled out his wallet and handed the girl several bills. "Now, leave before you ruin my daughter's wedding."

"Gladly." Gloria looked at Billie, and her expression softened. "To tell you the truth, I was going to quit that dumb job anyway." She started to turn away, then thought of something, and turned back. "Oh, and congratulations on your marriage."

Billie saw the organist craning her head as though wondering what was holding them up. The minister stood there, looking as bewildered as the guests. The organist began replaying the wedding march and Billie waited for her cue.

"Okay, Christie, I believe we're ready," she said, trying to sound calm when her insides were jumping about like popcorn on a hot skillet. It was then that she noticed her daughter's forehead, but it was too late to do anything about it. She sighed and watched Christie walk forward, and then Deedee, on the arm of Frankie's manager, Bucky. Billie caught a glimpse of Nick waiting for her at the altar. He looked handsome, and only slightly concerned as to why the wedding party had taken so long to get started. A small private smile lit his face when their eyes met.

Nick watched Billie walk the length of the improvised aisle on the arm of her father. She was beautiful in a cream-colored suit that was as simple and unpretentious as she was.

She looked worried.

Nick took his place beside her and wondered if she was just nervous. He glanced around quickly and almost groaned aloud at the sight of Snakeman with his boa. He looked at Christie, saw three wrestlers' signatures on her forehead, and winced. He considered himself to be flexible, but, he had to admit, this wedding was somewhat unusual. And what the hell was that clacking sound? One look at Deedee and he had his answer. He'd never seen so many beads on a woman. What could she have been thinking when she'd purchased such an outfit?

Poor Billie. He'd wanted everything to be so perfect for her.

The minister's smile looked forced as he began a short speech about the bonds of marriage. Billie could barely hear him over the jangling beads. "Could you speak up?" she whispered.

The minister shot her a look of apology, then glared at Deedee. He cleared his throat and started over in a louder voice.

Nick glanced at Christie, who looked as though she wanted to crawl under a rock. The door to the solarium slammed and almost everybody present glanced over their shoulders to see Max running down the aisle, his hair uncombed as usual, his glasses askew. He pulled up at Nick's elbow and tried to straighten his tie.

"Sorry I'm latc," hc said.

The minister arched one brow in question.

"I'm the best man," Max said.

Billie thought the boy looked tired and pale, but she couldn't question him at the moment.

The minister began again. "As I was saying—"

Just then there was an explosion, followed by the sound of shattering glass. Several women screamed; the crowd bolted to their feet, craning their heads to see what had caused the blast. Billie glanced in the direction of the largest tent where tables had been set up for the reception that was to follow. The elaborate wedding cake had been blown to smithereens, the food splattered on shards of what had once been champagne glasses. The champagne bottles had burst, spewing champagne in all directions.

A sense of dread and disbelief clouded her head. She stood motionless as reality set in.

"Everyone clear the area now!" a detective yelled, even as the guests scattered toward the long driveway that led to the road.

Billie grabbed Joel and Christie and led them away quickly, depositing them with her parents in case her help was needed. An employee from the catering service had obviously been injured in the blast; several security guards and plainclothes detectives were kneeling beside someone on the ground.

Billie searched out Nick. He and Max were helping an elderly couple to safety. They joined her a moment later.

"Thank God you're okay," Nick said, his eyes combing Billie for signs of injury. "Where are the kids?"

"My parents have them."

"Is everyone all right?" Nick called out to the stunned crowd. They looked about and finally nodded.

"I need to talk to you, Nick," Max said, sounding desperate.

Nick turned to him, the look on his face almost menacing. "Are you responsible for this?" he demanded.

Max's expression changed from concern to anger. "Hell, no. And I'm tired of you accusing me for everything."

Nick met his gaze. The boy seemed as frightened as everyone else. "Then help me check the guests. I want to make sure nobody was hit by flying glass."

The boy spun on his heels and headed in the opposite direction. "Go to hell."

Nick glared at Max's retreating back, but he didn't have time to do anything about the kid just yet. He had to check for injuries.

Billie noted the wedding guests standing around quietly, most of them still in shock. Many were her family members—simple, down-to-earth people who'd never been in a house the size of Nick's or rubbed elbows with famous people, and had certainly never had to run from a bomb blast. They looked toward Billie and Nick, obviously searching for answers.

All at once, Billie spied Sheridan Flock heading toward them. The woman looked angry enough to take off Nick's head. She planted her hands on her hips. "Oh, gee, I hope I haven't come at a bad time. I had no idea you were getting married." Her eyes were cold, almost flashing with hatred as she took in the sight of Billie in her dress. "Don't you look sweet?"

"Actually, your timing couldn't be worse," Nick said. "Someone set a bomb off. People could have been killed."

"Somebody obviously despises you as much as I do," Sheridan replied. She stepped closer, so close she was no more than an inch from his face. "Just who the hell do you think you are, sending the police to question Daddy and me? You're lucky he didn't come here personally. Isn't it bad enough that you ruined my life?"

"Your life hasn't been ruined, Sheridan, and I didn't say anything to the police. The stable hands saw the temper fits you pitched over here; you threatened to do everything but shoot me at close range. I'm sure they reported it when they were questioned."

"My father is going to sue you—"

"I'd hoped we could remain friends, Sheridan."

"Screw you *and* this poor creature who thinks you're such a hot catch." She slapped him hard and stomped away.

Billie put her finger to her eye. It was twitching again. And she had a headache. "I need a moment of quiet," she said.

"And I need to restore some order," Nick told her.

Billie wandered over to one of the limos. It was empty, and it looked dark and peaceful inside. She crawled in and closed her eyes.

Someone tapped on the car's window. She glanced up and found Raoul's face pressed to the glass. She opened the door.

"I have to get you out of here," he said. "You're in danger."

"What?" Billie almost shrieked the words.

"I'll tell you on the way," he said.

"Tell me now!"

"Get out of the limo fast. It may be rigged."

"Rigged? You mean with a bomb?" Billie almost fell from the limo getting out of it. Raoul grabbed her arm, shoved her into his truck, and squealed away.

"Where are we going?" Billie cried, watching the limo grow smaller as Raoul drove away like a madman.

"Someplace safe."

"How do you know I'm in danger?"

Billie heard a loud explosion and turned. The limo literally flew apart before her very eyes and burst into flames. All she could do was stare in mute disbelief. Another thirty seconds, and she could have been killed! Her children had almost lost their mother. And what if they had been with her? The thought was too much to bear.

A wave of dizziness swept over her as the realization of what could have happened hit with such a force, she thought she might be sick.

A horrified Nick raced blindly toward the burning limo; Max was right behind him. "Nick, wait!" the boy cried.

"Mr. Kaharchek, stop!" the detective ordered. "It's not safe."

"I've already called 911," one of the caterers yelled out.

Nick couldn't hear for the steady roar in his head. He had to know if Billie was in the car. He fought the blazing heat without a thought for his own safety, tried to reach the door, but the flames made it impossible. Max and the detective grabbed him and literally tackled him.

"Get your hands off me!" he shouted. "I have to see if she's in there! I have to know."

Several of the security guards were at the scene with fire extinguishers. One of them was able to get a good look at the interior of the limo.

"Mr. Kaharchek, your fiancée is not in the car," he said.

"Are you sure?"

"Yes. There's no one in the car."

"Raoul, would you please tell me where we're going?" Billie insisted, once they'd left the city limits behind and turned onto a dirt road.

"I'm taking you to a safe house," he said, reaching over and patting her hand. "Try to calm down."

"What do you mean, safe house?"

"You need to know something about me," he said softly. "I'm not a bug man."

Which explained why he hadn't been able to kill the spiders in her house, she thought. "I don't understand."

"I'm an undercover police officer, and I've been posing as a pest-control man for a year, due to a string of burglaries in Loudoun County. Recently, I was assigned to protect you."

"From whom?"

"Nick Kaharchek, and now his crazy cousin, Max."

Billie gaped in total disbelief. "What are you talking about?"

"He isn't what he seems, Billie, you have to trust me on that one. And now that his crazy cousin Max is on the scene, it only makes my job harder."

Everything suddenly felt even more disjointed. "I don't understand."

"I'm not at liberty to discuss the details, but Kaharchek is involved in a number of shady deals headed up by some, um, unsavory figures."

Billie just looked at him.

"Nick's a player in a variety of money-making scams run by some of the most important people in the country."

"Are you saying Nick is involved with the Mafia?"

"That term is a little outdated, but the men he deals with will stop at nothing to get what they want, and they all operate under the guise of respectable businessmen, just like Nick." He paused. "Why do you suppose Nick refuses to print anything against the new developers who plan to build a damn city on prime marshland? That land has been preserved for hundreds of years, but all of a sudden it's up for grabs? Nick's behind the whole thing, and he stands to make a lot of money."

"I don't believe you."

"You will when he's indicted."

Billie felt the blood rush to her ears. She could taste the disappointment in her mouth. Nick involved in illegal activities? It was hard to swallow. Had she let love blind her?

"Is Max involved? Did he bomb Nick's car and start the fire in the stables?"

Raoul looked at her. "Max knows all about Nick's

business dealings, and he's just crazy enough to do whatever he can to stop them. He's like a kamikaze pilot who is so caught up in a cause he'd strap dynamite to his body and crash a plane into a crowd of innocent people, just so he can make a statement. The only reason Max is interested in hurting you is to get back at Nick."

Billie was quiet as they turned onto yet another dirt road. "What about my children?" she said, a lump of fear forming in her throat. "How do I know Max won't try to harm them in my place?"

"Your children and family are under protection as well. It's you we're most concerned about."

Billie tried to let it all sink in.

A few minutes later, Raoul pulled into the driveway of a ramshackle house and parked. "This is it," he said.

Billie frowned. "You're kidding."

"It's the best we could do on such short notice. Besides, you won't be here long."

Billie followed him inside a musty room that smelled of old food and dirty clothing. She turned and found Raoul locking dead bolts with a key. "What are you doing?"

"Securing the place. Nobody's going to get in if I don't want them to."

Billie watched him put the keys in his pocket. Nobody was going to get out, either, she told herself.

Nick stood, hands on hips, his face streaked with soot from the fire. If Billie wasn't in the car, then where the heck was she? He'd been all·through the house and she didn't seem to be on the grounds.

"Are you looking for the bride?" one of the caterers asked. "I saw her leave with a man. He was driving a truck."

"Raoul!" Max said. "I bet it was Raoul. That's why I was late to the wedding. I think Billie's bug man has her."

"Bug man?"

"His name is Raoul Hernandez."

"You mean the pest-control man? I use his service. Why the hell would *he* have Billie?"

"I think he's got a thing for her. Why do you think she has spiders all over the house?"

Nick remembered Billie mentioning spiders to him the first time they'd met, and how she hated to enter a room with a spider in it. "Billie is scared of spiders," he said, thinking out loud. "At least she used to be."

"And who better than Hernandez would know that? I think he's been bringing spiders into her house so Billie will keep calling him for service. As dumb as it sounds, I think he feels it'll make him look like a hero or something."

Nick shook his head impatiently. Billie was missing, and Max was going off in God only knew what direction. "Get on with it, Max," he said.

"I sort of got suspicious when Hernandez was unable to kill harmless spiders after numerous attempts, then I caught him looking at Billie when he didn't know anybody was looking. I'm telling you, Nick, the guy has it bad for her. I analyzed a canister of bug spray he left behind. It's sugar water and what I think may be granulated hamster food. Nobody in their right mind would ever spray that stuff to get rid of bugs. In fact, it's a primo bug banquet. Also, Raoul works on household repairs for Billie, simple things, but it takes him forever. I think he never gets around to fixing Billie's stuff right because it's an excuse to be with her. And I think he's created an entire epidemic of spiders and other insects in the neighborhood just so Billie won't get suspicious about the bugs in her place."

Nick shook his head. "That sounds insane."

"That's not all. After I found out that Hernandez has the keys to half the houses in the neighborhood, and that there have been a couple of break-ins around here in the past few days, I did some digging. He's only been in the business for a year or two, but all of the neighborhoods he services have experienced a recent rash of minor break-ins. Hernandez is a con man. He builds people's trust and confidence, and next thing they're giving him the keys to their places and asking him to pick up their mail and newspapers while they're away."

"Then he robs them?"

"Not right away. I think he has duplicate keys made and robs them at a later time so they won't suspect him."

This time Nick frowned. "Why don't I know anything about the burglaries in Billie's neighborhood? I run a newspaper, dammit. My reporters do a column on police blotter stuff in the local section. Why haven't I seen anything in the newspaper, and why hasn't Billie mentioned it?" Then Nick realized he'd only scanned the front page since the bombing of his car, because he'd been so preoccupied. He'd been away from the office more in the past few weeks than he had in years, so he hadn't talked to the reporters on the local beat lately. And minor burglaries didn't make headlines.

"Billie probably didn't want to worry you," Max said. "But she accused Deedee of leaving the doors unlocked, and she said a set of spare house keys went missing for a day or so. Billie found them again, so she didn't get the locks changed, but there was a day or two there where she was really worried about it. Deedee told me that on the way over.

"If Raoul took the keys, he'd have had time to make spares and return them. And he's capable of doing something like that. I don't think anything was actually taken during the burglaries, except for maybe the last one. I think they were committed by Raoul in hopes of scaring Billie so she'd maybe turn to him for help."

"How do you know all this?" Nick said, eyeing Max suspiciously.

"I know my way around a computer, and I know how to hack into a system and break through a few firewalls here and there. For a good cause, mind you. Raoul Hernandez has spent years working construction, where he learned to use explosives."

The color drained from Nick's face. "What else?"

"He's a career con man. He's got a rap sheet that would knock your socks off, and has spent time behind bars on burglary, arson, and fraud charges. His background also includes a stint in a mental health facility, so he's probably unstable to boot."

"Where does he live?"

"I don't know. He's moved from his old place, probably in the last day or so, and he didn't leave a forwarding address. It isn't easy catching up with this guy, Nick. He has about ten aliases. I typed in every one of them, mixed them around, played with them for hours before I hit pay dirt and found his old address. I called him, and the phone had been disconnected. His landlady said he moved out in the middle of the night. He receives his mail through a post office box. I checked it early this morning, but it was empty."

"How did you get into his post office box?" Nick held up his hand. "Never mind, don't tell me." Nick pressed his fist against his forehead. Think, he told himself, but nothing sprang to mind. "Dammit to hell!" he yelled, drawing looks from the others. "Does it get any worse?"

Max nodded. "I'm pretty sure he's got Billie. That's about as bad as it gets."

CHAPTER SIXTEEN

Billie tried to act as normal as she could, even though her pulse raced so frantically she could feel it at her throat. She did not know what to believe anymore. Raoul had sounded so convincing, almost too convincing, but the Nick Kaharchek he'd described to her was not the man she had fallen in love with. Even with all the crazy things going on around them, bombs and burning stables, Billie had had no reason to believe that Nick was not who he seemed to be. He was honest and hardworking and shared the same beliefs as she.

Had she simply been so much in love with him that she'd failed to see him as he really was? If Raoul had meant to harm her, he would never have ordered her from the limo before it exploded. But how did he know the limo had a bomb in it to begin with?

"What's wrong?" Raoul said.

Billie looked up. Instinct told her to keep her mouth shut and her questions at bay for the moment. She needed answers, but she didn't even know the questions. For the time being, she would have to play along. "I was just thinking," she said. "You saved my life back there. If it weren't for you—" She shuddered.

"You don't think I'd let anything happen to you, do you?"

Another question for which she had no answer. "Of course not. I'm just terribly shaken."

"How about a cup of coffee? I have your favorite brand."

Billie smiled, even as she wondered why Raoul would have purchased her favorite brand of coffee unless he'd known ahead of time she would be there. He hadn't shown her a badge, and she hadn't thought to ask. Now she was afraid to.

"I'd love coffee. Where's the kitchen? I'm probably better at making it than you."

It was the first smile he'd given her since he'd ordered her into his truck. "The kitchen is through that doorway. Let me show you."

Billie walked into a filthy room. The counters and sink and metal table were cluttered and piled high with dirty dishes. Raoul would expect her to notice.

Billie turned to him, hands on hips. "Why is this place such a mess?"

He looked embarrassed. "The other guys obviously didn't bother to pick up after themselves."

Billie thought he sounded calmer. "Well, I can't tolerate a dirty kitchen. As soon as I make the coffee, I'll straighten up." He looked happy to hear it. The thought of cleaning the kitchen was not a pleasant one, but Billie knew she'd go crazy if she didn't find something to do. Besides, cleaning helped her think, and she had a lot of thinking to do. It would also give her a chance to look around for some kind of weapon, something to protect herself with, if the need arose. Kitchens were always chock-full of sharp objects. It was up to her to find a few.

She glanced at the window, noting that it was rigged with some sort of battery and wired to what appeared to be a plugged test tube. Two needles pierced the stopper, each connected to a different wire. What did it mean?

"What are you looking at?" Raoul asked, coming up behind her.

Billie felt the hair prickle on the back of her neck. "Is that some kind of security device?"

"Yeah. Just ignore it and make the coffee, okay?"

Billie winced when she opened the old metal percolator. No telling when it had last been cleaned. She scrubbed it thoroughly before putting the coffee on. Behind her, Raoul paced.

"You seem nervous," she said. "Are you afraid Max will find this place?"

Raoul chuckled. "Nobody is going to find us. But if they do, they won't live to regret it."

*   *   *

"I need to speak to the detective in charge," Nick told a tall man with thinning sandy-colored hair. He wore a dark suit and a serious expression.

"You're talking to him. I'm Detective Ferrell."

"You need to hear this."

Max repeated his story quickly while the detective looked on in awe. Nick wasn't certain the man believed Max or not. As far as the police were concerned, Max was probably their main suspect. Nevertheless, the man asked questions and took brief notes as Max's tale unfolded, jotting down the numerous aliases Raoul Hernandez was known to have used. Ferrell phoned the station and waited as the person on the other end of the line fed information into the police computer. He made more notes.

"Have someone run the data over here."

Ferrell hung up the phone and looked at Nick. "I'll get right on it. By the way, we've checked airlines, train, and bus stations. We've questioned all the neighbors, and spoken with Mrs. Pearce's friends—"

Nick met his gaze. "My fiancée would never leave town without her children."

"That is our assessment, as well. Unless she was forced. Sounds like that's a possibility." The cop put his hand on Nick's shoulder. "We'll find her."

Nick took a deep steadying breath. "How long will it take?"

"I can't answer that, but we're doing everything we can." The detective hurried to his car and got on the radio.

*   *   *

Billie knocked the stack of pictures from the top of the refrigerator as she tried to dust. They scattered to the floor. Raoul glanced over at her. "Sorry," she said. "I didn't see these."

He shrugged. "They're just pictures of my kids."

She knelt down and began to pick them up. Her hand froze in mid-air when she noted the little girl with the dark hair. It was Julie Favor, the girl from Nick's neighborhood.

"That's my daughter," Raoul said.

Billie felt a sinking sensation in the pit of her stomach. "Yes, you've shown me her picture before. She's lovely."

Raoul put the photographs back on top of the refrigerator. "I like to carry pictures of my kids with me on assignment. Keeps me company."

Billie smiled, even as a chill of fear crept up her spine. She'd been had. Tricked. As she cleaned, she began to put together the pieces of a puzzle that had been bothering her for days.

Raoul had only pretended to be her friend, spraying her house almost daily since her pest control problems had appeared, making home repairs that never truly got fixed. He obviously wasn't a good bug killer, because the spiders had continued to invade her home.

Raoul knew she had once feared spiders. When she'd hired him, she'd told him how her brother had been bitten by a brown recluse when they were kids. He still had a terrible scar. It had taken her years to get past the sheer terror of seeing even a tiny harmless spider. Raoul had confessed his fear of the dangerous arachnids, as well.

"I would rather face a rattlesnake than a brown recluse spider," he'd said the day she'd confided her old fears to him. Which had made her wonder why he'd gone into the pest control business to begin with.

But what about the infestation that had occurred in the neighborhood? she wondered. Maybe it was too much of a coincidence to be a coincidence. Had he been doing the same thing to her neighbors, pretending to fight the war on bugs when, in fact, the bug population was growing? If so, why?

Did Raoul have some sort of fixation on her? He'd certainly hinted that she needed a good man in her life, but he hadn't actually made a play for her. Besides, he had a family. Or so he'd said. Now she knew differently.

Nevertheless, her mind reeled with more unanswered questions.

If Raoul did have feelings for her, and he knew she didn't share his sentiments, what would he do to try to win her over? The answer was suddenly clear. Raoul had been trying to scare her, and the spiders were only the beginning. She thought of the sounds outside her bedroom window that had kept her awake much of the night when her children were gone. Was Raoul responsible for those as well? And what about the burglaries in the neighborhood? A single mother with two children would certainly be afraid of break-ins on her street, and Raoul had access to some of the homes. People trusted him.

She had trusted him.

When Nick Kaharchek appeared in her life it surely must've put a damper on Raoul's hope of winning her heart, if he had indeed hoped to do so.

Another chilling thought hit her. Raoul serviced Nick's place, as well. That's how he'd ended up with pictures of Julie. Nick's sudden appearance in her life had blown all Raoul's plans for a relationship with her. Had he blown up Nick's car and set fire to the stable in return? And what about the cake at the wedding reception?

The security guards would have thought nothing of letting Raoul spray the lawn for bugs the morning of the wedding, especially a man who came and went in the Kaharchek household and was well known throughout the community. And they would have been way too busy to follow him around. Raoul could easily have placed a bomb beneath the table where the cake was to sit. And, as devious as he was, he could have put a bomb in the limo when he saw her sitting in the back seat. Then he'd pulled her out of the car before it detonated. There was no other explanation for why the limo she'd climbed into, the one she and Nick were supposed to ride away in after the wedding, had exploded.

Billie's stomach knotted, her anxiety growing with every breath she took. If she was right, that could only mean one thing. Raoul would rather see her dead than married to another man.

She pushed the thoughts aside, at least for the moment. It was too much to consider at once, and she had to try to act natural if she wanted to survive. If

Raoul even suspected she knew what was going on, she was a dead woman.

She filled the sink with hot water and began putting dirty dishes in it. Finally, she walked into the living room to check for more dirty dishes. Raoul sat on the faded sofa, obviously lost in thought. She picked up several coffee cups and found a plate on a far table, crusted with old food that was unrecognizable. Something fishy, now rancid, the smell that had greeted her the minute she'd walked through the door. The odor hit her hard, and she gagged.

"What's wrong with you?" Raoul said.

Billie covered her mouth and shook her head. Her stomach pitched, and her jaw muscles ached. She was going to be sick. Quickly, she turned for the kitchen, but her shoe caught the table leg and she tripped. Coffee cups crashed against the floor and shattered, but she continued to hold the plate, almost falling face first into the food.

Raoul groaned on the sofa. "Do you need help?"

Fighting dry heaves, Billie tried to raise her head. It was then that she saw them, several gallon-sized jars beneath the table, a large spider pressed against the glass of one. She screamed.

"Jesus Christ!" Raoul shouted, coming to his feet. "What is wrong with you?"

Billie was too sick to get up at first. She stared at the jars, all housing various insects and spiders, from the small black spiders she often found in her house to the small brown German roaches. One jar contained several brown recluse spiders. She screamed again.

"Get away from there," Raoul snapped. "What's

wrong with you, have you lost your mind? Look at this mess."

Billie's throat began to close on her. "You're—" She paused and gagged once more. "Storing insects in here."

"I'm not *storing* anything," he said angrily. "I'm conducting experiments." He looked agitated. "I've, uh, been working on a new insect spray. Actually, it's better than anything you can buy on the market. I'm looking to have it patented. I expect to make a ton of money on it."

Billie's stomach continued heaving. The filth and stench, and finally the insects, had gotten to her. She needed air. She turned for the front door and reached for the doorknob.

"Don't touch that!" Raoul yelled so loudly that Billie snatched her hand away as though she'd just burned herself. He grabbed her wrist and yanked her away from it.

"What's wrong?" she cried.

"You'll blow up the place."

Billie glanced over and saw something wired to the front door—it looked like the thing on the kitchen window. What did it mean? "What is that?"

"Something to keep people out," he said harshly. "Someone even tries to come through that door, and that baby will take off their head."

Billie looked at the door, then at Raoul. "But how do *we* get out?"

He met her gaze. "We don't."

* * *

Nick felt more helpless as the day wore on, and the afternoon sun sank into the horizon. He was not a man accustomed to sitting around doing nothing, or depending on others for help. He was a mover and a shaker, a man who got things done no matter what. As he listened to Detective Farrell discuss his strategy with a local FBI agent named Dwight Hawkins, he realized the likelihood of finding Billie was growing dimmer with every second that passed.

They needed to move now.

Nick motioned for Max to follow him outside to the garden Billie loved. Her gardening tools and gloves sat on a patio table, waiting. He wondered if she would ever again get to do any of the simple little things she loved. If she lost her life it would be his fault, and he would spend his own life blaming himself. He wouldn't blame her if she no longer wished to marry him, but he wanted her alive more than he wanted his next breath.

"This isn't going to work," Nick said. "I'm going to lose it if something doesn't happen soon."

Max nodded. "That's my feeling exactly. At the rate they're going, it'll take forever for them to find Billie. *If* they find her."

"You got any better ideas?"

"I might have one or two."

They were interrupted when Detective Ferrell stepped out with Agent Hawkins. "I know what you must be going through," he told Nick. "I'm sorry."

Nick didn't think he looked sorry at all. This was just another case to the law-enforcement personnel, and Ferrell's only reason for solving it was so he could close the file. Nick realized he was probably being overly cynical, but he couldn't help himself. He had to stay angry in order to maintain any control over his emotions. "Thanks," he muttered.

Agent Hawkins stepped forward. "One of our agents entered all of Hernandez's aliases into our main computer and came up with a driver's license that Ms. Holt positively identified as the man we're looking for."

"We have an APB out on this Raoul guy," Ferrell said, "and I've got half the force flashing his picture and questioning people at convenience stores, gas stations, and fast-food restaurants near the neighborhoods he worked." Ferrell paused and looked at Agent Hawkins. "We've since had some disturbing news."

Nick steeled himself for the worst. "Billie's dead?"

"No, Mr. Kaharchek, we have no information on Mrs. Pearce at this time, although we're doing everything possible. We ran Hernandez's prints through our automated fingerprint identification system and got a hit. Mr. Hernandez is wanted by the FBI for questioning in an unsolved murder case. An old girlfriend of his has been missing for close to five years. The family says she walked out on Hernandez after having been battered by him numerous times." He paused once more. "The family suspects foul play."

Nick tried to listen to what the man had to say after that, but he could barely keep his impatience hidden. He'd heard enough. It was time to take matters into his own hands. He waited until the two law officers disappeared inside before turning to Max.

"Tell me your idea, Max."

"It's kinda illegal."

"I'm listening."

"If Raoul just moved somewhere new, he would have to notify the utility companies and get the electricity and water turned on. And I bet he'd use one of his aliases. I figure the police will check it out soon enough, but it'll take them a while to get the info. They gotta go through channels, and stuff."

"Any delay, and it could be too late."

"Right. But I could do it now."

Nick looked at him. "How?"

He shrugged as if it were no big deal. "Simple. I break into the water company's computer. I've done it before. Not in this town, of course. I was protesting a bogus rate increase by the water and sewer department back home, and I needed vital information to prove how unnecessary—"

"You hacked into the water company?" Nick asked. "Did you get caught?"

"Yeah, they busted me, but I was only eleven years old at the time. Didn't take the necessary precautions." He smiled. "Still managed to get the information I was looking for, though. It'll be fastest if we can do it on-site. I bet they don't have any security for the on-site computers—maybe not even a decent firewall on the system—if we access it in-house."

"What about the security on the building?"

"I can disarm most security systems, and I can pick a lock if I have to. I just need to get to the server."

Nick couldn't hide his amazement. "What the hell is that?"

"It's the computer file that lists everybody's name and address who uses water in this town, and the list of new accounts. If I cross-check that list against Raoul's aliases, I bet we'd find him."

"Just like that?"

"I might have to figure out some employee's password to get in, but like I said before, I'm pretty handy with computers. I was a killer hacker once. I liked the challenge of it. Now I only do it if it's for a good cause."

Finding Billie was definitely a good cause. "Let's go," Nick said.

The two walked inside. Nick found Ferrell and Hawkins studying a map of Nick's property. "We're going to grab something to eat," he said.

"Mr. Kaharchek, we've found Arnie Bates."

Nick paused. "Yeah?"

"There's an old abandoned well on your property?"

Nick nodded. "It hasn't been used in years."

"One of the officers checked inside. Found Mr. Bates lying in the bottom. He's been dead several days."

Nick swallowed. "Hernandez?"

"We don't know for sure. Mr. Bates may have seen Hernandez skulking about the property. Since the well was boarded up we know it was no accident."

Nick's mind reeled. Had Bates come back on the property once he'd been fired? Could he have torched the stable out of spite, or had Hernandez been trying to punish him for what he saw as Nick taking Billie away from him? He no longer knew *what* to think. At least he didn't suspect Sheridan or her father anymore. She might wish he was dead and frying in hell, but she loved horses more than she hated him.

"So we're dealing with a cold-blooded murderer for certain," Nick said, thinking out loud. He started for the door, knowing he and Max had no other choice but to make their moves. "Keep me posted—I want to know the instant you've got something useful."

Ferrell nodded. "I have your cell phone number if I need you." He waited until they'd walked out the front door before motioning for a plainclothes detective. "Follow them."

Billie tried to keep her voice light as she finished wiping the kitchen counters down. She had found a bottle of pine cleaner—the label was so faded it was obvious it hadn't been used in years—so the stench of old food was not as noticeable now. "I'd complain to your superior if I were you," she said, still playing along with Raoul, although she wasn't sure he was falling for it. "You should not have to work in a place like this."

He didn't answer. He merely sat at the kitchen table watching her every move.

Billie handed him a fresh cup of coffee and winced inwardly when she found her hands trembling. She couldn't afford to screw up now that Raoul knew she suspected the implications of the traps he'd set for her. Or did he? She did not take him for a smart man, but he was clearly dangerous. How she had managed to miss seeing that side of him the past year was beyond her.

"You nervous?" Raoul asked.

Billie gave a snort. "Wouldn't you be, after all that's happened to me? I housed a madman bomber under my roof; in fact, I allowed him to sleep on my son's twin bed. My wedding cake blew up in the middle of the ceremony, and I was almost blown to bits in the limo. I arrive here, only to find we're surrounded by—" she shuddered "—insects. Not only that, I have no idea where my children are. Hell, yeah, I'm nervous."

Billie thought she sounded convincing, but fatigue was wearing her down. She'd seen no possible way of escape, not even when she'd gone to the bathroom. Every window was rigged with some kind of device, as were both doors. Judging by all the explosions lately, Raoul knew what he was doing. She believed him when he said they'd blow up if she touched them. If, by some miracle, anyone found them, they'd die trying to get in, and she and Raoul would most likely die, as well. Which confirmed what she'd thought earlier. Raoul would take them both down, and Nick, too, if possible. He'd never let her go, even if it came to a murder and suicide between them. She tried not to think of Joel and Christie.

Yes, Raoul had fooled her and everyone in the neighborhood.

"You're the one who wanted to marry Kaharchek against my advice," he said after a moment. "I tried to warn you."

Billie sighed heavily. "I know."

"You don't know what you've put me through, Billie. How many nights I lay awake, just thinking—" He didn't finish the sentence.

Thinking what? she wondered. She could tell by the clenching and unclenching of one fist that Raoul was getting upset, and that's the last thing she wanted. She suspected, from the wild look in his eyes, that he was near his breaking point. Her affair with Nick had set him off, and the wedding had pushed him right over the edge.

"I was infatuated with Nick," Billie said, trying to keep Raoul calm. "You have no idea what it's like to catch your husband cheating on you. It was devastating to think I wasn't woman enough to keep my marriage alive. I was rejected by my own husband, the one person I thought I could trust more than anyone else." She sniffed and glanced away as though the thought were too painful to consider.

Raoul stared at the toes of his boots. "I know all about rejection. You think I haven't suffered? I was in love once. I wanted to marry a girl and raise a family with her." He paused and took a sip of his coffee. "That was back in Texas. She was the prettiest thing I'd ever laid eyes on." He raised his head, studied her face, and cocked his head to the side. "You remind me a lot of her. Same eyes and upturned nose. The two of you could have been twins. I noticed it the first time I saw you."

Billie felt her gut tighten. "What happened?"

"Caught her cheating on me. Took me a while, but I was able to forgive her the first time, once my anger passed." He shook his head. "And I'm here to tell I was one angry son of a bitch.

"Second time I caught her—" He paused and gazed ahead at nothing in particular, as if his mind were someplace else.

Billie wondered what he was seeing. His eyes still had that faraway look. "What happened the second time?"

"I figured the bitch wasn't worth marrying."

"You're probably right," Billie said, wondering where his mind had wandered. His expression was vacant, and looking into his black eyes was like looking through the windows of an empty house.

"Where is she now?"

Raoul frowned slightly, and his expression became dazed. When he spoke, his voice sounded different somehow. "I don't remember where I put her." Very slowly, he turned his head until he was looking directly into Billie's eyes.

Without thinking, she took a step back.

"I heard you and Nick together in bed that night. I heard what the two of you said to one another. Heard it all."

Billie's heart began to pound steadily; she could feel every measured beat. Her gaze locked with his. "I made a mistake," she said softly. "Nick was a mistake."

"Some mistakes are worse than others."

Billie gripped her coffee cup. She glanced away, afraid to look at him. "Nick is rich and powerful. My children could have had everything, Raoul. I wouldn't have to pinch pennies anymore."

He slammed his fist against the table. "Are you saying you prostituted yourself?"

Billie didn't know how to answer.

"There are no excuses for what you did. You knew how I felt about you."

Billie looked up, her eyes glistening with tears. She was afraid he had gone over the edge, and she no longer knew how to play him. "Y-you never said anything. Besides, you're married."

"None of that was real. Don't try to make a fool out of me. You know the girl in that picture. She was at the wedding today."

"What does any of it matter now?" Billie said. "It's all in the past. Nick and I are finished."

Billie added coffee to her cup. She turned slowly, giving him a half-smile. "Nick asked me to sign a prenuptial agreement." She gave a rueful laugh. "Do you really think I would have married him after that? I just wanted to see the look on his face when I turned and left him standing at the altar."

Suddenly, and without warning, she threw her coffee cup in the sink, and it shattered. "But Max ruined it all by setting off the bomb."

Raoul stood and crossed the room to where she was standing. "I don't believe you."

She looked at him squarely. "I'm not asking you to."

He raised one hand and touched her cheek lightly.

Billie remained calm as he moved closer, pressing himself against her, slipping one leg between her thighs, pressing. She met his gaze unflinchingly, her lips parted. She thought of Nick, of the joy his nearness had brought her. And her children, their warm bodies smelling so sweet as she tucked them in bed each night.

"You don't know what I had to go through to plan this whole thing," Raoul said. "I would kill for you, Billie. I have killed for you."

Billie felt as though her breath had been cut off. "I'm sorry."

He raised his hand and cupped her breast. "Kiss me."

Billie wondered how far she would have to go to save her own life. To see her children play again and hear Nick's soft voice in her ear.

She lifted her lips to his.

Nick and Max headed for the Loudoun County Water Company, stopping briefly at a hardware store so Max could pick up the items he needed, a box to carry them in, and a couple of flashlights. The building was in town, just off Main Street, tucked between a dentist's office and City Hall. The Purcellville Police Department sat right across the street. Nick and Max exchanged looks as Nick drove to a doughnut shop a couple of blocks away and parked. Nick glanced across the street to where the Holiday Inn sat, and he wondered how Billie's family was holding up.

"I hope to hell you know what you're doing," Nick muttered. "I don't have time for one of your harebrained schemes."

Max shook his head. "You don't like me, do you, Nick?"

"I never said that."

"But I'm a pain in the ass as far as you're concerned."

"Yes, Max, you *can* be a royal pain in the ass at times, but I'm really not in the mood to discuss it."

"Yeah, I know. You're too busy."

Nick stopped walking. "Yes, as a matter of fact, I am a little busy right now. The woman I love has been kidnapped by a madman," he said. "I don't know if she's dead or alive or—" He paused. He couldn't think along those lines or he'd lose it, go stark raving mad. Right now he had to remain in total control. "I'm a little preoccupied at the moment."

They began walking again. "You've always been too busy for me," Max said glumly.

"Perhaps we could have this conversation later."

"And I've looked up to you all my life. You've been like a father to me."

Nick shot him a funny look.

"It's true. Why do you think I asked to visit every summer?"

"Because I let you run wild, and I let you set up all that lab equipment at my place and blow up my stuff."

"And because you're the only person in the world who doesn't really believe I'm insane when I do the crazy things I do."

"There are moments, Max," he said, "but I knew the first time I held you as an infant that you were different. Special. I knew you would one day make a difference in the world. I still believe that."

Max shoved his glasses up his nose and glanced at

his cousin, but didn't speak. He simply squared his shoulders and continued walking.

They stopped in front of the water department building and looked around. "The security system is not going to be a problem." Max pointed to a decal on the front door with a familiar logo on it. "My folks use them. I've worked with that company's stuff before." He glanced back toward the police department where a patrol car pulled from the parking lot and turned onto Main Street. "Let's try it from the back."

Nick followed. "How long will it take you to get what you need?"

Max shrugged. "Depends how long it takes me to figure out the employee password. When I was hacking in from my home computer, it took me almost eight hours."

"Eight hours!" Nick glared at him. "We don't have eight hours."

"I had to get through the firewall, and I was only eleven years old. I'm a lot better at this stuff now," Max said. They stopped at the back door. The place was dark, and Nick couldn't see any signs that anyone was working inside the building. Max opened his toolbox and went to work. Nick shone the flashlight on the security box while Max removed the front cover plate and reached for the wires.

Beads of sweat dotted Nick's brow as Max peered closely into the alarm box, muttering to himself as he began working on it. A couple of snips, a few mutters, a couple of tugs on the wiring, and a green light flashed on, the lock clicked open, and they were inside the door.

They hurried down a hall, checking each room where signs were posted on doors that read "H_2O is Our Business." Finally, Max grinned. "Bingo."

Nick followed him into a room filled with computers and monitors. Max sat down before one and cracked his knuckles. "Okay, baby, talk to me."

Ten minutes later, and Max still had not come up with the password. He and Nick brainstormed. "This is a bugger," Max said, obviously accustomed to the frustrations associated with uncooperative computers.

Nick paced. He wondered what Billie was doing, whether she was okay. Whether she was even alive. How would he tell her children?

Stop it, he told himself. If he allowed himself to think along those lines he'd never make it. But the thought of having to give Christie and Joel bad news filled him with a sense of fear and dread that he'd never before experienced.

No matter what, he would see to the care of Billie's children. He would raise them if necessary, and he would raise them right.

Just as Billie would want it.

Nick squeezed his eyes closed, then opened them, because he couldn't bear to see the images in his mind. His only hope right now for finding Billie alive was knowing that Raoul loved her. Would he hurt the woman he loved? He tried not to think about Raoul's missing girlfriend. Raoul had obviously had no trouble killing Bates, so the odds were he'd killed before. Would he kill Billie to keep her from loving someone else?

Finally, he pulled a chair next to Max and began

doodling on a message pad with the company's logo and the words "H_2O is Our Business." Anything to take his mind off Billie, he told himself, but he could feel himself getting closer and closer to the snapping point. The clock ticked loudly, drawing his nerves tighter and tighter. His molars were sore from gritting his teeth, and the back of his shirt was sweat-drenched.

He colored in the logo. Patience, he told himself. If he could only hold out a little longer.

"Dammit!" Max said, wiping his eyes beneath his glasses. He blinked several times.

"H_2O," Nick muttered.

Max glanced at him. "What?"

"Try it."

Max frowned. "That's too easy. Nobody could be that stupid." He typed it in, and the screen lit up. They looked at one another. "How'd you know?"

"I didn't."

Max reached into his pocket and pulled out the list of Hernandez's aliases. He began typing them in, mixing and matching names. All at once, the name Raoul Santos came up on the screen. "Here he is," Max said. "That's his old address." He pointed. "This is his new one."

Nick's hands trembled as he jotted down any information he could find, including the address. Max backed out of the computer, leaving the monitor's screen just as they'd found it, and they left the building. The boy put the wires back into their original places, screwed the plate to the front of the alarm system, and they took off.

*   *   *

Deedee was on her cell phone with Billie's mother when Ferrell's phone rang. Standing just off the kitchen in the hallway leading to the garage, she stopped talking and tried to hear what he was saying.

"You think they found something?" Ferrell said. "Uh-huh. Okay, where are they headed? The doughnut shop across from the Holiday Inn? Okay, follow them and keep me posted. I'll get the men together."

Deedee slipped into the half-bath and relayed the information to Billie's mother. "They're headed for the doughnut shop," she whispered. "It's just across the street from where you are. I'll keep my cell phone with me and call you on yours when I know something."

Nick and Max arrived back at the doughnut shop in record time. "Shouldn't we notify the police?" Max said.

Nick shook his head. "I'm afraid to risk it. I'm betting Raoul isn't too fond of cops. If they scare him, he might go off the deep end and hurt Billie." *If she weren't already hurt or worse.* "I think we need to check things out first."

They climbed into Nick's car and started down the street. "How far is it?" Max said.

"Normally it takes a half hour to reach that area. It's out in the country. I'll make it in twenty minutes. Fasten your seat belt." He squealed from the parking lot of the doughnut shop, leaving long skid marks in the road.

They hadn't gone more than a mile before Nick frowned into his rearview mirror. "Aw, shit."

Max glanced up. "What is it?"

"There's a damn police car and tour bus several blocks behind us. I think it's Billie's family."

Max turned in his seat and watched for a moment. As they turned a corner, he caught a better look. "Yep, that's it. And that's not all. There's at least half a dozen limos following the bus."

Billie had cleaned the kitchen and bathroom and was trying to pick up newspapers in the living room when Raoul looked up from the sofa. "Don't you ever stop?"

"The place needed a little cleanup work. And I like to keep busy, or I get bored." Actually, she was more frightened than bored. Having been kissed by Raoul once, she'd decided the only way to avoid him was to stay busy and keep as far away from him as possible.

He gazed at her, and it was clear what he was thinking. "There's a solution to that, you know?"

Billie suppressed a shudder. Instead of showing fear, she put on a look of annoyance. "You're just like every other man I've ever met," she snapped.

He frowned. "What's that supposed to mean?"

"You don't care what I've been through today or that my nerves are shot. I'm disappointed in you, Raoul. I thought you were more sensitive than—" She shook her head. "Never mind."

"I'm a helluva lot more sensitive than Nick, if

that's what you mean. Shame you waited until it was too late to find out."

Too late to find out?

She planted her hands on her hips. "You told me you were married, remember?"

"I didn't want to risk scaring you off. I'd hoped in time something would happen between us."

"You lied to me."

He looked at her a long moment before getting up. "I could make it up to you."

She waved him aside. "I don't want to talk about it."

He suddenly looked sad. "Oh, Billie." He stepped closer. "I fell in love with you the first day I met you. There's been nobody in my life since."

She shot him a rueful look. "More lies."

"Listen to me, Billie. We can still be together."

She blinked several times. "What? How?"

"I can get us out of here safely. We still have plenty of time."

"What are you saying?"

"Come away with me."

"Do you mean that?"

"Yes."

She stepped closer as if to embrace him, then came to a halt. "My children. What about my children?"

"I can get them. It'll take a little planning, but you'll have to trust me."

Billie gazed up at him. "Trust is hard for me right now, Raoul."

"I know. But you'll see. In the end, we can all be

together, a big happy family." He smiled and pulled her into his arms once more.

Billie heard a noise and felt Raoul stiffen immediately. "What was that?" she said.

Raoul released her, pulled a gun from beneath a chair cushion, and peeked out the window. "Dammit to hell!"

"What is it?" Billie raced to the window. Vehicles, lots of them, not to mention the police cars, as far as the eye could see, were headed down the long dirt road in their direction. Even the tour bus her relatives had rented. There had to be a hundred people on the way. Relief flooded through her. "What in heaven's name?"

Raoul shoved her away from the window. "Your boyfriend has found us."

Billie could not hide her joy. Nick was on his way; he had found her!

Raoul turned, took one look at the smile on her face and slapped her hard. Blood spurted from her nose as Billie collapsed on the floor.

"Bitch. You been screwing with my head the whole time, haven't you?" He pressed his fist to his forehead. Finally, he raised his gun and aimed it at her.

Billie froze. The moment of truth had arrived. Somehow, she had managed to hang on this long; now her time was up. But she had to stay alive a few minutes longer so she could warn the others about the doors and windows.

"Go ahead and kill me," she said. "Isn't that what you've wanted to do all along? But guess what? The minute you pull that trigger, you've lost me for good."

Raoul's face became distorted with rage, his stare so filled with hate that his eyes seemed to burn right through her. "No!" he cried like a wounded animal. His face crumbled.

Billie sensed the change in him, the total break from reality. His eyes were those of a madman. He would kill her, all right, and then he'd turn the gun on himself, just as she'd suspected.

A voice suddenly shouted Billie's name from the other side of the door. She recognized it immediately. In one fluid move, she was on her feet.

"Nick, stop! Don't touch the door."

Raoul grabbed her and tried to cover her mouth, but she bit him hard enough to draw blood. He cried out and released her for a second.

"The door is rigged! Don't touch the door!" Billie shrieked the words so loudly that it felt as though her vocal cords had been ripped from her throat.

Raoul grabbed her and shoved the pistol against her head. "Come on in, folks," he taunted. "Hey, Nick, I've enjoyed your girlfriend. You're welcome to her. What's left of her." He started laughing. "You get it? What's left of her?"

On the other side of the door, Nick heard every word. He felt as though all the blood had drained from his veins. What had Hernandez done to Billie? He was filled with such rage that it left him immobile for a minute.

"He's bullshitting you, Nick," Max said. "Didn't you hear what Billie said? The door is rigged. He *wants* you to come after her. You could be killed."

Nick looked at Max. "It doesn't matter anymore.

I've already died a hundred deaths today. There's no telling what that lunatic has done to her." He closed his eyes and the pictures he saw were horrific.

"If you go through that door you could kill her," Max said. "She's still alive. That's what counts, right?"

Nick steeled himself. Max was right. As long as Billie was alive everything would be okay.

Detective Ferrell and several other officers examined the door. "Shit, it's booby-trapped," Ferrell said. "Call the bomb squad."

Nick stepped closer. "There's no time, dammit! He could be doing anything to her in there."

Ferrell turned to him. "What do you expect us to do, burst through the door and get blown to hell and back?"

"I can get you through that door," Max said.

The men jerked their heads in his direction. Nick grabbed the boy. "Are you sure?"

Max nodded. "Yeah, I can disarm that thing. I'll need something from the tool box to cut the wires."

Ferrell was already on the phone to headquarters. Agent Hawkins stepped closer to Max. "I can't let you do that, son. Please move away from the door."

Deedee called out. "Max, I have my manicure kit with me. Will that work?" Behind her the whoosh of a bus door opening caught Agent Hawkins's attention. Deedee tossed a black leather case to Max, who opened it and pulled out a pair of gold clippers.

"Stop!" Hawkins ordered. "You are unauthorized to touch that explosive device."

"Go to hell, man," Max said. "I make my own rules."

Nick put his hand on Max's arm. "Listen to me, Max," he said gently. "You've done enough."

"This is not a sophisticated device, Nick. It's a simple tilt fuse. Anybody can make one; all you need is a battery, a test tube or plastic pill container, a little wire, and a ball bearing. Hernandez was simply counting on the element of surprise. We rush the door, turn the knob, and blam!"

"We could try the windows."

"He's rigged the windows as well, so we may as well go through the door." He pointed to the doorknob. "See what I mean? All you have to do is cut those wires. That'll break the circuit, and we're in."

Nick grabbed his arm. "Wait. Let me cut them."

"The bomb squad is on its way," Ferrell said. "Both of you back off. Now."

"Why don't you shut up, you giant turd?" Deedee said to Ferrell. "My brother is smarter than the whole bunch of you."

Inside, Billie screamed as Raoul, his arm locked around her throat, tightened his grip. "Come on in, Kaharchek," he called out. "I'm waiting for you."

Billie was fast losing oxygen. Her head fell to the side and she sank to the floor, falling at Raoul's feet in an amorphous lump. He laughed out loud.

"You're missing the party in here, Nick, old boy. I just strangled your girlfriend."

On the other side of the door, Nick panicked. He grabbed the clippers from Max. "Back away!" he shouted to the crowd, putting the clippers to the wire. "Get back, Max."

"Let me help you, Nick."

"For God's sake, Max, listen to me. I can't lose you, too. I love you, kid."

Billie's family stepped back silently, as did the half-dozen or so wrestlers who had arrived in the limos behind the bus. Ferrell and Hawkins motioned for the officers to take cover, as well.

Raoul pressed his ear closer to the door. "They're going to disarm the damn thing," he muttered angrily.

Nick stood alone at the door. Once he saw that everyone was a safe distance away, he took a deep breath and very carefully clipped the wires. He turned the knob carefully. Seconds ticked by. Nothing happened.

Max grinned. "Told you so. It's safe now."

On the other side, Raoul tucked his pistol inside his waistband and reached for a shotgun.

Ferrell stepped forward with half a dozen police officers, all holding guns and big riot shields. "You're under arrest, Kaharchek," he said. "You, too, squirt," he told Max. He looked at his men and nodded.

One of the officers tried the doorknob. It turned, but the door didn't budge. "It's locked tight," he said. "Maybe he's got it braced shut."

Frankie seemed to step out of nowhere, surrounded by five other wrestlers. "Move out of the way and let us professionals handle this."

Ferrell arched both brows as he took in the size of the men. Frankie grabbed two shields and handed one to Snakeman. "Let's go." The two wrestlers slammed against the door. The wrestlers took turns. The dead bolts held fast, but the door splintered.

Inside, Raoul let out a loud hysterical laugh as he aimed his weapon. "Come on in, Kaharchek. Come to papa."

Behind him, Billie pulled herself to a standing position and reached for one of the gallon-sized jars. Adrenaline gushed through her body as she raised it over Raoul's head and slammed it down with every ounce of strength she could muster. Glass shattered in all directions. The shotgun fell to the floor. It fired, and a hail of lead splintered the baseboard.

Raoul sank to the floor as the door burst open and the wrestlers came through, Frankie leading the way. Frankie grabbed the shotgun from the floor and the pistol from Raoul's pocket, and handed them to a police officer.

Nick rushed in, eyes wild with fear at the sound of the gunshot. He saw Billie, looking much the worse for wear, but still alive. Ignoring the drying blood at her nose and on her suit, he took her in his arms. She burst into deep sobs.

Raoul opened his eyes. Several wrestlers stood over him, their looks menacing. Raoul flinched. "I have spiders on me," he cried. "Oh, shit, they're brown recluses! One of them bit me. Somebody help me."

The wrestlers took one look at the skittering spiders and raced from the house. "You don't want to mess with a brown recluse," Frankie told Deedee once he reached her side. "You ever see what they can do to a man?"

"Oh, Frankie," she said on a sigh. "You were so brave."

Raoul was crying as a police officer wearing thick gloves hauled him to his feet. "Please help me," he sobbed.

Billie shuddered and Nick led her outside where her large audience of family and friends cheered. Her parents raced to her side and hugged her. "Where are the kids?" she asked.

"Back at the hotel," her mother told her. "They're safe."

Nick took Billie in his arms once more, choking back the emotion he felt now that she was safe. "They're okay, baby. Everything's going to be okay."

Two hours later, Billie was seated on her sofa, her children on one side, Nick on the other. Her parents sat in chairs across from them. She was clean, and Nick had personally tended her wounds. Her house and backyard were packed with relatives and wrestlers, all of whom had dined on a truckload of pizzas and submarine sandwiches Nick had ordered from a nearby deli. Neighbors had streamed in with food, including more than a dozen desserts. Deedee and Frankie had already left to catch a chartered plane to Vegas where they planned to be married upon arrival.

Nick and Billie were oblivious to most of what was going on around them. All they could do was gaze at one another and remind themselves how lucky they were to be together.

"I thought I'd lost you," Nick whispered.

Billie raised her hand to his cheek. He looked exhausted. She had already heard how he and Max had broken into the water company in order to find Raoul's house, and she couldn't have been prouder of them.

"You saved my life," she said. "You know what that means. I'm responsible for you. For the rest of your life," she added with a smile.

Billie's minister, who had spent the past hour with the family, shaking hands and making certain everyone knew how blessed they were that everyone had come through the ordeal without serious injury—except Raoul, of course, who'd suffered multiple spider bites and was in critical condition in the hospital—stepped up to the couple.

He took Billie's hand as he prepared to leave. "This has been a long day for you," he said. "If I can be of help, please call me."

Billie smiled. "There is one thing you can do for us, Reverend Bennett," she said softly.

Ten minutes later, Billie and Nick said their vows before a full house of relatives, neighbors, and wrestlers. Nick kissed Billie tenderly as soon as they were pronounced man and wife. He hugged her tightly against him, then pulled Christie and Joel close. He motioned for Max, and the kid joined in. They were greeted with more cheers.

"Does this mean you're going to adopt me?" Max asked hopefully.

"You can stay as long as you like," Billie said. "You're part of this family now." She and Nick exchanged smiles.

"Do we get to go on the honeymoon with you?" Joel asked.

Nick and Billie looked at one another. "Honeymoon?" they said in unison.

"I completely forgot," Nick confessed.

"You can leave tomorrow," Max said. "I'll baby-sit."

Once again Billie and Nick exchanged looks.

"You've done enough, Max," Nick said. "We wouldn't think of imposing."

Billie nodded emphatically. "Besides, the kids want to spend a couple of weeks with their grandparents."

Joel opened his mouth to object, but one look from Billie made him close it.

"Then I'll stick around and watch the house while you're gone," Max offered. "I still have a few more things to repair, and I need to get back to work on that marshland project."

Nick shook his head. "I have a feeling that our lives will never be the same." He kissed Billie full on the lips as Christie and Joel giggled and Max rolled his eyes. In the background, the ice maker dumped another load.

CHAPTER ONE

My name is Stephanie Plum and I've got a strange man in my kitchen. He appeared out of nowhere. One minute I was sipping coffee, mentally planning out my day. And then the next minute . . . *poof*, there he was.

He was over six feet, with wavy blond hair pulled into a ponytail, deep-set brown eyes, and an athlete's body. He looked to be late twenties, maybe thirty. He was dressed in jeans, boots, a grungy, white thermal shirt hanging loose over the jeans, and a beat-up, black leather jacket hanging on broad shoulders. He was sporting two days of beard growth, and he didn't look happy.

"Well, isn't this perfect," he said, clearly disgusted, hands on hips, taking me in.

My heart was tap-dancing in my chest. I was at a total loss. I didn't know what to think or what to say. I didn't know who he was or how he got into my kitchen. He was frightening, but even more than that he had me flustered. It was like going to a birthday party and arriving a day early. It was like . . . what the heck's going on?

"How?" I asked. "What?"

"Hey, don't ask me, lady," he said. "I'm as surprised as you are."

"How'd you get into my apartment?"

"Sweet cakes, you wouldn't believe me if I told you." He moved to the refrigerator, opened the door, and helped himself to a beer. He cracked the beer open, took a long pull, and wiped his mouth with the back of his hand. "You know how people get beamed down on *Star Trek*? It's sort of like that."

Okay, so I've got a big slob of a guy drinking beer in my kitchen, and I think he might be crazy. The only other possibility I can come up with is that I'm hallucinating and he isn't real. I smoked some pot in college but that was about it. Don't think I'd get a flashback from wacky tobacky. There were mushrooms on the pizza last night. Could that be it?

Fortunately, I work in bail bond enforcement, and I'm sort of used to scary guys showing up in closets and under beds. I inched my way across the kitchen, stuck my hand into my brown bear cookie jar, and pulled out my .38 five-shot Smith & Wesson.

"Cripes," he said, "what are you gonna do, shoot me? Like that would change anything." He looked more closely at the gun and shook his head in another wave of disgust. "Honey, there aren't any bullets in that gun."

"There might be one," I said. "I might have one chambered."

"Yeah, right." He finished the beer and sauntered out of the kitchen, into the living room. He looked around and moved to the bedroom.

"Hey," I yelled. "Where do you think you're going? That's it, I'm calling the police."

"Give me a break," he said. "I'm having a really shitty day." He kicked his boots off and flopped onto my bed. He scoped out the room from his prone position. "Where's the television?"

"In the living room."

"Oh man, you don't even have a television in your bedroom. Someone's really sticking it to me."

I cautiously moved closer to the bed, and I reached out and touched him.

"Yeah, I'm real," he said. "Sort of. And all my equipment works." He smiled for the first time. It was a knock-your-socks-off smile. Dazzling white teeth and good-humored eyes that crinkled at the corners. "In case you're interested."

The smile was good. The news was bad. I didn't know what *sort of real* meant. And I wasn't sure I liked the idea that his equipment worked. All in all, it didn't do a lot to help my heart rate. Truth is, I'm pretty much a chicken-shit bounty hunter. Still, while I'm not the world's bravest person, I can bluff with the best of them, so I did an eye-roll. "Get a grip."

"You'll come around," he said. "They always do."

"They?"

"Women. Women love me," he said.

Good thing I didn't have a bullet chambered as threatened because I'd definitely shoot this guy. "Do you have a name?"

"Diesel."

"Is that your first name or your last name?"

"That's my whole name. Who are *you*?"

"Stephanie Plum."

"You live here alone?"

"No."

"That's a big fib," he said. "You have *living alone* written all over you."

I narrowed my eyes. "Excuse me?"

"You're not exactly a sex goddess," he said. "Hair from hell. Baggy sweatpants. No makeup. Lousy personality. Not that there isn't some potential. You have an okay shape. What are you, 34B? And you've got a good mouth. Nice pouty lips." He threw me another smile. "A guy could get ideas looking at those lips."

Great. The nutcase who somehow got into my apartment was getting ideas about my lips. Thoughts of serial rapists and sex killings went racing through my mind. My mother's warnings echoed in my ears. *Watch out for strangers. Keep your door locked.* Yes, but it's not my fault, I reasoned. He's a crazy alien. How do you keep aliens out?

I took his boots, carried them to the front door, and threw them into the hall. "Your boots are in the hall," I yelled. "If you don't come get them, I'm pitching them down the trash chute."

My neighbor, Mr. Wolesky, stepped out of the elevator with his arms loaded up with bags. "Five days to Christmas and the stores are picked clean," he said. "And they all say everything's on sale, but I know they jack up the prices. They always gotta gouge you at Christmas. There should be a law. Somebody should look into it."

Mr. Wolesky unlocked his door, slid inside, and slammed the door after himself. The door lock clicked into place, and I heard Mr. Wolesky's television go on.

Diesel elbowed me aside, went into the hall, and retrieved his boots. "You know, you have a real attitude problem," he said.

"Attitude this," I told him, closing my door, locking him out of the apartment.

The bolt shot back, the lock tumbled, and Diesel opened the door, walked to the couch, and sat down to put his boots on.

Hard to pick an emotion here. Confused and astounded would be high on the list. Scared bonkers wasn't far behind. "How'd you do that?" I said, squeaky-voiced and breathless. "How'd you unlock my door?"

"I don't know. It's just one of those things we can do."

Goosebumps prickled on my forearms. "Now I'm really creeped out."

"Relax. I'm not going to hurt you. Hell, I'm supposed to make your life better." He gave a snort and another bark of laughter at that. "Yeah, right," he said.

Deep breath, Stephanie. Not a terrific time to hyperventilate. If I passed out from lack of oxygen, God knows what would happen. Suppose he was from outer space, and he conducted an anal probe while I was unconscious? A shiver ripped through me. Yuck! "What are we looking at here?" I asked him. "Ghost? Vampire? Space alien?"

He slouched back into the couch and zapped the television on. "You're in the ballpark."

I was at a loss. How do you get rid of someone who can unlock locks? You can't even have him arrested by the police. And even if I decided to call the police, what would I say? I have a *sort of real* guy in my apartment?

"Suppose I cuffed you and chained you to something. What then?"

He was channel-surfing, concentrating on the television. "I could get loose."

"Suppose I shot you."

"I'd be pissed off. And it's not smart to piss me off."

"But could I kill you? Could I hurt you?"

"What is this, twenty questions? I'm looking for a game here. What time is it, anyway? And where am I?"

"You're in Trenton, New Jersey. It's eight o'clock in the morning. And you didn't answer my question."

He flipped the television off. "Crap. Trenton. I should have guessed. Eight in the morning. I have a whole day to look forward to. Wonderful. And the answer to your question is ... a qualified no. It wouldn't be easy to kill me, but I suppose if you put your mind to it, you could come up with something."

I went to the kitchen and phoned my next-door neighbor, Mrs. Karwatt. "I was wondering if you could come over for just a second," I said. "There's something I'd like to show you." A moment later, I ushered Mrs. Karwatt into my living room. "What do you see?" I asked her. "Is there anyone sitting on my couch?"

"There's a man on your couch," Mrs. Karwatt said. "He's big, and he has a blond ponytail. Is that the right answer?"

"Just checking," I said to Mrs. Karwatt. "Thanks."

Mrs. Karwatt left, but Diesel remained.

"She could see you," I said to him.

"Well, duh."

He'd been in my apartment for almost a half hour now, and he hadn't done a full head rotation or tried to wrestle me down to the ground. That was a good sign, right? My mother's voice returned. *It means nothing. Don't let your guard down. He could be a maniac!* Frightening, right?

"What are you doing here?" I asked him, curiosity beginning to override panic.

He stood and stretched and scratched his stomach. "How about if I'm the friggin' spirit of Christmas?"

My mouth dropped open. The friggin' spirit of Christmas. I must be dreaming. Probably I'd dreamed I'd called Mrs. Karwatt, too. The friggin' spirit of Christmas. That's actually pretty funny. "Here's the thing," I said to him. "I have enough Christmas spirit. I don't actually need you."

"Not my call, Gracie. Personally, I *hate* Christmas. And I'd prefer to be sitting under a palm tree right now, but hey, here I am. So let's get on with it."

"My name's not Gracie."

"Whatever." He looked around. "Where's your tree? You're supposed to have a stupid Christmas tree."

"I haven't had time to buy a tree. There's this guy I'm trying to find. Sandy Claws, wanted for burglary, and now he's failed to appear for his court appearance, so he's in violation of his bond agreement."

"Hah! Good one. That's a prize-winning excuse for not having a Christmas tree. Let me see if I've got the details right. You're a bounty hunter?"

"Yes."

"Very sexy."

I did another eye-roll.

"And you're after Santa Claus because he skipped."

"Not Santa Claus. Sandy Claws. S-a-n-d-y C-l-a-w-s."

"Sandy Claws. Cripes, how would you like to have *that* name? I bet he uses kitty litter."

This was coming from a guy named for a train engine. "First, I have a legitimate job. I work for Vincent Plum Bail Bonds as a bond enforcement agent. Second, Claws isn't such a weird name. It was probably Klaus and changed at Ellis Island. It happened a lot. Third, I don't know why I'm explaining this to you. Probably I had a stroke and fell down and hit my head and I'm actually in ICU right now, dreaming all this."

"You see, this is typical of the problem. Nobody believes in the mystical anymore. Nobody believes in miracles. As it happens, I'm a little supernatural. Why can't you just accept that and go with it? I bet you don't believe in Santa Claus either. Maybe Sandy Claws didn't have his name changed from Klaus. Maybe he had his name changed from Santa Claus. Maybe the old guy got tired of the toys-for-kids routine and just wanted to go hide out somewhere."

"So you think it might be Santa Claus living in Trenton under an assumed name?"

Diesel shrugged. "It's possible. Santa's a pretty shifty guy. He has a dark side, you know."

"I didn't know that."

"Not many people know that. So if you could catch this Claws guy, you'd get a Christmas tree?"

"Probably not. I haven't got money for a tree. And I haven't got any ornaments."

"Oh man, I'm stuck with a whiner. No time, no money, no ornaments. Yadda, yadda, yadda."

"Hey, it's my life and I don't have to have a Christmas tree if I don't want one."

"Everyone wants a Christmas tree. If you had a Christmas tree, Santa would bring you stuff . . . like hair curlers and slut shoes."

"Give it up. I'm not getting a tree. End of discussion. And you're going to have to leave because I have things to do. I have to work on the Claws case and then later I promised my mother I'd be over to bake Christmas cookies."

"Not a good plan. I have a better plan. How about we find Claws and then we shop for a tree? And on the way home from the tree, we can see if the Titans are playing tonight. Maybe we can catch a hockey game."

I did yet another eye-roll and brushed past him. I was doing so many eye-rolls, they were giving me a headache. I'd planned to take a shower but there was no way I was getting into the shower with a strange man sitting in my living room. "I'm changing my clothes, and then I'm going to work. You aren't going to pop into my bedroom, are you?"

"Do you want me to?"

"No!"

"Your loss." He returned to the couch and television. "Let me know if you change your mind."

An hour later we were in my Honda CRV. Me and Supernatural Man. I hadn't invited him to ride along with me. He'd simply unlocked the door and gotten into the car.

"Admit it, you're getting to like me, right?" he asked.

"Wrong, I *don't* like you. But for some unfathomable reason, I'm not totally freaked out."

"It's because I'm charming."

"You are *not* charming. You're a jerk."

He flashed another one of the killer smiles at me. "Yeah, but I'm a *charming* jerk."

I was driving, and Diesel was riding shotgun, flipping through my folder on Claws. "So what do we do here, go to his house and drag him out?"

"I stopped by his house yesterday and his wife said

he'd disappeared. I think she knows where he is so I'm going back today to put some pressure on her."

"Sixty-seven years old, and this guy broke into Kreider's Hardware at two in the morning and stole fifteen hundred dollars' worth of power tools and a gallon of Morning Glory yellow paint," Diesel read. "Got caught on a security camera. What an idiot. Everybody knows you've got to wear a ski mask when you pull a job like that. Doesn't he watch television? Doesn't he go to the movies?" Diesel pulled out a file photo. "Hold the phone. Is this the guy?"

"Yes."

Diesel's face brightened, and the smile returned. "And you stopped by his house yesterday?"

"Yes."

"Are you any good at what you do? Are you good at tracking down people?"

"No. But I'm lucky."

"Even better," he said.

"You look like you've had a revelation."

"Big time. The pieces are beginning to fit together."

"And?"

"Sorry," he said. "It was one of those personal revelations."